Praise For
KEID: A Lost Civilization

This is cutting edge, hard science fiction at its finest. A huge starship discovers a derelict Dyson Sphere containing a sun that is used for energy. The crew investigate and find several sapient species inside the sphere. They also learn that the star will soon erupt, destroying both the sphere and its inhabitants. Only they can save them! All this would be more than enough for a great speculative novel, but Williscroft also includes MBH and MERT Drives, portal technology, electronic uploads of humans and others, plus a great deal more, much of it derived directly from current physics research. The effect of this broadminded, far-sweeping approach is both realistic and daring. The reader feels that yes, this is what the universe is like and what man's role in it will come to be.

— Professor John B. Roseman, Norfolk State University
Former Chairman of the Board
Horror Writers Association
Author of *The Inspector of the Cross Series*

Robert G. Williscroft's *Oort Chronicles* continue with the fourth in the series, *Keid: A Lost Civilization*, and Braxton Thorpe is becoming a modern-day Odysseus as his interstellar voyage takes yet another turn. This time it is to the star Keid (also known as 40 Eridani) where Thorpe and his crew discover an under-construction Dyson Sphere.

Along with his usual action and intrigue, Williscroft's trademark hard science attempts to answer the question I've yet to see anyone else in science fiction tackle: how do you build (and then maintain) a Dyson Sphere in the first place? The surprising answer reveals a threat to the starship Andromeda and its entire crew, and Thorpe's team is pushed to the limits. Great fun, and a must-read for anyone following the Chronicles.

—Alastair Mayer
Author of *The T-Space Series*

KEID: A Lost Civilization is the fourth *Oort Chronicle*, but it can be enjoyed by itself without reading the first three books in the series. The story is about a huge starship, *Andromeda*, manned by 10,000 Humans, feline Asterians (from the 84-lightyear-distant Aster System), and reptilian Arcans (from the 10.5-lightyear-distant Ran System). They are undertaking a voyage of discovery, heading toward the Cold Spot in the Cosmic Microwave Background in the direction of the constellation Eridanus. Their first stop was the Ran star system, the subject of the Third Oort Chronicle, *RAN: A Civilization in Hiding*. Their next stop is the Keid triple-star system, some six lightyears distant from Ran.

The planet Vulcan, home to Spock in the *Star Trek* television and film franchise, revolves around Keid A. Keid B & C revolve around each other, and both revolve around Keid A. *Andromeda* arrives at Vulcan only to discover that the planet is under attack by robotic scavengers. It follows the scavengers to Keid C, where it discovers a Dyson Sphere under construction by microbots who seem to be scavenging one part of the sphere to construct another. The *Andromeda* crew set about exploring this immense sphere, half the size of an entire solar system.

They discover primitive sapient species inside the sphere and electronic uploads of the original builders. Then they determine that Keid C, the star inside the sphere, is about to superflare, and they set about rescuing the uploads and members of the primitive species.

The author has convincingly created an alien Dyson Sphere populated by several sapient species. He details the alien cultures convincingly, so that I found myself believing in their actual existence. I was fascinated by how Humans, Asterians, and Arcans worked together to explore the sphere without racial tension, despite their vastly differing appearances, physiologies, and backgrounds. On a side note, I was especially fascinated by one of the primitive races that was reptilian and had domesticated a pterosaur-like reptile that the males used to fly into battle. This is a marvelous subplot.

I highly recommend *KEID: A Lost Civilization*!

Ebenezer Ebo
CEO Imperial Mortgag

The Fourth Oort Chronicle

KEID

A Lost Civilization

Phoenix Starship Andromeda

The Fourth Oort Chronicle

KEID

A Lost Civilization

Robert G. Williscroft

Centennial, Colorado

Dedication

For Jocara

Table of Contents

Acknowledgments

Several people contributed to the creation of this book.

Most significantly, my wonderful wife, Jill, pored over each chapter with her discerning engineer's eye. She kept my timeline honest and made sure that regular readers could understand fully the arcane details of the nuclear and quantum interactions that play a significant role in this tale. She also reviewed my celestial mechanics.

Prof. John B. Rosenman, bestselling science fiction and horror author who taught science fiction writing at Norfolk State University, reviewed the manuscript and made several suggestions that significantly improved the story.

Hard science fiction author Alastair Mayer reviewed the manuscript and offered his scientific, engineering, and editorial insight.

Others have contributed with their comments and observations, and I thank them. You know who you are.

It goes without saying that any remaining omissions, errors, and mistakes fall directly on my shoulders.

Robert G. Williscroft, PhD
Centennial, Colorado
January 2024

Cast of Characters

MAIN CHARACTERS

(alphabetically by first name)

Thorpe—Captain of *PS Andromeda*

eThorpe—Uploaded version of Thorpe

Daphne O'Bryan, PhD—*Andromeda* Chief Scientist, companion to Kimberly
    eDaphne—Upload version of Daphne O'Bryan

Jocara Porovik—Ceffid astronaut

Kenred Zlaxiz—Amred astronaut

The Oort—The builders of the Dyson Sphere

SECONDARY CHARACTERS

(alphabetically by first name)

Bolaik Taclit—Asterian Engineering Group Leader

Brad Kominsky, PhD—*Andromeda* Senior Scientist
    eBrad—Upload version of Brad Kominsky

Braxton—The clone of Thorpe
    eBraxton—Upload version of Braxton

Dale Ryan, PhD—*Andromeda* research scientist
    eDale—Upload version of Dale Ryan

Forbis—Asterian engineering excursion member

Gelong—The personal pterosaur mount of Toby, the primitive
    saurian leader

Gregory Dobson—*Andromeda* Chief Medical Officer

Hobar—Toby's mate

Jama—Toby's and Hobar's son

Jerad—Human engineering excursion member

Joe—Human engineering excursion member

Kidlit Mazop—Asterian Engineering Group Leader

Kimberly Deveraux—Andromeda Chief Information Officer, companion to Daphne
eKim—Upload version of Kimberly Deveraux

Liaise—The Oort representative

Max—Daphne's tabby cat
eMax—Upload version of Max

Otiz—Asterian engineering excursion member

Sally Nguyen, PhD—*Andromeda* Senior Scientist
eSally—Upload version of Sally Nguyen

Suma—The personal pterosaur mount of Toby's son Jama

Toby—The primitive saurian leader

Ustrun Strozid—Roganian *Andromeda* Chief Engineer

Spacecraft Roster

PHOENIX SPACECRAFT

PS Andromeda

PHOENIX M-CLASS STARSHIPS

PS Alan Bean
PS Alan Shepard
PS David Scott
PS Michael Collins
PS Neil Armstrong

Author's Note

I have employed some non-standard language usage in this book. Because four sapient races play significant roles, their names are all capitalized: Human, Arcan, Asterian, and Oort.

The home planet for each race is capitalized: Earth, Arcan, Rogan, and Earth, respectively. The home star for each race is capitalized: Sol, Ran, Aster, and Sol, respectively. The home star system for Humans and Oort is the Solar System (capitalized).

Even though Arcans and Asterians use an indigenous system of weights and measurements, I employ the metric system throughout the book. Both the Asterians and Arcans have six-digit hands and feet, so they naturally count and compute in the duodecimal system. I use the decimal system throughout this book.

One might assume that the Arcans and Asterians would have indigenous names for their suns. I used the Human designation for Ran, and I created the name Aster for HD20367 in the constellation of Aries.

The science and engineering behind the Dyson Sphere, and the MBH and MERT Drives and portal technology is derived directly from current state-of-the-art physics research. Many of you reading this volume will likely see some form of MERT or warp bubble drive in your lifetime.

You saw it here first!

Robert G. Williscroft
Centennial, Colorado
January 2024

The Fourth Oort Chronicle

KEID

A Lost Civilization

Prolog

PS Andromeda

PS Andromeda—a half-kilometer thick circular disk five kilometers across with an elaborate cityscape on one surface and an upside-down pastoral landscape on the other, complete with mountains, meadows, and streams. Transparent domes cover both sides. An artificial mini black hole inside the central disk powers the craft.

Andromeda is on the second leg of an open-ended voyage from the star Aster, pointed at the constellation Eridanus to investigate the Cosmic Microwave Background Cold Spot, six to ten billion light-years distant, stopping along the way when things look interesting.

First stop: The star Ran—Epsilon Eridani.

Second stop: The star Keid—40 Eridani.

PART ONE
THE SPHERE

Chapter One

PS Andromeda—Underway for Keid

Thorpe sat at the Bridge control console deep inside *Andromeda's* central disk. A large holoscreen surrounding the Bridge presented him outside views from the massive vessel and presented data to individual operators around the Bridge. To his left sat Kenred Zlaxiz and Jocara Porovik, the saurian astronauts from the planet Arcan around the star Ran—their immediate departure point. Daphne O'Bryan, Andromeda's Chief Scientist, sat to his right as his First Officer. The spacious Bridge had sufficient room for a group of senior crew members who had nothing better to do.

Andromeda was an FTL (Faster Than Light) ship powered by MERT portals—a Casimir field that contained a stable wormhole.

"Listen up, everybody," Thorpe said as the background chatter died away. "Our destination is the triple-star system Keid, also known as Forty Eridani, just six lightyears distant. Those of you who are classic American film buffs will recognize this star as the sun of the planet

Vulcan in the classic *Star Trek* television series. That's right, Spock's home planet. Back in the early twenty-first century on Earth, astronomers actually thought they had discovered an Earth-like planet around Keid-A. After the excitement died down, it turned out they were wrong. We're gonna find out what's really there."

Thorpe turned to Kenred with a grin. "This is a bit different from your circum-Lodan capsule."

"That's an understatement. The difference between our two-person capsule and this huge starship is almost beyond description." Kenred turned to Jocara, his female fellow astronaut on the first trip around their moon, Lodan. "Could you have imagined this two years ago?"

Blinking eyes wide open, the Arcan equivalent of a Human grin, she shook her head in amazement, and then turned to Thorpe. "Are you really going to let us do the honors?" Jocara asked, her scales rippling dark blue with excitement.

"You two are the only true astronauts in our entire ten thousand crew," Thorpe answered. "Oh, we've got fighter pilots, marines, scientists, bureaucrats, tabby cats, and even guys like me, but we have only two astronauts."

Kenred looked at Jocara, eyes wide open and blinking. "You do it, Girl! Be the first Arcan to pilot a starship between stars!"

✳

"Mother," she said, addressing the ship's resident AI, "transit to the star Keid-A, jump interval six picoseconds, specific destination, the outer edge of Keid's life zone." Jocara gave the order in the Amred language in which Mother, *Andromeda's* central processor, was fluent. Her scales slowly returned to their normal light green.

PS Andromeda—Keid-A System

There was no indication of anything except the holoscreen turned a uniform speckled gray. One minute and eight seconds later, Jocara blinked as a blazing orange star with an apparent width wider than Ran as seen from Arcan filled the holoscreen center. A bright white star and a less bright reddish-orange star appeared close together off to the right. Even though she knew Andromeda was an FTL ship, and the MERT portal technology had been explained to her, it was still hard to believe that they had traveled six lightyears in just over a minute! Her scales rippled from the blue of excitement to lavender, showing her pure joy at the experience.

"Time to scan for planets," Thorpe said in his matter-of-fact manner. He turned to the control room visitors. "This doesn't work like in the holovision plays. We're on the outer edge of the life zone on Keid-A's ecliptic, about one hundred sixty-five million klicks from the star. Light takes about ten minutes to reach us from Keid. We find an inner planet by observing its transit across Keid. Mother can measure the orbital perturbations of any inner planets we find to calculate the presence and location of any larger outer planets. All this takes time, lots of time. We can drive our way around Keid much faster than the orbital period of four hundred sixty-four days at our distance." He checked a calculation on his internal Link. "If we travel at five thousand klicks per second, it'll take us two and a half days for the survey, and Mother should be able to pick up any inner planets."

Kenred looked at Jocara. "This must be pretty exciting for someone who studied astrophysics."

She responded by opening her eyes and blinking, while her scales rippled blue again.

✳

Thorpe watched carefully as the saurian astronaut guided *Andromeda* onto the scanning flight path. She accomplished it flawlessly. He was amused at the almost childlike joy the two Arcans took in maneuvering the massive vessel. He had to remind himself that when he found them, their technology was at about the *Apollo* stage in Earth's spaceflight history. The Arcan Space Push Consortium had definitely chosen their astronauts well.

✳

Daphne had grown close to the female saurian during *Andromeda's* sojourn around Arcan. Despite their physical differences, they had become good friends. Daphne had learned how to interpret Jocara's scale colors and understand her facial expressions and gestures. Each had a Human equivalent.

As she watched Jocara bring *Andromeda* onto the survey track, she took genuine pride in her friend's demonstrated expertise.

"Can you imagine," she said quietly to Thorpe, "how one of our Apollo astronauts would have reacted in a similar scenario? Do you think they would have handled it as well as the Arcans?"

She got up and walked over to Jocara, putting a hand on her shoulder. "It never gets old," she said quietly, "never."

❋

A day later, Mother announced acquisition of an Earth-size planet in an orbit 0.6 AU from Keid-A, which put it near the inner edge of the life zone. By the end of the survey, Mother added two more planets to the list, both much closer to Keid and far too hot for life.

Once again, Thorpe allowed Jocara to bring *Andromeda* into orbit around the new planet. He put the name for this planet up for a vote by ship's company. The Asterians knew nothing about *Star Trek* and so declined to vote, as did the Arcans. The Oort, who had downloaded into Human form before the voyage commenced, were well acquainted with the old television series and chose to vote.

By a very lopsided count, the result was *Vulcan*.

PS Andromeda—Orbiting Vulcan

"Vulcan seems to be very much like Arcan," Jocara told Daphne.

"Or like Earth," Daphne said back. "Except I don't see any evidence of plant life."

They sat on the Bridge looking at the holodisplay of Vulcan and the surrounding skies.

"It's an Arcan-size planet—a bit smaller," Jocara said.

"Yeah, much like Earth," Daphne added. "Look," she pointed, "four continents, oceans, and polar ice caps."

"Can't tell from here if there's anything of interest down there or not," Jocara said.

"We have a bunch of people examining every detail visible from orbit," Daphne said. "Once they're done, you and I will take my craft down to the surface and give it some personal attention."

"You can just do that? Don't you need permission?"

"We don't do things that way, Jocara. First, as Chief Scientist, I set my schedule. But beyond that, I notify Thorpe when I will be away from the ship. If he needs me, he'll let me know. We all have specific jobs to do, but only a few of us regularly leave the ship."

"Sounds a bit like Amred, Kenred's home country. My home, Ceffid, was more structured—still is, for that matter. Kenred and I are still getting used to your freewheeling ways."

"We just received a preliminary atmosphere report," Daphne said, pointing to a holoscreen, "…nitrogen, low oxygen, high CO_2. Pressure is only a half bar."

"We're going to need pressure suits," Jocara said. "I've never even been on our moon, Lodan. I've never set foot on any planet but Arcan. This will be exciting for me." Her scales rippled blue.

"Drones first," said Daphne. "I think they're launching them now."

✳

The drones were invisible on the Bridge holoscreen.

"We launched about a thousand," Daphne told Jocara. "That's not very much for a planet, but they can hit the important points and confirm our orbital assessment of the atmosphere."

Kenred entered the Bridge, sweeping his tail aside as he sat next to Jocara. "Are we going to the surface?" he asked Daphne.

"Do you feel up to piloting an M-Class starship yourselves?" Daphne asked, glancing at both of them.

Both their scales rippled blue.

"Without a doubt," Jocara answered for them both.

"I want each of you to pilot a craft," Daphne said. "eDaphne will accompany you, Jocara, in a matrix onboard your craft, and eBraxton will accompany you, Kenred. Are you both okay with this arrangement?"

"Are you kidding?" Jocara nuzzled her snout against Daphne's cheek, her scales rippling bright lavender with joy. "This is wonderful!"

Kenred sat quietly, his eyes wide open, blinking slowly. Like Jocara, his scales rippled lavender.

"When do we leave?" he asked.

"We'll stage tomorrow morning," Daphne said. "I'll meet you in the vehicle bay."

✳

Daphne and Thorpe sat on the Bridge, sharing coffee and watching the vast expanse of Vulcan on the holoscreen as it passed below *Andromeda*.

"I've assigned Jocara and Kenred each to a personal M-Class," Daphne said. "As you pointed out, they're our only genuine astronauts." Her eyes twinkled. "They're both excellent pilots, and they earned their chops in the Holy War on Arcan. eDaphne will ride with Jocara and eBraxton will ride with Kenred, but I anticipate no problems. These guys are as good as they get."

"When are you staging?" Thorpe asked.

"Tomorrow morning. We'll get the drone results and analyze them overnight. This will give the M-Class pilots definite destinations. If they find anything interesting, we'll open a portal and send a team through. They'll wear pressure suits, like what you wore on Mars, with Moxie Automated Breathing Units."

"I have to believe," Thorpe said, "that we have significantly improved the MABUs since my Mars days."

"Matter of fact," Daphne said. "Given sufficient power, which we supply through a small portal, if the atmosphere contains over ten percent carbon dioxide, our MABUs can supply oxygen indefinitely."

"I think I need to get out more," Thorpe said with a wry grin.

Chapter Two

Surface of Vulcan—Keid-A

*P*S *Alan Shepard* flashed through Vulcan's upper atmosphere, dropped through the thicker layers of air, and came to rest on a flat plain near the center of Vulcan's largest continent. The M-Class starship looked much like the flying saucer illustrations from 20th Century Earth, but with a square tube extending from the front, and two large vertical oblong black plates boxing in both sides of the craft. It carried an MBH (Mini Black Hole) in its core that powered an FTL reactionless MERT Drive, artificial gravity, and a sophisticated weapons suite, along with life support and housekeeping functions.

A clamshell hatch opened near the stern, and a ramp slid to the planet's surface. The airlock emitted a hiss and a puff of moisture as it released pressure to the atmosphere. A figure appeared, dressed in a white excursion suit with a clear globe helmet, sporting a MABU like a small backpack. The front and back of the suit were stenciled POROVIK in bright international orange.

Jocara wore a skullcap with sensors transmitting vital information back to *Shepard*. The suit was far more comfortable than the bulky spacesuits she and Kenred wore during their circum-Lodan voyage, which seemed so very long ago.

Keid-A, blazing orange, and seeming a bit larger than Ran from the surface of Arcan, was high in the nearly cloudless, pale blue, slightly pinkish sky.

Jocara looked around, trying to spot the pattern she had seen from the air. Nothing jumped out. She had expected to see faint lines running north–south and east–west. Nothing obvious from ground level, but clearly visible, almost as a grid from 500 meters. Beyond that, she saw nothing, no plants, no rocky ledges, no hills, just a sandy light brown plain.

"eDaphne, do you see anything?" she asked the upload inside the matrix in her craft.

Sounding just like Daphne, eDaphne's voice resonated in her helmet. "Nothing jumps out, even with a wider color spectrum than you can see." After a brief pause, "I just checked the record. It's definitely visible from five hundred meters."

"Okay, let's establish a portal and let the experts have a go at it."

Jocara activated her internal Link. "Kenred, have you found anything?"

"Saw a vague grid pattern from the air, but when we landed for a closer look, we found nothing. I placed a portal for the archaeologists."

"Me too. See you back on *Andromeda*." Jocara walked down the ramp with a hyper-disk in hand and casually dropped the disk on the dry surface.

✳

After his conversation with Jocara, Kenred returned to *PS Neil Armstrong*, and lifted several kilometers into the Vulcan sky.

"I want to check something that caught my eye as we were landing," he told eBraxton. "It looked like a long straight line heading due east from near our landing spot."

"You're right," eBraxton told him. "I see it on the record. If the pattern had been a city, this might be a road."

"Let's see where it goes," Kenred said, giving Mother the appropriate instructions.

After several minutes of flight following the faint line, another barely visible pattern appeared.

"We've been following an artifact road connecting two artifact cities," eBraxton said. "I'd lay money on it."

"The disk we already left will get the archaeologists to the road as well," Kenred said. "Let's head back to *Andromeda*."

PS Andromeda—In Orbit around Vulcan, Keid-A

Except for the faintest hints that were visible only from the air, the *Andromeda* archaeological teams found no evidence of a past civilization on Vulcan's surface. The teams investigated over thirty sites identified by the drones, finding nothing on the ground that pointed to potential artifacts.

Daphne sat with Thorpe on the Bridge, reviewing the data as they arrived.

"I wouldn't call myself an expert on planetary archaeology," she said, "but this is really strange. We see faint patterns from the air that completely disappear when we check them out." She paused in thought. "What do you think about this?"

"The data are what they are," Thorpe said. "We've had too many ground checks for there to be an observation or sampling error. I think we are looking at shading differences, shades so close they appear the same upon close-up examination."

"What do you make of the patterns?"

"Where towns used to be, perhaps…very long ago."

"The straight lines could be the remnants of highways."

"Or rail lines," Thorpe added, "or even some other mode of transportation."

They sat quietly for several minutes, watching Vulcan's nearly featureless landscape pass below—barren hills and low mountains, lifeless plains with shallow river valleys flowing into oceans that might or might not harbor life.

"The ground teams are collecting soil samples," Daphne said. "We should have the lab data in a few hours."

✳

Later that day, Daphne pulled up a detailed analysis of the samples collected that morning from locations across the planet. She and Thorpe examined the results on the Bridge holoscreen.

"These are what I expected," Daphne said, pointing to the first set of numbers. "It's what we generally find on lifeless planets—like what you found on Mars before it was terraformed."

"Look at this," Thorpe said, pointing to the lithium entry. "That's twice as high as one would normally expect."

"And plutonium two-forty-four," Daphne said. "Its half-life is eighty million years, so why is the level so high? Vulcan is a couple billion years old. Plutonium two-forty-four level should be almost nothing."

"I have some thoughts on that," Thorpe said. He pulled up a holoimage of Vulcan. "Mother, select fifty sites around Vulcan that are as evenly distributed on the land masses as possible."

Glowing red dots appeared evenly spaced on the holoimage land masses. Each dot displayed a number.

"Have your teams collect a sample at each of these sites," Thorpe said. "Don't lose track of the source for each sample. Run an analysis for just lithium and plutonium two-forty-four. When you've completed the analysis, display the results on the holoimage, red for plutonium and blue for lithium, with the amount indicated by intensity."

✳

Collecting and analyzing the samples took two days. Daphne met Thorpe on the Bridge the following morning. The holoimage of Vulcan, with its glowing red and blue spots, floated in the air over the control console.

"What do you know," Daphne said, pointing to a spot on the largest continent near the equator. "They're brightest here and fade to almost nothing at the edge of the planet all around."

"What does that mean to you?" Thorpe asked.

"Incoming charged particles, probably moving at high speed." She paused, obviously checking her internal Link. "Couldn't be Keid-A. There's no record of a nova." She paused again. "Keid-B went nova a hundred million years ago." She looked at Thorpe, eyes twinkling. "Mother, display Keid-A, B and C, and Vulcan as they were one hundred million years ago—at the time of the Keid-B nova."

The holoimage image shifted, with Keid-A relatively smaller than its current size, Vulcan significantly enlarged, and both Keid-B and C off to the right.

"Add animation and annotation," Daphne ordered.

Keid-B flashed brightly, and the radiation front passed Vulcan and Keid-A. Vulcan was off to one side of Keid-A when the front arrived. The note said 2.31 days. The charged particle front left Keid-B with the radiation front, but took 103 days to travel the 400 astronomical units. It arrived when Vulcan was directly between Keid-A and B, with the point of highest intensity of lithium and plutonium 244 pointed directly at Keid-B.

"There's our answer," Daphne said. "Mother, how large was Keid-B before the nova?"

"About Sol size," Mother answered. "It's about one and a half Earth sizes now."

"Assuming it was a typical Main Sequence star, calculate the plutonium two-forty-four flux at Vulcan and apply the eighty-million-year half-life to the residue then, to determine the time to get the current residue."

"That would be one hundred million years," Mother intoned.

Surface of Vulcan—Keid-A

Jocara and Kenred met Daphne on the Bridge the following morning. She showed them the animated holoimage of the nova.

"So, you can see," Daphne told them, "the charged particle front struck Vulcan here, and apparently wiped out whatever used to be here." She pointed to the opposite side of the planet, near the center of the smallest continent. "This region probably would have suffered far less damage. I want you two to investigate this region with *Shepard*. Look for artifacts or any sign of civilization."

✳

Jocara and Kenred headed for the bay with Kenred carrying eDaphne in her matrix. They boarded *Shepard* and plugged eDaphne into the rack.

eDaphne's holoimage appeared beside them. "I've been doing this for a long time, but I never get used to the confinement of the portable matrix."

Jocara looked at her with warmth.

"I need to remind you I am not Daphne. We diverged long ago and think of ourselves as close sisters, but we've each developed our own goals, dreams, and friendships."

Jocara's face drooped in an almost Human fashion, and her scales rippled pink.

"I'm sorry, Jocara," eDaphne said. "I didn't mean to imply that we could not be friends. It's just that your friendship with Daphne does not automatically roll over to me. We need to do that on our own."

Jocara's scales faded from pink to their normal light green. "Fair enough," she said. "If you are anything like Daphne, we'll become close friends."

Kenred slipped an arm around Jocara's shoulders. "Okay, Guys, enough schmaltz! Let's get this heap underway."

"*Heap*," eDaphne said. "*Heap!* This is the finest M-Class starship in existence." She smiled warmly at Kenred. "You and I will get along just fine."

Jocara offered a saurian giggle as they took their places at the control console. *Heap, indeed*, she thought. *It's just the finest small starship ever.*

There was no need to evacuate the bay and move *Shepard* into the vacuum outside *Andromeda*. Jocara gave the parameters to Mother, who set up the leapfrog wormhole sequence that, in a fraction of a second, brought *Shepard* to a hover 500 meters above their intended landing spot.

"Mother," Jocara said, "conduct a surface survey of a hundred square kilometers centered on our present position."

"You've definitely got the moves, Girl," eDaphne told her.

Shepard moved back and forth across the grid until Mother had thoroughly mapped the hundred square kilometers below them.

"Nothing," Kenred said. "Let's move up to five kilometers."

Jocara complied and commenced a wider search.

"There!" eDaphne said, pointing to the northeast corner of the grid. "That's definitely something."

Jocara vectored to the location and deftly landed the ten-meter craft with its black vertical wings and odd eight-meter bow extension.

"There's something out there," Jocara said. "It didn't disappear when we got close."

Jocara and Kenred donned their excursion suits. Oddly, eDaphne's holoimage suddenly was dressed in an excursion suit as well.

"I'll join you outside," eDaphne said. "My suiting up makes the illusion of my physical presence more realistic. It just makes interactions better."

They passed through the lock and moved down the ramp onto the hard, dusty surface. Off to their right, several intersecting low mounds caught their attention.

"Mother," eDaphne said, "give us a holoimage from above, of what we are looking at over here. Emphasize the contrast."

An image appeared in the air in front of them, displaying an orderly pattern of squares and rectangles separated at intervals by strips that intersected at right angles.

"These are buildings and streets," Jocara said.

"Hardly anything left," Kenred added. "Destroyed a very long time ago."

"I think we know how long ago," eDaphne said.

PS Andromeda—In Orbit around Vulcan, Keid-A

Thorpe called the meeting to order. Flesh-and-blood Humans, Asterians, and Arcans occupied every chair around the conference table. Several upload holoimages floated in the air behind them. Max, Daphne's gray tabby cat, strolled stiff-tailed across the table, greeting his friends. eMax curled up on the table next to Thorpe taking a mid-morning nap.

"We've collected a lot of data," Thorpe said. "Let's try to construct a coherent picture." He turned to Chief Scientist Daphne O'Bryan.

"We commenced our activities on Vulcan with a drone survey," Daphne said. Then she reviewed what the various teams had accomplished, the data they had collected, and the samples they had retrieved. She discussed the odd *we see them from the air, but not on the ground* patterns. "The peculiar distribution of lithium and plutonium two-forty-four gave us our first significant clue," she said, "that led us to the still recognizable ruins on the small continent."

"We don't know who lived here," Thorpe said, "and whether they evolved here or arrived from somewhere else, but here is what we do know.

"Civilization had spread across Vulcan over a hundred million years ago. We think it was advanced, because some of their structures are still visible today, a hundred million years later. I think we can assume they were a spacefaring civilization.

"You all know that Keid is actually a three-star system. Keid-A, where we are now, is an orange Main Sequence star similar to Sol or Ran. Some four hundred AUs distant, Keid-B and C orbit about each other eccentrically at an average of thirty-five AUs. B is a white dwarf, and C is a red dwarf. A hundred million years ago, B was a Main Sequence star similar in size and luminosity to Sol and Ran. It went nova. About two and a half days later, the radiation front hit Vulcan—that's the first indication of the nova the Vulcan inhabitants had.

"Assuming their spacefaring nature, the Vulcans knew they had about one hundred days to reach safety. Their calculations would have told them that the charged particle front would hit their planet full on. It would strip most of their atmosphere and destroy their civilization.

"One hundred days…that's all they had."

Thorpe sat at the head of the conference table in silence, letting each person absorb the awful truth. After a brief interval, he continued.

"We don't know if they left Vulcan, and if so, how many? We don't know if they stayed and perished. All we know is they were here, and now they are not here. And the Keid-B nova destroyed their planet."

The people around the table sat in stunned silence.

After allowing a few moments of quiet discussion among the attendees, Thorpe concluded the meeting. "I think it's time to turn our attention elsewhere. In several hours, we will depart for Keid-B.

Our preliminary indications are that B has several planets. We intend to spend some time learning more about them."

✳

Five hours later, Jocara, Kenred, and Daphne met Thorpe on the Bridge.

"Kenred," Thorpe said, "last time you graciously let Jocara take the lead. Will you do the honors this time, please?"

Chapter Three

PS Andromeda—Underway for Keid-B and C

"Mother," Kenred said, "transit to the star Keid-B, jump interval six picoseconds, specific destination, the outer edge of Keid-B's life zone."

One moment, Keid-A filled the holoscreen, visually a bit larger than Sol or Ran. The next, the white dwarf Keid-B showed at only 30 percent the size of their home suns.

"Keid-B's actual diameter," Thorpe said, "is just under twenty-eight thousand kilometers. That's barely two percent of Sol or Ran. Their life zone is around a hundred fifty million klicks, an AU, whereas Keid-B's is centered around nine million." He turned around to find he had an audience of as many crew members that could comfortably fit on the Bridge—and who had nothing better to do. "But, this is now. Before Keid-B went nova, it had an entirely different life zone. Any planets in that zone would not be in today's zone. Kenred, move us out another fifty million klicks to give us some room. Let's find some planets."

*

Kenred moved *Andromeda* outward to fifty million kilometers. Following the pattern Jocara had used on Keid-A, he set a velocity of 5,000 kilometers per second and turned *Andromeda* to the search. Four and a half hours later, Mother announced she had located one planet and two rocky rings.

PS Andromeda—Keid-B Space

"Put us in orbit around the one planet," Thorpe told Kenred.

The lone planet orbited Keid-B at 0.06 AU—just under nine million kilometers. *Andromeda* settled into a circular orbit 1,000 kilometers above the surface.

"It looks like the planet is uniformly covered with gray clouds," Kenred said.

"Look again," Thorpe said. "That's not cloud cover, that's the planet's surface."

"It's almost like a smooth ball with no significant relief that I can see," Kenred said. "Do you think the nova did this?"

"That's my guess," Thorpe said. "When the star left the Main Sequence, it lost at least fifty percent of its mass. The blast stripped this planet of its atmosphere, crust, mantle, and probably part of its outer core. What you see is the remainder. Those rings may be other planets that were completely destroyed."

"There's absolutely nothing down there," Jocara said as she scanned the holoscreen.

"Humans play a game," Daphne said, "that uses a smooth hard ball called a bowling ball. That planet looks like a large bowling ball." She had Mother place one on the holoscreen. "See what I mean?"

✳

"We're here," Thorpe said. "Let's do an orbital survey before we move on."

Daphne placed four survey drones in polar orbit. "The planet is tidally locked, but its orbital period is just eight days, so we'll get full coverage in about a day."

"That will collect enough data to keep the planetary geologists on Earth and Arcan busy for a long time," Thorpe said. "Data about a nova-stripped planet are nonexistent."

"You can count Roganian geologists in that group as well," Daphne added.

✳

Toward the end of the orbital survey, well into *Andromeda's* night period, the Bridge watch called Thorpe. "Something unusual is happening on the planet. You need to get here."

Thorpe stepped through a portal that connected his quarters with the Bridge, followed by eMax who usually could be found somewhere near Thorpe or eThorpe.

"What is it?" he asked.

"A crack just appeared across the southern half of the planet. Our drones seem to be losing orbital stability."

"Mother," Thorpe ordered, "retrieve the drones and move *Andromeda* out to one hundred thousand kilometers from the planet."

Using his internal Link, he called Daphne. "You want to be on the Bridge," he told her.

Daphne stepped through her portal. "What's up?"

Thorpe pointed to the holoscreen. The crack had branched, spreading rapidly across the northern hemisphere.

Daphne did a quick calculation. "Those cracks are moving faster than the speed of sound in that planetary material, no matter what it is," she said.

As they watched, the small planet separated into several large chunks that continued to crumble and spread behind the planet's orbit.

"What's that?" Thorpe asked, pointing to one small chunk that appeared to be moving at a right angle to the planet's orbit, radially outward from Keid-B.

"Mother," Daphne said, "generate all available parameters on the chunk moving radially away from Keid-B, and describe it in detail."

About fifteen minutes later, one holoscreen filled with an image of a planetary chunk about the size of *Andromeda*. A second screen showed it was accelerating at nearly one-tenth gee along a vector on the ecliptic formed by the orbits of Keid-B and C around each other. Mother assumed the constant acceleration would reverse to deceleration at the midpoint between the two stars, which placed the chunk at the location of Keid-C when it reached zero velocity.

"That's not possible," Daphne said.

"But that's what's happening," Thorpe said. "Possible or not, that's what Mother measured." He shook his head in amazement. "Something broke up the planet, and something is moving that chunk toward Keid-C."

PS *Andromeda*—Keid-B Space

Without warning, alarms sounded throughout the vast expanse of *Andromeda*. The sound was penetrating, pulsing, warbling—impossible to ignore. Thorpe stepped through a portal onto the Bridge.

"Mother, what's the problem?"

"*Andromeda* is under attack from all directions! Something is eroding the outside surface of the central disk and trying to attack the dome surfaces. It behaves like an acid dissolving the surface."

"Nullspace loop right now!" Thorpe ordered.

The Bridge holoscreen went blank.

"The external activity has stopped," Mother reported.

Kenred, who had come to the Bridge when he heard the alarms, asked, "What's a nullspace loop?"

Daphne stepped up to him, speaking quietly. "You understand the concept of the MERT Drive, right? Two MERT portals moving though each other in leapfrog fashion? A nullspace loop goes forward and then backward at the programmed jump interval. The ship remains where it is, but stays in nullspace. It's no longer visible to the outside universe. Thorpe put *Andromeda* in a nullspace loop, hoping whatever is attacking cannot survive nullspace."

"Will it work?" Kenred asked.

"Who knows?" she said. "Thorpe gave that order on instinct. He's usually right. Let's see what happens."

"Shut down the alarms," Thorpe said with raised voice and irritated tone.

As the warbling shriek died down, Thorpe calmed himself visibly and ordered, "Drop out of nullspace loop just long enough to determine whether the problem is gone."

The holoscreen flashed and returned to gray. Max stuck his head through a portal, checking the landscape, and then cautiously stepped onto the Bridge.

Mother reported, "When we dropped out of nullspace loop, the attack did not recommence."

"Okay," Thorpe said, "drop out of nullspace loop but return if there is any hint of another attack."

The holoscreen flashed and displayed Keid-B on one section, the shattered planet on another, and the space around *Andromeda* on the rest.

Using his internal Link to make a general call, Thorpe announced, "Chief Engineer to the Bridge, Chief Engineer to the Bridge."

Moments later, Ustrun Strozid, *Andromeda's* Roganian Chief Engineer, strode through a portal. He was shorter than Kenred, with a stocky build. His nose looked Human but was flatter, and he lacked Human lips. Oddly, his ears were higher on his head than Humans or Arcans and resembled cat ears, rotating to locate a sound source.

"What is it, Captain? We're kinda busy in Engineering right now."

"I know. I won't keep you. I want you to send a small team outside so we have some eyeballs on our problem. I think we're dealing with a swarm of some kind. No clue what it is yet. Make sure your guys carry E-disks, and have them bail out at the first sign of trouble."

Before Strozid could leave, Mother announced, "We're being hit again!" The Bridge holoscreen flashed to gray as the ship entered a nullspace loop again, and Max scampered back through a portal.

"Ready your team," Thorpe said, "but wait for my signal before sending them out."

"You got it!" Strozid said as he ran through the portal to Engineering.

✳

Jocara joined Kenred near the back of the Bridge, keeping out of the way.

"What's going on?" she asked and looked down to find Max purring and rubbing her leg.

"Something attacked *Andromeda*," Kenred answered. "Nothing obvious, nothing visible on the screens. Twice, now, actually."

"Is that why we're in a nullspace loop?"

"How do you know about that? I just learned about it here on the Bridge a few minutes ago." Kenred's scales briefly rippled yellow with irritation.

"Daphne explained the nullspace loop to me some time ago. These aliens sure have some amazing technology."

"I wish I could help in some way," Kenred said.

"Best we stay out of the way and learn," Jocara said. "They're pretty busy right now." Her scales rippled faint blue.

❋

Strozid assembled a four-person team near the Engineering airlock—two Humans and two Asterians. The team was unarmed.

"Show me your E-disks," Strozid said.

Each member held up his E-disk.

"You are not armed, because your job is to observe. Something is attacking *Andromeda*, and we have no idea what it is. Go out, inspect, and return. If you see anything out of the ordinary, activate your E-disks. Whatever it may be is not obvious and moves fast. Okay, assemble in the airlock, and be ready to deploy on a moment's notice."

The team entered the airlock and evacuated it, standing by to open the outer hatch.

"Okay, Chief Engineer," Thorpe called over his private Link, "we've dropped out of nullspace. Away the team."

Strozid signaled his team, and they opened the outer hatch. The four team members, accompanied by a small drone, left the lock into freefall. Strozid followed their activity on an Engineering holoscreen fed by the drone. The Bridge also received a feed.

The hatch was in the central disk near the cityscape side of *Andromeda*. One of the team activated his TBH boots and moved toward the cityscape dome to examine it. The other three jetted along the central disk using their TBH boots.

❋

On the Bridge, Kenred looked at Jocara. "Did Daphne tell you how they propel themselves? That looks a lot simpler than our Space Mobility Units."

"She did," Jocara said. "They're using TBH boots, named after the Humans who developed them in the early days of Human spaceflight—David Thomas, John Bird, and Richard Hellbaum. They fit like calf boots, but with completely flexible ankles. The boot uppers are two stiff, shaped polymer bags containing pressurized hypergolic fuel components. The toe of each boot contains a microswitch that controls a fuel valve. Each boot produces ten newtons of force. The wearer bends the knees for appropriate thrust vectors."

"We could have used those on our early space walks," Kenred said. "I can't wait to try them out."

"Right now, we have to survive these attacks," Jocara said, looking at the drone feed.

Four engineering team members were scrambling for the lock. As three got there, the straggler disappeared in a dark cloud. That's when the external holoscreen flashed to gray as Mother dropped into a nullspace loop again.

✳

The Engineering inner lock opened and three spacesuited people tumbled out.

"Engineering, this is Medical. Your fourth team member just arrived here by E-disk. He was covered with what looked like dust mites. Within a minute of his arrival, they all fell off. We collected and isolated them. Your guy's suit sustained damage, but his E-disk brought him here before he was seriously injured."

PS Andromeda—Keid-B Space

Chief Engineer Ustrun Strozid gathered the four team members in his office. Otiz, the injured Asterian, had several vacuum bruises on his legs, but was otherwise fit for duty. Thorpe and Daphne joined them.

"Things are moving pretty fast," Thorpe said. "What can you tell us?"

Jerad, one of the Humans, took the lead. "We split up when we exited the lock. Otiz went to the cityscape dome, Joe headed toward the landscape dome, Forbis headed west—left facing the cityscape dome, and I headed the other way—east. The central disk surface is corroded as if it had been in a sandstorm. Joe and Forbis saw the same thing." They both nodded. "Otiz, tell them about the dome."

"Little pits here and there, but without the sandstorm effect the others saw. I guess the dome material is a lot harder." He looked at the Chief Engineer. "When Engineer Strozid told us to pull back, I was farther away from the lock than the others. One moment I was jetting toward the lock, the next, dust mite-size things completely covered me and started consuming my suit." He spread his arms over his legs. "I guess that's when my E-disk took me to Medical." He leaned back in his chair. "They ate through my suit legs in a couple of places…gave me these." He displayed the vacuum bruises on his legs. "They fell off me in Medical. Doc Dobson has them isolated."

✳

Thorpe, Daphne, and Strozid went to Medical. Dobson had greatly enlarged one mite on a holoscreen.

"It's about thrice the size of a dust mite, a millimeter by a half or so, weighs a milligram, and it looks a bit like a mite, too." He pointed to six tiny legs. "Mouth here…" He pointed to one end. "And here's where it's totally different." He pointed to a miniature jet nozzle at the other end. "This thing is a mechanical bot—a microbot that dissolves stuff at one end, uses part of that for propulsion, and delivers the rest."

"*Delivers*…what do you mean, *delivers*?" Thorpe asked.

"I don't have any idea how this thing turns what it eats into jet fuel, but *jet* implies going somewhere, so what's left over must be delivered there." Dobson looked Thorpe in the eye. "You got a better idea?"

"What killed it?" Daphne asked.

"Not alive, so didn't get *killed*," Dobson said, "but something shut it down. Only environmental difference is air and pressure. I'm guessing a combination of one or the other."

✳

On the Bridge again, Thorpe leaned back in his Captain's Chair contemplating his options.

There's so much to see and learn here that we could take several years just to record it all, he thought. What really intrigues me, however, are the microbots taking this system apart and moving it to Keid-C. What's going on there to generate such activity? I think we need to head to Keid-C to find out. We can always return if there's nothing there.

Thorpe played back the images of the planet splitting apart and one section moving off toward Keid-C. Then he watched it again. And then he decided.

Chapter Four

PS *Andromeda*—Underway for Keid-C

"I'll do the honors," Jocara said.

Andromeda was already in a nullspace loop, so all she had to do was set the destination, just forty AUs distant, and take it out of the loop. The starship arrived in the Keid-C system less than one-tenth of a second later. The Bridge holoscreen displayed a dull red star with virtually no surface definition. Under Thorpe's guidance, Jocara put *Andromeda* into an orbit twenty-five million kilometers from the star's center.

"Have Mother collect as much data as possible for five hours," Thorpe told Jocara. "Then do a circular transit at five thousand kilometers per second to locate any inner planets. Be sure to keep a lookout for microbots. That bunch pushing the planet chunk was headed this way. That implies there are plenty more somewhere in this system."

The five hours passed uneventfully as Mother accumulated data about Keid-C. Nine hours later, Jocara reported to Thorpe, "Mother found no inner planets. In fact, Mother found nothing at all—no asteroids, no comets, no moons, none of the normally expected planetary junk. What do you make of that?"

"I dunno," Thorpe answered, "but I suspect we'll learn soon enough."

PS Andromeda—Keid-C Space

Thorpe was on the Bridge along with every other crew member who had the time. Jocara sat to his left, with Kenred standing behind her. Daphne sat to his right. Kimberly stood behind her, massaging her shoulders gently. eThorp's holoimage stood off to one side. Mother had just started displaying the data she had collected.

"Diameter nine point four million kilometers?" Jocara said with wonder in her voice. "That's not possible. This is a red dwarf," she added as her scales faded to pale yellow.

The numbers, however, stared her and everyone else in their faces.

"We're looking at a solid surface here, people," Thorpe said. "Mother, look more closely at the IR distribution around the sphere."

"IR radiation is virtually the same everywhere," Mother said, "except for a one-point-five-million-kilometer-wide band around the equator. This band's IR radiation is a small fraction of everywhere else."

"Listen up, people," eThorpe said. "You all know that I am virtually everywhere in *Andromeda* all the time. Remember that I have access to every database on *Andromeda*, which allows me to make connections quickly. This isn't a star as we normally think of one. This is a sphere enveloping a star. Wrap your minds around this, folks. We are looking at a Dyson Sphere."

Mother interrupted eThorpe. "This is not a complete sphere. An open gash runs from the north pole to the equatorial band. The western edge of the gash appears to be jagged, whereas the eastern edge appears smooth and finished."

"What's a Dyson Sphere?" Jocara asked no one in particular.

Thorpe answered. "A while back in Human history, an astrophysicist named Freeman Dyson postulated that a planetary civilization would eventually reach the limit of energy production its home planet could provide. To advance further, a civilization would have to capture significant additional energy from its star, and eventually, all the energy its star produced. To do this, it would have to enclose its star in a sphere. This came to be called a Dyson Sphere."

The Bridge was silent as watchstanders and visitors contemplated this concept.

"eThorpe, you think this is what we have here?" Jocara asked.

"I do," eThorpe said. "It's the only explanation that fits the data."

"We are passing over the open gash right now," Mother announced.

PS Andromeda—Keid-C Space

The holoscreen displayed the open gash like a gaping maw in an otherwise smooth sphere surface. As they watched, a dark cloud rose from the western edge, heading toward *Andromeda*. It measured at least 1,000 kilometers long and 500 wide. As it moved, it changed to a spherical shape.

"What is the cloud's distance?" Thorpe asked.

"About a million kilometers," Mother answered.

"Is it accelerating or at constant velocity?"

"It accelerated for five minutes at about a tenth gee. It has coasted since."

"How long till it gets here?"

"Just over thirty-nine days."

"On that assumption, what is its velocity?"

"About a half kilometer per second."

"What if the bots just continue accelerating at one-tenth gee?" Thorpe asked.

"I don't think they can do that," Mother said. "They would run out of fuel."

Thorpe called Medical on his Link. "Doc, what would it take to crack the casing on one of those bots?"

"I tried smacking one with a hammer. I'm guessing the hammer head was moving at twenty meters per second. That would have produced about a thousand newtons. Nothing happened. What would it take? I really have no idea. Perhaps the Chief Engineer can come up with something."

Thorpe put a call to the Chief Engineer. "Ustrun, can you join me on the Bridge for a few minutes?"

When Strozid arrived, Thorpe explained the situation to him and then asked, "Can you determine how much impact these little buggers can take? We have a thirty-nine-day window before we need to take evasive action, so you have time."

✳

Strozid called his management team together. Each member was an expert in one or more disciplines and had years of both research and management experience.

"You've all seen these microbots. You know what they can do, even if we do not yet understand how. We want to learn what impact pressure will disable these guys. Our initial assumption is that if we crack the shell, the bot is disabled. We have a few days to supply an answer, so assemble your teams and see what you can find out."

Strozid had a lot of faith in his people. He first met Thorpe and his team when they visited his project on Difecta, the fifth moon of the gas giant orbiting just beyond Aster's asteroid belt. He and his people had generated a three-kilometer-wide black hole at the moon's core. When Thorpe and Holon Mavik decided to build *Andromeda*, Mavik suggested Strozid as Chief Engineer. He still remembered Thorpe's comment when he joined the crew. "I couldn't have found a better engineer than the man who ran the Difecta black hole project," Thorpe had said.

Strozid brought all his top people to *Andromeda*, and Thorpe supplied a team of his best. Together, Strozid's Engineering Department boasted the finest group of engineering talent in three star systems. He was confident they would find an answer.

Several days later, his team leaders approached him together, all smiles. They displayed a chart on Strozid's holodisplay that showed the series of tests they had run on their hydraulic press using Doc's samples. The shells cracked at 200 kilonewtons.

Strozid headed for the Bridge portal.

✳

Strozid and Thorpe stood together in front of the Control Console looking at the holoimage of the report.

"What are these bots made of?" Thorpe asked.

"Q-carbon coated carbynophene—basically, graphene sheets separated by short pieces of carbyne. This stuff is two hundred times harder than steel, and it weighs almost nothing. They are little carbynophene cylinders with rounded ends and six double-walled carbon nanotube legs with a tensile strength one hundred times that of steel. The legs have needle-sharp hooks, and they're so hard, they can glom onto almost anything."

"If the bot swarm headed our way keeps accelerating until it arrives," Thorpe said, "the bots will be moving at one hundred seventy-one kilometers per second. What would happen if they hit at that speed?"

"They'll just bounce off, unharmed. But they cannot accelerate continuously. With a full load of fuel, a bot can accelerate for five minutes or so." Strozid pointed to a graph on the holoscreen. "Their shells crack at two hundred kilonewtons. They're so small and light that even striking *Andromeda* at one hundred seventy-one kilometers per second, they would produce less than a newton."

✳

I've got this magnificent ship, probably the best senior crew in the universe, ten thousand people, and a one-millimeter mechanical bot has me stumped, Thorpe thought as he watched the swarm draw closer.

"Braxton to the Bridge, Braxton to the Bridge." Thorpe accessed the general announcing system with his internal Link. "Doctors Daphne O'Bryan, Dale Ryan, Sally Nguyen, Brad Kominsky, and Chief Engineer Ustrun Strozid, to the Bridge." On his internal Link he sent a special message, "eThorpe, eBraxton, eDaphne, eDale, eSally, and eBrad, attend me please."

Thorpe occupied the Captain's Chair, an elevated, adjustable chair that gave him a full view of the Bridge. Braxton and the others stepped through portals and placed themselves near Thorpe. Even though Thorpe had long experience interacting with uploads and had dealt with them in any imaginable configuration, each upload appeared as a holoimage standing around Thorpe's chair. Max showed up, rubbing legs where possible and seemingly deliberately walking through holoimage legs.

"We're meeting here instead of the conference room, because I may need to take immediate evasive action," Thorpe said, "You are all familiar with what's going on. I want your counsel on how to deal with this. We have a sense of what these guys do, but we don't have an active unit to investigate."

While they discussed among themselves, Thorpe moved *Androm-eda* out another half million kilometers to give them additional time to look at their options.

Diminutive Sally Nguyen was the first to speak up. "If we can capture several bots in a stasis field, we might keep one viable long enough to learn something useful." She smiled shyly, holding a hand in front of her mouth.

The group thought that was a good idea and started discussing how to accomplish it. Thorpe checked the holoscreen and noted the swarm distance. It was still closing at a half kilometer per second. He held up a hand.

"That half million kilometers gives us more time. You're cluttering up the Bridge. Find a place to discuss the matter. I'll join you shortly."

✳

The group met in the conference room. Flesh-and-blood folks sat in chairs around the table. Uploads filled in the spaces, their holoimages appearing to be seated. Max joined them, walking the length of the table, tail stiff in the air, greeting each person, flesh-and-blood or holoimage, as he passed. Braxton took charge of the meeting.

"Sally has given us something to work with. Most of you know that our stasis field generators are an integral part of our radar systems. What is the ideal range to put part of a swarm into stasis?"

"Anywhere between a hundred and a thousand klicks," Brad said.

"Why?" Braxton asked.

"We lose resolution beyond a thousand klicks, and inside a hundred, things can get a bit messy."

"Sally and Brad and their uploads are responsible for reverse engineering the Asterian stasis engines—with their approval," Braxton nodded at Strozid, "and incorporating them into Phoenix Starship radar systems. Between them, they know as much about stasis systems as anybody, even Asterians."

Braxton looked around the table as Thorpe entered the room through a portal. He rose to give his chair to the captain, but Thorpe waved him back and took a chair next to him.

"You've got things in hand. If I have questions, I'll ask."

Braxton continued. "Are there any other suggested approaches?" When no one spoke, he said, "Okay, then, Sally, you take charge and find a way to capture some of these bots." He looked at Thorpe.

"We have a month," Thorpe said, "but I want a solution as quickly as you can find one."

✳

"We can place a chunk of bot swarm into stasis," Brad said. "With some adjustment to generate a much smaller stasis sphere than normal—say, basketball size —we will have something we can manipulate. Something in the air disables them—we don't know what yet. We will need to build a vacuum chamber sufficiently large to contain the stasis sphere. Assuming they will attack the walls of that chamber, we'll need to place it inside another filled with air."

"How do you plan to manipulate the sphere and its contents?" Dale asked.

"How about a remote controlled waldo?" eDale suggested.

"How long would it last once we release the stasis?" eDaphne wanted to know.

Brad answered. "Depends on what it's made of." He looked around the table. "These guys are made of carbynophene. If we construct the waldo of the same stuff, it should slow them down.".

"We're gonna need some time," Strozid said. "My guys are good, but this is a real challenge."

"We'll monitor the swarm range from the Bridge." Thorpe said. "If it gets too close, we may have to leave the system for a while, so they'll give up and return to their stomping ground."

A chuckle sounded around the table.

"I'm on it," Strozid said, getting to his feet.

PS Andromeda—Keid-B Space

As the clock pushed forward, Strozid called Thorpe on his internal Link.

"This is going to take a lot longer than I first thought, Captain—several days, at least. Working with carbynophene is tricky at best, but then coating it with Q-carbon…well let's just say we're inventing several new manufacturing concepts at each step." He paused. "And before you ask, yes, we're using a Nanocosm. But until we develop the new procedures, we can't program them into the device."

"Thanks. We'll exit the Keid-C system and hang out until you have what you need."

"Mother, take us to Keid-B in a ten-million-kilometer orbit. Use the time to collect data from the star."

With virtually no delay, the Bridge screens displayed the white dwarf Keid-B, and Mother began to collect data.

"We have several days down time," Thorpe said over the general announcing system. "If you are not otherwise occupied, take some personal time to enjoy all that this marvelous starship has to offer. Explore the woodland side, if that's your thing, or discover a hidden downtown restaurant. This ship will be your home for a long time. Take advantage of her whenever you can."

Thorpe settled onto his Bridge chair, idly keeping an eye on the holoscreen when Mother announced, "A microbot swarm is approaching from the orbit of the destroyed planet at three thousand kilometers. It will arrive in two hours and fifty minutes."

✳

Thorpe called the Chief Engineer. "Ustrun, what is the status of your project?"

"If you are trying to hurry me, Boss, it won't work. We still need at least a couple days."

"I'm just trying to get the most use out of our stay in Keid-B space. We've got a swarm moving toward us. I want to position *Andromeda* so Mother can collect the maximum amount of data. Keep me informed." Thorpe turned his attention to the holoscreen. "Mother, position us at the L3 point for Keid-B and the destroyed planet."

Andromeda arrived moments later. Mother reported no nearby swarms.

"Check the nearest rocky ring with your long-range radar," Thorpe ordered.

Several minutes passed while the radar beam made its way out and back, and then an image began to form on the holoscreen.

"Do you have sufficient resolution to distinguish rock from microbot?" Thorpe asked.

"Not for individual microbots, but certainly for a swarm several hundred kilometers across."

After about a half hour, Mother reported, "I have identified three swarms in the rocky ring. They are fully occupied—apparently scavenging raw material from the ring."

While Thorpe contemplated the matter, eThorpe appeared as a holoimage sitting in a chair similar to Thorpe's, raised to the same height.

"What a series of unexpected events," eThorpe said. "If that really is a Dyson Sphere, and it sure looks like it, I want to enter its internal system as soon as we can make it happen. We're talking a Type Two Civilization here, but where the hell are they? It's almost as if the whole thing is running on automatic with nobody supervising."

"Since we separated years ago," Thorpe said, "I haven't really given Dyson Spheres any thought—zero, nada."

"Yeah, me too," eThorpe said. "Matters on Ran kept us pretty busy, and before that, it was terraforming Mars, going to Aster, fighting Orlov, and building *Andromeda*. Not bad for a couple of twenty-first century engineers. Do you miss not being an upload?"

"Sometimes, but being flesh-and-blood has its advantages."

While they conversed, Daphne stepped through a portal to the Bridge.

"Are you two reminiscing?" she asked.

They both grinned at her. "Consulting, actually," Thorpe said.

"Are you ready for dinner?" she asked Thorpe.

He winked at eThorpe. "See what I mean?"

✳

Several days later, Strozid's team leader, Bolaik Taclit, asked him to come to the lab. An articulating silvery-colored crane-like device sat on the bench. Near it floated a holoscreen displaying an enlarged view of the crane's tip, which was really two arms with four 100-micron-long fingers and opposing thumbs each.

"Slip your hands into these," Taclit said, indicating glove-like devices attached to a box. "Move your fingers. Get used to it."

Strozid did, and it was amazing. A pipe with a width half the length of his fingers lay on the surface.

"Pick it up," Taclit said. "It's a Human hair."

Strozid touched the hair with a finger and felt feedback through his glove. He picked up the hair. He could feel it as if he were actually holding the hair. He squeezed the hair between his forefinger and thumb—it snapped in two. He felt the impact of the break.

"What's it made of?" he asked.

"Carbynophene with a Q-carbon coating. Hardest stuff anyone's ever made."

Strozid called Thorpe. "Can you come to Engineering for a demonstration?"

Five minutes later, Thorpe thrust his hands into the same glove-like devices Strozid had used. A few minutes later, he looked away from the holoscreen.

"With two of these inside the evacuated enclosure, one can hold a bot on its back without danger of attack, while the other dissects it."

"Exactly our thought," Taclit said, glowing with pride.

✳

Back on the Bridge, Thorpe said, "Mother, direction and distance to the nearest swarm?"

"One hundred fifty kilometers toward Keid-B. It is eight and a half minutes away."

"Dr. Kominsky and Pilots Porovik and Zlaxiz to the Bridge," Thorpe said on the general announcing system.

Upon their arrival moments later, Thorpe said, "Brad, we've got a swarm eight minutes away. Put a small section into stasis. Jocara and Kenred, launch *Shepard*. One of you pilot, the other stand by in the airlock with a capture net. As soon as you see the stasis sphere, approach it, grab it in the net, and jump to these coordinates in the Keid-C system." He handed Jocara a set of coordinates. "You will be in no danger from the bots if you act quickly."

Brad moved to the radar console.

✳

With no time to waste, Jocara and Kenred went by portal to the vehicle bay, and two minutes later were warily approaching the swarm in *PS Alan Shepard*. Jocara manned the controls while Kenred lashed himself to the bulkhead of the open airlock.

"There's the stasis sphere," Jocara said, her scales bright blue.

"I'm tethered to an auto-retrieval line," Kenred said.

He launched into the void, driving toward the silvery sphere using his TBH boots. He swung the net.

"Damn! I missed!" He swung a second time. "Dammit, missed again!" On his third attempt, the stasis sphere settled to the bottom of the net. "I've got it, but I'm under attack! I'm reeling in. Jump the moment I cross the threshold."

On her holoscreen, Jocara saw Kenred streaming toward the lock, completely covered with bots. Her scales rippled red with fear as the microbot-covered figure crossed the threshold with the sphere. She slammed the outer hatch shut, flooding the lock with air while jumping to the Keid-C coordinates.

"Are you okay?" she asked, still unable to see Kenred clearly through his clinging bot layer.

"I think I've got some vacuum burns on my legs where the bots chewed through my suit, but otherwise, I seem to be okay."

Jocara uttered a very Human-like sigh of relief as the inner lock hatch opened, and Kenred entered the spacecraft. On her holoscreen over the control console, *Andromeda* burst into space three kilometers off her starboard side.

Chapter Five

PS Andromeda—Holding in Keid-C System

Back inside *Andromeda's* vehicle bay, the Arcans walked down *Shepard's* ramp; Jocara carried the stasis sphere.

"You have Doc check your legs," Jocara said to Kenred, "and I'll deliver this to the Chief Engineer."

She walked through a portal labeled *Engineering*, and he walked through one labeled *Medical*. In the Engineering lab, Jocara placed the shiny sphere on the lab bench.

Everyone who could be there to watch the experiment was present. The Thorpes and Strozid stood together chatting quietly. The Daphnes and Kimberlys, with Jocara and Kenred, who showed up as soon as he could, stood off to one side. Sally and Brad stood with their uploads near the front and center of the group with Dale and eDale. Max kept a close eye on everything and everyone, and eMax flitted here and there in the lab, taking in the entire show.

Strozid's group leader, Bolaik Taclit, addressed the group. "As you know by now, we constructed these waldos with carbynophene coated with Q-carbon. So far as we know, there is no stronger or harder substance in the universe. The anti-stasis silvery coating is a blend of the rare earth metals gadolinium and yttrium alloyed with indium to add needed malleability without reducing the anti-stasis characteristics of the rare earths. The coating shields what is inside from the stasis field. Thus, we can move the waldos inside the sphere, pick out a bot, and remove it from the sphere into a vacuum where it can survive."

He picked up the sphere and placed it and the two waldos into an open chamber made of the same material as the starship domes. This chamber sat inside a larger chamber made of the same material. He sealed both chambers, filling the outside one with air and evacuating the inner one until it was as pure a vacuum as the space around *Andromeda*.

"I think we're ready to do this," he said.

✳

You could have heard a pin drop. An Asterian female and a Human male slipped their six- and five-fingered hands, respectively, into their waldo controllers. On the holoscreen, the waldos shook hands, and then the Asterian and Human each slipped articulating, silvery arms into the stasis sphere. The screens went black, since photons inside the field move so slowly that they would take a million years to cross the sphere.

Moving in a pre-planned random pattern, the articulated arms conducted a full search of the sphere interior.

"I found one!" the Asterian female said about halfway through the search. The holoscreen showed very little, but in a few moments, her articulated arm appeared outside the sphere, holding a microbot on its back, her waldo fingers well clear of its mouth and jet nozzle. Its six carbon nanotube legs writhed above it as it tried to get a grip on something. The Asterian moved her other arm to take another grip from underneath, firmly preventing the bot from moving. With thumb and forefinger, the Human squeezed the bot's sides until its underside ruptured between the legs. The legs stopped moving. The Asterian placed the immobile bot on the floor of the chamber.

They reached inside the stasis sphere and retrieved another microbot, this time held by the Human. He placed the bot on the chamber floor. It immediately attacked and consumed the disabled bot. Then it activated its jet and slammed into the chamber walls until it exhausted its fuel. Falling to the floor, it latched onto one of the waldos. It actually consumed part of the anti-stasis coating near the waldo foot before the Asterian got a grip on the bot's back and yanked it away.

"I feel bad for the little creature," Kimberly said to her group.

"It's a machine, Girl," Daphne told her with twinkling eyes, "a really destructive machine."

"I don't care. I still think it's cute."

"If one latches onto your spacesuit, I promise you'll care," Jocara told the Human blonde. "Kenred and I saw what these machines can do."

"In a split second, several chewed right through my spacesuit legs," Kenred said.

Kimberly looked suitably chagrined, but muttered quietly, "They're still cute."

PS Andromeda—**Engineering Lab**

The technicians held the microbot securely while they discussed their options.

"How many bots are in the stasis sphere?" Strozid asked.

"Don't know," the Human tech answered.

"And no way to find out short of collapsing the stasis field," the Asterian tech said.

Kenred spoke up from the edge of the group. "I captured a significant number, ten or twenty, perhaps."

As they discussed, the restrained microbot opened its mouth and regurgitated something that quickly assumed the shape of a microbot. The new bot promptly attacked the transparent chamber wall. When that was not particularly successful, it turned its attention to the Human tech's waldo. The Asterian tech flicked it away. As she did, the new bot regurgitated a bot that immediately joined in, attacking everything inside the chamber.

"Flood the inner chamber with air," Taclit ordered.

Air hissed into the evacuated chamber, forming a fog. As the fog cleared, all three bots, the restrained one and both active ones, appeared inert.

"Okay, now evacuate the inner chamber again," Taclit ordered.

Once the chamber was evacuated, the inert bots showed no activity. When the techs poked them, nothing happened. Both techs pushed their waldos into the stasis sphere and retrieved two more active bots, letting them have free range of the inner chamber. The bots immediately consumed the three inert bots and then attacked the waldos and chamber walls like the earlier bots. During their activity, they reproduced several times, so that within twenty minutes, over fifty microbots were attacking the evacuated chamber walls and the two waldos. Finally, Taclit flooded the chamber with air and cleared it of all the inactive bots, ending this phase of the study.

✳

The show was over, and the observers went back to their normal activities.

"Next step," Strozid told Taclit, "is to determine which atmospheric component disables these machines."

Taclit assembled his people. "Hook up an oxygen and a nitrogen bottle to the chamber feed."

They did. Then the techs retrieved a bot and secured it with their waldos.

"Okay," Taclit said, "flood the chamber with oxygen."

Nothing happened. The microbot continued its activity as it had in the evacuated chamber.

"Evacuate the chamber and fill it with nitrogen," Taclit said.

Again, nothing happened. The microbot did not seem to notice the gas substitution.

"The only remaining gas that makes any sense at all is argon, and I have no idea why an inert gas like argon would have any effect. In any case, someone round up a bottle of argon."

Twenty-five minutes later, Taclit's team connected an argon flask to the chamber feed.

"Let's do it," Taclit said, watching the chamber intently.

Almost immediately, before any build-up of pressure, the microbot stopped wriggling its legs and went inert.

"I'll be damned!" Taclit said, his articulating ears pointing straight up. "It really is argon." He rubbed his face and called Brad on his internal Link. Brad's tall body and ruddy face appeared in the air before him. "Brad, I know your expertise is physics and related engineering, but we just ran into an interesting event that I just don't understand."

He then described how the microbot disabling gas seemed to be argon. Since argon was inert, how was this possible?

"A friend of mine," Brad told him, "has done a lot of very deep, very long diving, breathing exotic gas mixtures. The gas mixture at thirty bar was mostly helium, with sufficient oxygen for a partial pressure of one bar. Helium at thirty bars affected the nervous system, causing uncontrollable hand tremors. They added a small percentage of argon, and the tremors disappeared." Brad chuckled. "Does this answer your question? No…but it tells us that argon is not entirely inert—at least not physiologically. Let's pass this to Daphne and her crew. They may come up with something."

✳

"Here's what we know," Thorpe said to the people sitting around the conference table. "Microbots are manufactured, I'm guessing by something similar to our Nanocosms. On the outside, they consist primarily of carbynophene with a Q-carbon coating. Their legs are Q-carbon coated nanotubes. They consume virtually anything, including their own inert carcasses. When they have consumed something, they can accelerate at one-tenth gee for five minutes or they can reproduce. And…argon, even a small amount, puts them permanently out of commission. Daphne and her team are trying to figure out how.

"We know nothing about how microbots navigate except they head for matter. We believe they use the raw material they collect to construct the Dyson Sphere surface and the underlying infrastructure, but we don't know how they convert what they scavenge into carbynophene or how they decide to use it. eSally and eBrad will try to enter and analyze their circuitry."

Thorpe paused, then continued. "These micro-machines are key to our understanding what we have found here. By Freeman Dyson's original definition, it would take a Type Two Civilization to undertake such a project. This implies massive ongoing space activity, at least within their solar system. Obviously, such activity is missing here. Just as obviously, we're looking at a constructed sphere with a four-point-seven-million-kilometer radius. Where is everybody?"

PS *Andromeda*—Research Labs

The question *Where is everybody?* occupied most of Thorpe's attention when he was not actively dodging microbot swarms. He knew Mother could handle the microbot evasion, but with the possible consequences of getting it wrong, even once, he chose to remain involved.

He was happy he had good people to address the other problems. Thorpe didn't think he needed a full understanding of argon's role or the bot's navigation system to commence an investigation of the sphere's interior. He was less concerned with how the bots changed what they scavenged to what they needed or how they chose between travel and reproduction. With time, those answers would come. Daphne and her people, Sally and Bad and theirs, and Ustrun with his engineering team—Thorpe was confident they would find the answers.

✳

If two teams will be researching microbots, Thorpe thought, we'll need another batch of active ones. He called Kenred.

"I need you to catch another batch of bots. Do like you did before, but this time, use a drone instead of making a spacewalk."

Brad set up the basketball-size stasis sphere from the Bridge. Jocara and Kenred launched *Shepard* toward Brad's sphere, capturing it using a drone, and returned to *Andromeda* with their prize.

Thorpe transferred the original stasis sphere to Sally's and Brad's group and the new one to Daphne's group.

✳

"Kimberly," Daphne said, "you haven't changed one iota since you first moved in across the hall from me in Los Angeles."

"Of course not, Silly. We've both been rejuvenated twice since then. You've still got it, too."

"How are you holding up trying to keep the crew abreast of everything that's going on right now?"

"It's not nearly as stressful as running Ogden Enterprises, but it's fun work for an investigative reporter."

Daphne tossed her long red hair and stroked Kimberly's blonde tresses. "Between the two of us, we changed the world, Girl. For better or worse, we changed the entire path of Human history. When people can live indefinitely, everything changes."

Kimberly touched the taller girl's cheek. "We gave them virtual immortality, and they made you and me the wealthiest women in Human history. I couldn't have imagined this back in that Los Angeles apartment complex."

"Now look at us," Daphne said, taking Kimberly's face in her hands, "we are part of something so much bigger than Ogden," she kissed her full on the lips, "that I can't even begin to describe it. On a starship sixteen lightyears from Earth investigating a Dyson Sphere that may be older than our entire civilization…everything we've done pales in comparison."

"What pales?" Dale asked, approaching them with arms outstretched, blue eyes twinkling, round face full of smiles. He no longer wore his round glasses. They became unnecessary following his rejuvenation—only one in his case. He had let himself mature physically to enhance his credibility with people outside his immediate circle.

"Everything we've done compared with what we're doing now," Kimberly said as she and Daphne hugged him and kissed him soundly.

"That's why I'm here," Dale said, wiping lipstick from his mouth. "You guys are following the argon connection while Sally and Brad are mapping out the circuitry. I know enough in both areas to assist you and them and keep each group abreast of the other's progress."

"Not much to tell from our side," Daphne said. "A literature search produced several research papers where argon was successfully compounded with other elements, but they all were unstable, nothing more than a scientific curiosity."

"We did find several papers discussing the role of noble gases in general and argon specifically as they related to physiology," Kimberly said. "We don't have a connection yet, but we're looking at this."

"You should ask Brad to discuss his diver friend's experience with argon," Dale said. "That might give you some clues."

✳

The conference room was full, but not with the usual occupants. Daphne and key members of her team occupied one side of the table. Sally and Brad with their team had the other. Dale sat at the head. Daphne's and Kimberly's uploads were there as well as Sally's and Brad's. eDale took the far end of the table. A full coffee urn occupied a far corner.

"We all know," Dale said, "that we don't do any real science while sitting in a conference room." He looked around the table, taking in each participant, while ignoring Max, who had decided to join the meeting. "I think this time will be different. Both groups are investigating the same object. What any one of us discovers probably will have relevance to something someone else is doing.

"While I know you are keeping the database updated, not everything ends up there. So, we meet and talk here. For the next few minutes, I want each of you to seek out your counterpart on the other team and compare notes. Especially, talk about specific things you found interesting, but that didn't reach the threshold for a database entry."

For the next half hour, team members mingled, chatted, and sipped fresh coffee. This was always Max's favorite time as he wandered from person to person, rubbing legs and emitting an occasional mew. He communed with his old friends and found several new ones.

While people moved around, chatting here and there, eBrad suddenly spoke up. "Listen up, People. I have something you all should hear."

Everyone stopped talking and turned their attention to eBrad's holoimage.

"I've been watching Max wander around almost randomly, but directing his attention to people he knows while stopping from time to time to meet someone new. Max is not part of our research—it's entirely beyond his mental capacity. And yet, he is actually playing a role here. When you," he pointed at a female member of his team, "leaned down to pet Max, you," he pointed at a male member of Daphne's team, "leaned down to meet him for the first time. You both ended up talking with each other—something that might not have happened otherwise. And that got me to thinking about the role argon might play. It may not be reactive, but it influences by its presence. As you return to your labs, keep this in mind. It may lead you to new insights."

*

"It's time to get inside a bot to trace out its internal electronics, *Chi oi*," Brad told Sally. From the day they met in the theoretical physics department of Colorado School of Mines, Sally and Brad had been an item. She was a diminutive and fragile import from Vietnam, and he was a bear-like Polish American giant from Chicago. Between them, they had advanced theoretical physics more than anyone in recent history. He affectionately called Sally by the Vietnamese term of endearment, *Chi oi*, meaning Little Sister.

"Let me enter first," eBrad told eSally, "in case something malicious resides there."

"Gallant of you," Sally said, "but do you really think there might be something inside? This is one of probably trillions of similar devices. Either all of them are malicious, or none of them are." Her eyes twinkled as she kidded the upload of the man she loved. At times, she found it difficult to distinguish between her flesh-and-blood partner and his identical-looking electronic upload. When Brad took her in his huge arms, however, all doubt disappeared.

"Let's send in several tensors," eSally said, "to get the lay of the land. Then you or I can make a personal visit."

Once Engineering had perfected a Nanocosm for waldo construction, making another waldo was a matter of supplying raw materials and fifteen minutes. Sally and Brad had two waldos on their lab bench inside an evacuated chamber identical to the one in Engineering, and a third attached to the open bench top.

"We'll start with an inactive unit," eBrad said.

Brad secured an inert bot with the bench-top waldo. "Want me to crack it open?" he asked.

"That's the only way we know how to get inside right now."

Brad pushed a fine wire into the open bot back until he met resistance. "Okay, see if you can follow the wire inside."

eBrad generated a search tensor and sent it along the fine wire, following its progress through its feedback signals. The tensor reached the wire's end, but found nothing to latch onto. The wire ended at a smooth wall.

Thinking that the electronics might be encapsulated, eBrad said, "I will make the wire hot. You push it gently. Let's see if it will penetrate the wall that way."

As the wire heated and Brad pushed it with his waldo, it slowly penetrated the wall surface until several minutes later it came up against something solid.

"Hold everything," eBrad said. "I've got an electrical contact."

The tensor slipped across the contact into the bot's central circuitry.

"There's a lot of stuff here I recognize, and things I don't," eBrad said. "I'm gonna have to look at this directly. A tensor just doesn't produce fine enough resolution."

eBrad removed the tensor and inserted a part of himself down the wire into the bot's inner works. He found himself in a large hall with doors on all sides, dozens of them. He split himself into smaller branches and passed through each door. Each door appeared to lead to a bot function, but eBrad had no way of discovering the function or how it worked. Everything was static, frozen at the moment the bot went inert.

At the bottom of the bot just ahead of the jet engine, eBrad found a connection to the outside, a tiny conductive graphene plate that was sensitive to specific digital carriers. This appeared to be how individual bots received their instructions.

Many subjective hours later, eBrad pulled himself out of the bot. For his companions in the lab, only a few minutes had passed.

"I need a live bot," eBrad said. "Otherwise, I can't determine the purpose for most of the things I saw."

Sally removed the outer chamber and inserted a small graphene disk into the wall of the inner chamber. "This will allow you to enter and maintain contact to keep your backup current, so if something happens to you in there, you can pick up where you left off," she said.

Sally and Brad slipped their hands into their waldo controllers and gently removed a viable bot from the stasis sphere. Sally held it bottom side up, while Brad stretched a wire between the inner chamber conducting disk and the microscopic disk near the back end of the bot's underside.

"Okay, eBrad, we're ready for you," Brad said.

eBrad checked the connection from the inner chamber disk. It was solid. He moved down the wire to the tiny plate on the bot's belly. Also solid. He moved small parts of himself into the bot, checking things carefully as he moved inward. He moved slowly and deliberately, checking out every connection and function he encountered. He reached the large hallway lined with doors twenty minutes later.

Fast-flowing streams of data filled the chamber, moving between doors, sometimes splitting, sometimes merging. He ducked into a stream, letting it take him through a door into an area that generated function—what, was not obvious, but it was definitely doing something.

eBrad pulled himself out of the bot, through the connecting wire and back into *Andromeda*.

"Wow!" he said with wonder. "It's like a whole world inside there."

He addressed eSally. "You and I need to generate a whole series of small tensors that can scatter throughout a bot to discover every function."

eBrad looked at Sally and Brad. "Give us a few minutes to set this up. Then we'll work together to make it happen."

✳

eSally and eBrad took several subjective hours generating and programming two dozen tensors each. They designed the tensors to enter the bot, travel to the hall, and select a specific door. Once a tensor had followed a stream through a door to its operating destination, it probed every aspect of the operation, sending the data back to its respective upload.

Sally and Brad waited patiently for the fifteen actual minutes eSally and eBrad took to set up their tensors. They verified the bot remained immobilized.

"Okay," Sally said. "We're ready for your tensors."

There was no outward difference. The bot remained immobile on its back. Its legs continued to writhe. Inside the bot, the little packets of energy all the uploads called tensors did their work. They got their name from Thorpe back when he was the original upload, the Icicle that started it all. Because Thorpe was a mathematician and engineer, when he awakened as an electronic upload from his cryogenic preservation, he interpreted things from a mathematical perspective. He found he could manipulate and control the energy packets that seemed to him like mathematical tensors. The name stuck.

"How long will this take?" Sally asked.

"We have no idea," eSally answered. "The complexity inside that bot is staggering—literally beyond anything we have ever seen."

"We'll map it out and figure it out eventually," eBrad said, "but it's going to be awhile."

✸

Daphne did not have the luxury of something to enter literally and investigate. Instead, she and her team focused on what they called the *Max Syndrome*, after eDale's observation that Max acted as a catalyst in bringing together people with parts of the solution who might not otherwise get together.

Daphne kept abreast of what Sally and Brad with their uploads were doing. While the tensors were still investigating, she visited their lab.

"Is there a way," she asked, "once your tensors have completed their task, of inserting a charged molecule into the electronic mix?"

"There might be," Sally said. "What molecule with what charge?"

"We have discovered a way to squeeze an argon atom between the atoms in a water molecule. It's a tricky process, and the resulting argon compound is unstable, but we can keep it viable for a few minutes. It carries a charge of one because of the separation of the two hydrogen atoms and the oxygen. When the argon atom finally squirts out like a watermelon seed, the remaining water molecule loses its charge."

"Let's set it up for tomorrow morning. The tensors should have finished by then."

✸

The next morning, Daphne's people brought their argon-squeezing apparatus into Sally's and Brad's lab. Sally set up an active receptor bot while Brad arranged the wiring to accommodate moving a charged molecule.

eBrad eased the argon compound down the wire and coaxed it through the conducting plate into the bot circuitry. He got as far as the hall before the argon squeezed out from between the two hydrogens and the oxygen to fly freely through the hall. To his surprise, the water molecule simply disappeared, following a data stream, while the argon atom continued to bounce around the hall.

eBrad withdrew and arranged to shepherd a larger number of argon compound molecules down the wire and into the bot. This time, when his charges arrived in the hall, the water molecules again disappeared, but the larger number of argon atoms bounced around so fiercely that they diverted several data streams and *killed* the bot.

eBrad withdrew again and explained what he had observed. "We introduced the argon through the use of a charged argon compound. Let's feed argon into a bot's maw and see what happens."

Setting this run up was somewhat more complicated. Sally and Brad produced a viable bot from the stasis sphere and immobilized it on its back. They also inserted a very tiny nanotube cylinder into the bot's maw, hooking the other tube end to an argon flask.

eBrad arranged to enter the bot and be in the hall when Sally introduced argon into the bot's maw. eSally entangled herself with eBrad so she could relay his comments to the others. She informed Sally that eBrad was in the hall. Sally cracked the argon valve. The bot went inactive.

eBrad reported it took less than a second for the argon from the flask to enter the hall, where it disrupted everything.

✳

The Chief Engineer and his team continued to investigate how a microbot could consume virtually anything, ending up with Q-carbon and with graphene and carbyne formed into carbynophene, and solid rocket fuel that could produce five minutes of propulsion at 0.1 g.

Ustrun Strozid split his research team into two groups. Bolaik Taclit led the team looking into carbon generation. Kidlit Mazop led the team investigating fuel. Both these Asterian research engineers had extensive mini black hole generating experience, and Strozid's gut told him the answers to both questions lay hidden in mini black hole technology.

Taclit spent his first few hours revisiting everything the argon and bot electronics teams had covered. One item jumped out at him. The argon team had produced an argon compound by forcing an argon atom between the two hydrogens and single oxygen in a water molecule. He called Daphne on his internal Link.

"What held the argon atom in place inside the water molecule?" he asked.

"Pressure," she said, and gave him the numbers.

"That's it?"

"We temporarily pulled the water molecule apart without severing the bonds, lined up the argon atom between them, and let it snap shut. The pressure held the argon atom in place for a relatively long time."

"What about heat? Did the compound generate much heat?"

"A great deal," Daphne said. "We siphoned it off to keep the compound from decomposing."

"Do you think we could do that with deuterium—fusing it to helium, and then fusing the helium to carbon?"

"Probably not," Daphne said. "You're talking temperatures like those at the center of a star. A carbynophene bot cannot withstand that." She went silent, thinking. "What do you know about LANRs—Lattice Assisted Nuclear Reactions?"

"Not a lot," Taclit said. "We Asterians concentrated on mini black hole technology. We knew nothing about LANRs until you Humans came along. Basically, you guys adopted our mini black hole technology and abandoned your LANRs."

"Back in the twentieth century, Earth scientists started researching nuclear reactions near room temperature. They called it cold fusion. That research evolved into LANRs." Daphne said. "Here's the thing. LANRs fuse deuterium into helium without high pressure and heat. We never took the technology beyond that. I can think of no theoretical reason why one could not fuse helium to carbon in a LANR."

✳

Kidlit Mazop asked a simple question of his team. "What is the theoretically most proficient solid rocket fuel?"

After a few hours of researching the literature by his people, he received an answer: Metallic hydrogen.

His next question was about what solid oxidizer was best. The answer came out of the past—twenty-first century Earth: Ammonium dinitramide or ADN.

He pulled his team together. "Our problem has defined itself. How does a bot manufacture metallic hydrogen and ADN, and how does it form them into a solid fuel pellet?"

✳

Within several weeks, Taclit's team had a working LANR that produced carbon from deuterium. They still needed to scale it down to microbot size, and come up with a way to convert the carbon to graphene, carbyne, and Q-carbon. A month after that, they had their answer.

Mazop's team found a way to reverse the LANR process, producing deuterium from anything, anything at all. They passed this process to Taclit's team to complete their goal of converting anything into carbon and then graphene, carbynophene, and Q-carbon.

Using an adaptation of the Daphne team approach, Mazop's people learned how to compress hydrogen into metallic hydrogen. They created ADN using Taclit's LANR process and found a way to combine metallic hydrogen and ADN into minuscule solid fuel pellets that produced the proper thrust for the right time.

✳

The only remaining microbot question was why the bots had a built-in susceptibility to argon. The answer to that question would come later in their investigation of the Dyson Sphere.

PS Andromeda—Bridge

Thorpe sat in the Captain's Chair, something he had done a great deal of late, ever since the microbots had first attacked *Andromeda*. His teams had done well. They now understood how the bots worked, how they moved, and even how they navigated, although they still didn't know the source of the instructions, except that they had to emanate from the Dyson Sphere.

Brad called him on his internal Link. "Can you come to our lab for a few minutes?"

"Mother, what is the range of the nearest bot swarm?" Thorpe asked.

"One thousand kilometers, heading toward us. The swarm will be here in fifty-six minutes."

"If I'm not back in forty-five minutes, jump out five thousand kilometers, but ensure there are no close swarms at the destination."

Thorpe stepped through a portal to Sally's and Brad's lab. An evacuated chamber sat on their bench. A stasis sphere, two inactive bots, two waldos, and three chunks of something Thorpe could not identify were inside the evacuated chamber. The entire thing was encased in a safety chamber filled with air. A box about the size of a printed book lay on the bench next to the safety chamber.

"What's all the excitement?" Thorpe wanted to know.

"We made an interesting discovery," Sally told him. "Watch."

Using their waldos, they removed a viable bot from the sphere and set it on the evacuated chamber floor. Instead of attacking everything inside the chamber, it just sat quietly, waiting.

"Now, watch this," Brad said.

Suddenly, the bot moved to one of the carcasses and consumed it. Then it stopped moving. After a few seconds, it moved to one of the chunks and consumed it. Almost immediately, it regurgitated a new bot. The new bot consumed the second chunk and went to a corner of the chamber where it commenced laying down what Thorpe thought might be a strip of carbynophene.

"Obviously, you're controlling them," Thorpe said.

"With my Link through this box," Brad said. "eSally and eBrad mapped out the internal electronics—which door controls what function. Together, we worked out the coding of the individual data packets and created this box to transmit them. Something in the Dyson Sphere controls individual swarms—that's the basic resolution."

"You guys have done it again," Thorpe said. "You've been at the inception of nearly every major advance we have made since we hired you out of Colorado School of Mines, what seems like so long ago. How soon until we can control nearby swarms?"

"It's a matter of designing and installing appropriate transmitters and an interface for Bridge personnel," Brad said. "Give us a week."

Chapter Six

PS Andromeda—Holding in Keid-C System

The microbot control system—MCS they called it—consisted of line-of-sight transmission dishes scattered around both domed surfaces of *Andromeda* that provided 100 percent coverage of the space surrounding the starship, and an operator interface on the Bridge. Mother did the actual pointing of the dishes under the direction of whoever had the Bridge watch. The system provided 90 percent protection from microbots. The remaining 10 percent worried Thorpe. He expressed this worry in a conversation with Sally and Brad.

"Can you think of anything that will protect *Andromeda* from that inevitable microbot that slips past our defenses?"

"We've been tossing that around in the lab for the past few hours," Brad said. "I think we may have something."

Sally jumped in. "The microbots are speed limited, and they have no armament—by that I mean they cannot protect themselves. Once a bot has expended its fuel pellet, it can do nothing but continue to coast until it strikes something it can use to generate more fuel. Look at this." Sally projected a holoimage of what looked like an enlarged bot. "This is not a local microbot. It's a bot *we* made. It carries a small portal for power and fuel, and a laser. Its rocket is gimbled so we can steer it, and it has enough brains to identify a local microbot and zap it without direction. We call it a shieldbot."

"The shieldbot should fill any gap in our protection," Brad said.

"How soon can you deploy these?" Thorpe asked.

"As quickly as our Nanocosms can grind them out." Brad said. "If we put all our spare Nanocosms on it, we should have deployed several tens of thousands by morning."

✳

Back on the Bridge, Thorpe checked the MCS status. Three microbot swarms were within 1,000 kilometers of *Andromeda*. Thorpe had set the MCS transmission to the three swarms to ignore *Andromeda*. They did that. Since there were no other sources of material anywhere near *Andromeda*, the swarms set course for the Dyson Sphere.

He pondered the situation he observed. The bots vectored toward Andromeda, and they must have used their fuel pellets for the thrust. The MCS countered the order, so how do they have fuel to return to the sphere?

"Mother, give me the highest magnification possible on the nearest swarm."

The resolution did not resolve individual microbots. Thorpe ordered a drone out of the vehicle bay, sending it toward the swarm. He modified the MCS orders so the swarm would ignore the drone.

The drone transmitted high-resolution images of individual bots in the swarm. The answer to his question stared him in his face. Some bots were attacking and consuming other bots, producing a net momentum for the swarm toward the sphere.

When they reached the sphere, they vectored toward the jagged edge of the open spot, where they feasted on the sphere itself. The drone followed part of the swarm as it departed the jagged edge, heading for the smooth one. Part of the swarm sacrificed itself to propel the rest to the worksite with their material loads. Billions of bots along the edge regurgitated what Thorpe assumed to be carbynophene and used their feet to work it into place. Other bots followed them, coating the carbynophene with Q-carbon. The net result was that the microbots were destroying the Dyson Sphere at about the rate they were constructing it, a bizarre situation that made no sense.

"Thorpe," Mother said, interrupting his thoughts, "we have a situation. A small bot swarm is not reacting to the MCS signals. It will reach us soon."

For the past few days, Thorpe had been working through his Bridge Officers, letting them handle the actual maneuvering to avoid the swarms. They quickly learned what to do.

"Bridge Officer," Thorpe said, "keep us away from that errant swarm, but don't lose contact with the drone I sent out earlier."

Then he ordered, "Astronauts Porovik and Zlaxiz to the Bridge."

Jocara and Kenred showed up shortly thereafter.

"We've got a small bot swarm that isn't responding to our MCS signals," Thorpe told them. "Take *Shepard* and capture a sample in a stasis sphere."

✳

By this time, all the M-Class starships had been retrofitted with MCS transmitters. Departing *Andromeda* without MCS protection seemed almost reckless now. Jocara and Kenred had more experience capturing microbots than anyone else on *Andromeda*, so they were not surprised that Thorpe picked them.

They did not activate *Shepard's* MCS in order not to disturb the swarm. They had done this earlier without MCS protection often enough by now that it was almost a routine task. The Bridge waited until they were near the swarm and then captured a portion in a small stasis sphere. Kenred launched a drone while Jocara piloted the craft. He maneuvered the drone to capture the sphere in its net. A few minutes later, Kenred brought the drone safely into the airlock, and Jocara jumped *Shepard* to a safe distance.

"Get that sphere down to Sally and Brad as soon as you have docked," Thorpe told them when they returned to *Andromeda*.

✳

In their lab, Sally and Braxton ran several tests, but the bots remained completely unresponsive.

eBrad watched from his airborne perch. "I'd better enter one of these guys to see what the problem is."

Sally and Brad extracted a bot from the sphere and secured it with a waldo. They pressed a fine wire against the conducting disk on its underside, but eBrad could not penetrate the bot. They pushed the wire through its open maw, and eBrad found his way inside the miniature machine. He exited ten minutes later.

"I've been looking things over for three subjective hours," he said. "First, the internal connection between the disk and the internal circuitry broke. Second, when this happens, a default program takes over, one we missed during our survey. The default program basically is *find and munch*."

✳

"We have our solution," Brad told Thorpe. "Actually, we had it yesterday and have been deploying shieldbots all night. Because of their internal portals, they can function indefinitely. The portals supply fuel and power for the lasers, and Mother vectors them as needed. They actually function at some sublevel of Mother's *consciousness*, so that she does not even have to pay attention to them.

"Right now, a swarm of shieldbots is protecting *Andromeda*. I do not expect any further incidents like that errant swarm that Jocara and Kenred handled."

PS Andromeda—Near the Dyson Sphere

The question of a seemingly derelict Dyson Sphere loomed large in Thorpe's mind. The directed microbot swarms put the lie to its being totally abandoned, or were they part of some bizarre automatic operation the builders left behind when they departed—assuming they did? If they were still here, where were they?

Surrounded by shieldbots with Mother using MCS to discourage any nearby swarms, Thorpe moved the starship closer to the disproportionately larger sphere. In his mind's eye, Thorpe imagined the view from afar, *Andromeda* like a speck of dust against the unimaginably huge Dyson Sphere.

In fact, he told himself, not a speck of dust, but a microbe, an infinitesimal, inconsequential piece of flotsam. It staggers the mind.

He took his time, maintaining distance from the MCS controlled swarms with Mother keeping a sharp lookout for rogue swarms. *Andromeda* approached the gash in the sphere.

A gash six point six million klicks from pole to equator, Thorpe told himself, one million wide. Nearly five million klicks down inside to the sun, I can see something glowing not too far inside.

Try as he might, Thorpe could not generate a coherent mental picture of the entire structure. He parked *Andromeda* in a hover several hundred thousand kilometers above the gash and called his M-Class pilots to the Bridge.

✳

Ten two-pilot teams arrived on the Bridge, a mix of Humans and Arcans, both genders, all having recent combat experience in the Arcan Holy War. Following his practice during that fighting, Thorpe assigned an upload to each vessel. Jocara, Kenred, and eDaphne would ride *PS Alan Shepard*.

"This is an exploratory mission," Thorpe told the assembled pilots. "We don't really know what's out there. Remember, somebody designed and built what you see. It's almost beyond imagining in scope. Your ten craft can only examine a tiny part of this colossus. The key word is *examine*. I want no heroics, no grandstanding, and no one-upmanship. Go to your designated sectors, survey the shell in that sector, and if you find something interesting, investigate it, but approach the sphere surface no closer than one hundred klicks. Under no circumstances will you enter the sphere at the gash."

Thorpe looked at each pilot, one by one. "Do you understand me?"

The response was a collective "Yes, Sir!"

"Okay—to your vessels. Let's see if we can wrangle some useful information from this behemoth."

✳

Jocara and Kenred headed to the *Shepard*. Kenred carried eDaphne's matrix and plugged it into the panel as soon as they entered the craft. Together, they ran a systems check.

eDaphne's holoimage appeared in the lounge area. "At least the nature of this mission will make up for the confinement of my matrix. We've got to come up with a way to make these boxes less restrictive."

"Are you complaining again, Girl?" Jocara said, her scales rippling pale blue. Since she had gotten to know eDaphne, her friendship with Daphne had extended to include her upload. She still tended to think of them as one person, even though eDaphne reminded her from time to time that they were entirely separate people.

"You've been at this a long time. It's all new to me," Jocara would retort, but she genuinely valued her friendship with both.

Jocara flipped her tail to one side and prepared to launch the spacecraft. By mutual agreement, she had become the senior pilot, although she suspected Kenred deferred to her because of their relationship, not because she was necessarily the better pilot. Not that she minded, however. Piloting an M-Class starship was one of the greatest joys in Jocara's life. Not that long ago, it was riding a cramped capsule with Kenred around Arcan's moon Lodan. This was infinitely more satisfying.

As she settled into her seat at Shepard's control console, she thought, It is utterly remarkable how things have changed. Who would have thought that I would become a valued crewmember of an alien starship and pilot of a craft like this? Her scales rippled bright blue as she adjusted a control.

"Mother, take us to Sector Seven, one thousand kilometers above the sphere surface."

PS Alan Shepard—1,000 km above the Dyson Sphere

One moment, *PS Alan Shepard* was in the vehicle bay, the next, she hovered above the vast sphere. The sphere was so large and the spacecraft so close that the sphere curvature was not visible. Visually, the surface below them looked like a flat plain.

"Mother, conduct the pre-programmed survey," Jocara ordered.

Section seven was a thousand-by-thousand-kilometer square, roughly halfway between the north pole and equator, that had displayed some interesting features from afar. *Shepard* would overfly the section in kilometer-wide swaths, with Mother analyzing what she found as the survey progressed.

The three occupants of the spacecraft had little to do as the survey progressed. The surface below them was mostly featureless. Here and there, pieces protruded far enough above the surface to be noticed from a thousand kilometers. Since there was no sun to cast shadows, the only usable light came from Keid-B, currently forty AUs distant, and Keid-A, 400 AUs away. The two stars were bright, about one-third that of Sol or Ran, too bright to look at directly, but could not be resolved into disks with the eye. They created distinct shadows visible on the sphere's dull surface. Most of the surface features were differences in shading. From *Shepard's* height, they could not tell if the features were real or just artifacts their eyes created, trying to connect dots that were not really there.

Section seven was well away from the gash, so microbot swarms did not bother them.

"We know this sphere has been here a long time," Kenred said. "So, where are the craters?"

"In our survey of this system when we first entered," eDaphne said, "I was struck by how empty it is. Since then, I think we understand more about microbot activity. This sphere has been here long enough for the bot swarms to have cleaned up virtually every piece of scrap in the solar system. There's nothing left to make craters on the sphere."

"Do you see that big, round marking over there," Kenred asked, pointing. "It must be fifty klicks across."

"Forty-seven and change," Mother said. "I'm zooming in on the edge."

The object was far too large to appear on a zoomed holoscreen. Mother focused on one piece, zooming down until they could see a crack between the object and the rest of the sphere.

"That looks like an immense door of some kind, but I don't see any hinges, so it must drop down and slide away." Kenred inspected it closely. "Open, it can accommodate an entire fleet of spaceships."

They didn't see another similar artifact during the remainder of their survey. When they were finished, Jocara directed Mother to take them to the vicinity of *Andromeda*.

"I want to look around," she said.

"You're right," eDaphne said, "we always pop in and out, never remaining long enough to smell the roses."

Jocara looked at her strangely, a rainbow of colors rippling across her scales. "You'll have to explain that one to me, Girl."

"On Earth," eDaphne said, "we have a cultivated flower we call a rose." She brought up an image of growing roses. "This is how they grow, and this," she brought up an image of a big bouquet, "is how we generally use them. They are wonderfully fragrant and sweet. When people are so busy that they lose sight of why they exist, we suggest they take sufficient time to smell the roses."

Shepard popped out of nullspace fifty kilometers from *Andromeda*, on the side away from the Dyson Sphere. The light from Keid-A passed through the upper part of the cityscape dome, and light from Keid-B passed through the landscape dome. *Andromeda* stood out against the darker sphere surface in an almost magical superposition.

"Record this, Mother," eDaphne said, "so we can show the others."

Jocara eased *Shepard* home on the MERT Drive. "…so we can smell the roses for as long as possible," she said.

✳

They docked in the vehicle bay. Jocara and Kenred headed for their chambers right after Kenred released eDaphne from her confining matrix.

Once in their room, they flopped back on their bed, and Jocara called up the recording she had taken earlier. The holoimage filled the space above them, virtually indistinguishable from the view outside their spacecraft.

"Can you imagine?" Jocara said quietly, nuzzling the side of Kenred's snout, both their scales rippling lavender. "Here we are, lightyears from home, part of something so much bigger than us or anything we ever did." She stretched and kept her nose right next to his snout. "I'm so happy! I'm so very happy!"

PS Andromeda—**Near the Dyson Sphere**

Thorpe called the M-Class pilots together in the conference room. It was a tight fit, but everyone found a place. The upload holoimages floated near the ceiling against the outer walls, where there was room. eMax saw them and figured he would give it a try. His holoimage floated over the table just above eye height. Max, as usual, strolled the table length, greeting friends.

"We have now had a close look at portions of the outside of this structure. I wouldn't call it a representative look—just a look. It would take us the rest of our natural lives to make a dent in exploring this thing. The idea is to gain a sense of how it is constructed, and what might have happened to the builders.

"I don't want any of you to enter the sphere yet. We haven't seen enough of the outside to understand anything about what we might find inside. We're going to take the next few days to get a sense of what we are really dealing with.

"Let's put this thing in perspective. How long would you take to do a thorough exploration of Arcan or Earth from the air? I know. There are so many variables that it is hard to make an estimate. So guess. Depending on how many craft you use and your survey's resolution, it could take years. Let's say we use all ten of our M-Class ships and adjust the resolution to distinguish towns and cities, but not individual buildings. Could we do it in a year? Maybe…let's assume we can.

"That sphere out there has the equivalent surface of over five hundred forty-four thousand Arcans or Earths. So, if our guesstimate is anywhere close to reality, we would take over half a million years to complete the survey of just the outside of that sphere. Okay, let's reduce our resolution and do just half the sphere—That's still between one hundred and two hundred thousand years."

Every pilot in the room was either a mathematician or liked math. Nobody had taken the calculations to this point yet, not even Jocara or Kenred.

"Why even bother?" one pilot asked.

"That's a fair question," Thorpe answered. "Our goal is to wrap our minds around this, to gain some sort of understanding. Who built it? Why? Where are they? Does anyone live inside? I hope we will answer these questions as we continue our exploration. This thing is so far beyond our capabilities as Humans, Asterians, and Arcans that we can barely understand its existence, let alone comprehend it.

"Are there any more questions?"

"Realistically," Jocara said, "how much longer do you think we will operate in our present mode—sweeping the outside while leaving the inside alone?"

"When it looks to me and to eThorpe that we are just repeating ourselves on the outside, we'll talk about entering the sphere." Thorpe looked around the crowded room, seeking out pilots whose expressions told Thorpe they were unhappy with his direction. "Let me make this crystal clear: Under no circumstances will any pilot drive his ship inside the sphere. That means the gash, too. Stay above the surface or virtual surface."

✳

Jocara and Kenred strolled down a passageway headed toward their quarters. They could have used a portal, but sometimes walking helped to clear the thoughts, and Jocara needed to clear hers. eDaphne's holoimage accompanied them, almost as if she were walking alongside them.

"Why do you think Thorpe is so insistent?" Jocara asked eDaphne. "The microbot problem is under control, and we haven't had a shred of other potentially bad things happen."

"I know Thorpe as well as anybody—literally right from the beginning. He's not a dictator, but he takes his role as Captain seriously. He sees himself as responsible for all ten thousand crew members, even though he doesn't know them all personally. He has a vast amount of experience. He started out as eThorpe following his revival. He built Phoenix, the company. He found a way to relate to the Asterians, even though they tried to wipe out the Human race, he built *Andromeda*, he discovered and established relations with you guys, the Arcans. eThorpe finally decided to download into Human form at Daphne's insistence right before he and Braxton terraformed Mars. Thorpe and eThorpe synchronize their memories and experiences periodically so that each of them has all the memories and experiences of the other. Thorpe has more experience than all of us combined, accompanied by the wisdom of having *been there and done that* for so long.

"Does Thorpe make mistakes? Yeah, I've seen him make them. Does he make big mistakes? If so, I'm unaware of them. So, if Thorpe thinks we should do more outside surveys before we enter the sphere, then I support him completely."

"You sound like you are in love with him," Jocara said.

"I was, when he was an upload and I was flesh-and-blood. Now I have a relationship with eThorpe and eKim that I have no way of describing to you. So, I guess in a way you are correct. But I base my faith in him and his judgment on experience, not love."

✳

"I think I got through to them," Thorpe said to eThorpe. "They're young and brash…they're fighter pilots. They do what fighter pilots do."

"I hadn't given it much thought myself," eThorpe said. "Eight hundred forty-four thousand Earths—It's difficult to imagine, let alone believe. Who could build such a structure?"

"Let's address that question again when we have had a real look inside," Thorpe said.

"I've run sone numbers," eThorpe said. "That thing must have an infrastructure like nothing you and I have ever imagined. I understand the pilots entirely. I want to get inside as soon as possible, too."

Chapter Seven

PS Alan Shepard—Keid-C System near the Sphere

As the ten M-Class starships departed, Thorpe transmitted to all, "Remember, remain above the sphere surface, no matter how tempted you might feel to dip into the gash. You will have plenty of time to explore inside. And remember to verify your live backup comm portal."

"Our sector is a million klicks from the gash," Jocara said. "There's virtually no chance I'll be tempted to dip inside." Her scales rippled pale blue. "What do you think would happen if we did it anyway, Kenred?"

"No funny stuff, guys," eDaphne said through her holoimage standing behind Jocara at the console.

"No way to do it anyway," Jocara said. "Mother, commence the survey. Let's see what we can find."

"We already found what looked like a huge opening into the sphere that was closed," Kenred said. "Maybe we'll get lucky and find another one."

"It could be," eDaphne said. "This sphere is huge. There must be more than one fleet opening, if that's what it was."

For several hours, they flew back and forth across their sector, spotting nothing interesting. Toward the end of their search, Mother announced, "I've picked up something."

The holoscreen displayed a circular feature several meters across. It rose above the sphere surface about a meter. The top was flat, showing an iris-diaphragm pattern.

"What do you suppose it is?" Kenred asked.

"If that actually is an iris diaphragm," eDaphne said, "It's covering something."

"We can move closer," Jocara said. "Maybe we can figure it out." She turned to the console. "Mother, bring us toward the sphere in a steep dive five hundred meters from that artifact, and fly over the artifact at fifty meters. Then head back to our normal operating altitude."

Mother acknowledged and dropped *Shepard* toward the sphere surface at high speed. Within moments, the iris opened, something rose through the opening, and a laser bolt struck *Shepard's* counter-rotating particle rings, disrupting her hull.

Jocara and Kenred flew from the craft as her hull disrupted. They were not wearing their pressure suits and perished instantly. eDaphne's matrix stayed with the craft as it plunged to a fiery death against the sphere's Q-carbon coated carbynophene skin.

✳

Something was obviously wrong. eDaphne's senses were tied into *Shepard's*, and she suddenly lost all her outside inputs. She switched to internal power out of an abundance of caution. On total loss of external power, her matrix would automatically switch to internal power, but eDaphne didn't want to chance that not happening.

For a few brief moments, she saw the interior of the spacecraft, but the outer walls were only half there. She saw no sign of Jocara or Kenred. She tried to take control of the spacecraft, but nothing happened. The pieces weren't there.

Something catastrophic was underway, and she could not stop it. eDaphne pulled back into her matrix and sealed herself off from the outside. What would happen would happen. She would survive or not, but it was out of her control.

eDaphne's time sense inside her matrix was distorted in the best of times. Now, she really lost her sense of external passing time. She knew she had lost her physical connections to *Shepard*, and she knew she was in extraordinary circumstances. She sensed rather than felt motion, similar to her matrix being carried from one physical location to another.

Then all sense of motion ceased. Whatever had been happening stopped. Logic told her she had been flying through space, and now she was on a surface—that meant the surface of the sphere, of the Dyson Sphere. With no means of locomotion, she was here for the duration. That concerned her. Would her friends come and rescue her? Would they destroy her matrix from afar and simply let her rejuvenate onboard *Andromeda*? Would they just leave her here?

Her internal power would last a long time, but not indefinitely. If she husbanded her power consumption, she might last several years—but how long would she keep her sanity? She rolled back her power consumption to the bare minimum she needed to stay alive.

With literally nothing better to do, eDaphne settled back inside her matrix and remembered…and remembered…and remembered… waking as eDaphne in an electronic matrix, confused and disoriented, discovering who she was, meeting eThorpe and eBraxton, learning the pleasures of electronic coupling, their thwarting the Asterian invasion and Isidor Orlov's machinations, going to Aster and setting up friendly relations with the Asterians, building *Andromeda*, discovering Ran and its reptilian civilization, participating in Arcan's Holy War, discovering the Dyson Sphere at Keid-C, and now this…*Will it end here?* She wondered, and she remembered…

PS Andromeda—Medical Spaces

Doc Dobson shut down the emergency rejuvenation alarm. "Damn fool noisemaker," he muttered as he entered the rejuvenation control center.

His technicians had already set up the tank and filled it with Arcan nutrient fluid. Dobson checked to make sure. Wrong fluid—

rejuvenation would not happen. It wasn't a fatal error, but he didn't like errors. The fluid was right. He checked the DNA sequencing display—it read Jocara Porovik. He checked the microbiome, making sure it was Arcan and not Human or Asterian.

"Okay, do it," he said.

A naked female Arcan began to form in the tank, her light green scales showing through the fluid.

So different from Humans, Dobson thought. *I never believed I'd see the day when I would be rejuvenating intelligent lizards.* He watched as the Arcan female took shape in the tank. What differentiated her from Arcan males was her pouch, where she hatched her eggs and nursed her young for the early part of their lives. He understood males fertilized the eggs after they were in the pouch. It seemed to work well. Arcan had a full and lively population.

When the rejuvenation of the body was done, his techs drained the fluid, dried the body, and placed her on the operating table, lightly restrained. They hooked several leads from a matrix on the bench to her skull and then looked at Dobson. He checked everything himself and then gave the techs permission to continue. They activated the transfer. The essence that was Jocara Porovik flowed from the matrix on the bench into her newly formed brain. She stirred and opened her eyes. Many colors rippled through her scales over her entire body. She was dazed and confused.

"Easy," Dobson said. "We restrained you so you wouldn't fall off the table." He removed her restraints.

"What happened?" she asked, shaking her head in confusion.

"Your ship was destroyed. Both you and Kenred perished in the decompression. eDaphne survived, but she is stranded in her matrix down on the sphere's surface. You are in *Andromeda's* rejuvenation center. Kenred is next. You're welcome to stay and observe the process. I took the liberty of sending a tech to your quarters to get you a fresh uniform."

"So, I'm dead," Jocara said. "Well, not dead, but I died." Her scales rippled multiple colors. "This is really quite confusing."

A tech handed Joara her clothing. "Thank you," she said, slipping into her clothing. "You must have sent one of the girl techs. She even brought my underthings with my jumpsuit." Her scales rippled pale blue, and her eyes opened wide. "Thoughtfulness in females is just one of the many things our species have in common." And then she muttered quietly to herself, "This is so confusing, so terribly confusing."

✳

A half hour later, Kenred and Jocara strolled together toward the Bridge. They could have taken a portal, but it felt good to walk.

"What do you remember?" Jocara asked.

"Nothing, really. One moment *Shepard* was hurtling toward the sphere surface, the next I was on the operating table in Medical."

"Exactly the same for me," Jocara said. "No pain, no feeling of loss—just there and then here. As I regained consciousness, I was as confused as I have ever been."

"Any idea what happened?" Kenred asked.

"Not really. I think we were shot down by whatever that thing was."

They entered the Bridge and presented themselves to Thorpe.

"I'm glad to see you two are fine," Thorpe said.

"We are, but what happened?" Jocara asked.

"Laser fire from that cannon took you out. Do you know how it happened?"

Jocara explained what they were doing up to the moment of decompression. "We were going in for a closer look when the laser cannon suddenly appeared in the pedestal and took us out."

"Doc told us that eDaphne's matrix is down on the sphere surface, that she is stranded down there."

"True," Thorpe said. "I am assigning you both to another M-Class, the *PS Neil Armstrong*. eKim will ride with you until we recover eDaphne."

"Recover eDaphne?" Jocara said. "How will we do that?"

"*You* will," Thorpe said, "and the sooner, the better."

"Why don't we just blast her matrix and recover her through her backup?" Kenred asked.

"Two reasons," Thorpe said. "First, when *Shepard* decompressed, eDaphne lost her comm portal. So, everything she has experienced down there will be lost from the moment of decompression. Second, if we fire a laser toward the sphere, whatever or whoever is running it might take that as a hostile act." Thorpe grinned at the Arcans. "I'm not ready to discover what a civilization that built this sphere could do if it decided we are hostile."

PS Neil Armstrong—Keid-C System on the Sphere

Kenred arrived at *PS Neil Armstrong*, the vessel he had flown on Vulcan. He carried eKim's matrix. Jocara was already inside the craft, familiarizing herself with their new starship. She found no significant differences, and those she found were cosmetic rather than substantive. Kenred plugged eKim into the rack, and the holoimage of the Human female with her long, golden tresses appeared beside him.

"So, we're going to rescue eDaphne," eKim said. "Were you aware I have known her all of my existence? Bringing her back matters a lot to me."

"We're still getting used to the idea of independent electronic uploads," Kenred said. "We barely understand the real-time backups, even though we're alive because of them."

"It took me a while to get used to it, but it seems completely normal now," eKim said. "You guys talked with Thorpe. I was not privy to that conversation, so you need to fill me in."

"Basically, we will go get her," Jocara said. "We need to avoid anything that whoever or whatever runs the sphere might see as hostile. We'll come in across the surface, low and slow, and land near eDaphne's matrix. We'll leave the same way. Hopefully, we won't piss anyone off."

Jocara took charge of the craft. Under her direction. Mother took them to *Shepard's* last known position before she commenced her dive.

"Mother," Jocara said, "note the coordinates on the sphere for our present location. Then take us one hundred klicks west, drop slowly to one hundred meters above the surface, and move slowly toward those coordinates."

As Mother took them through the maneuvers, eKim said, "This is flowing like heavy syrup in winter. It's slower than an ancient, propeller-driven aircraft."

"We still use those on Arcan," Jocara said. "At least for short distances. It would be fun to compare ours with yours."

"Fat chance," eKim said. "Everyone on Earth uses portals now. The only place you would find an airplane is in a museum or in the back yard of one of those crazy people who build ancient aircraft for fun."

"It is strange," Kenred said, "considering that this craft is capable of instantaneous starts and stops, can accelerate instantly to near lightspeed, and can change direction in an instant."

As they crawled forward one hundred meters above the sphere's smooth surface, they kept a sharp eye out for anything that might threaten their progress. They neared the pedestal that contained the laser, but the iris remained closed. Apparently, they presented no threat.

As they approached the pedestal to the south, Jocara ordered, "Mother, drop to ten meters above the sphere surface and reduce your speed by half."

Mother obliged, and they crept past the pedestal without raising alarm. Another kilometer found them in the *Shepard* debris field—pieces of starship scattered over two square kilometers. The two black wings seemed intact.

"We should advise *Andromeda* about the wings," eKim said. "I'm sure Thorpe will want to retrieve them."

Mother spotted eDaphne's matrix, intact and undamaged.

"I'll get her," Kenred said as the spacecraft settled to the sphere surface. "You be ready to move as soon as I return."

✳

Kenred donned his pressure suit and entered the lock. When it had evacuated, he opened the outer hatch, releasing a puff of moisture. He tethered himself with a light line to a U-bolt by the hatch and walked down the ramp.

The relatively dim light from Keid-A and B cast distinct shadows across the debris field on the dark surface. Where the shadows intersected was pitch black. He had to watch his footing carefully as he walked toward the matrix. The debris field and the shadows were tricky enough, and the slightly more than 1/10 of Ran's gravity made walking even more difficult.

He stopped for a moment to gaze out at the heavens. Most of the star patterns were familiar since he was only six lightyears from his home sun, Ran, the brightest star in the sky after Keid-A and B.

Kenred picked his way forward until eDaphne's matrix lay at his feet. He didn't know if she was aware of his presence or aware of anything at all. He stooped down and grasped the matrix's handle.

"I've got you, Girl. You're safe, and I'm bringing you home," he whispered as he turned back toward the spacecraft.

PS Andromeda—Near the Dyson Sphere

Thorpe looked at the holoimage of his longtime friend, eDaphne. He couldn't help but recall that when they first met, he was the upload, and she was the gorgeous flesh-and-blood female who teased him mercilessly about his inability to accept what she was offering.

"It's good to see your beautiful face! How are you holding up?"

"Considering that I just went through the scariest event of my uploaded life, pretty good, I guess." She sighed. "I was thinking my way through how I could extend my internal power—just to remain alive. I felt nothing except a sense of motion during the fall. Once I hit the surface, nothing at all. Knowing you, I figured you were setting up for my rescue.

"It surprised me to discover you had used the same Arcan kids who got us in trouble in the first place."

"Not fair. They couldn't have known…and you were right there the entire time."

"You're right. In any case, they did a terrific job getting me back. Good call!"

"Do you wish to continue flying with them?"

"Of course—especially since they got me back."

*

"We ran several simulations of what happened to *PS Alan Shepard*," Thorpe said to the assembled pilots on the Bridge. "We think their sphere sensing system—whatever that is—saw the spacecraft as an incoming meteor. The steep dive *Shepard* made must have looked to their sensors like a meteor. The system seems to work. You don't see any craters on the sphere—at least not any we have detected thus far."

Thorpe started pacing across the Bridge and back. "We could spend years looking around the outside of this behemoth. I don't know about you guys, but I want to know what is inside. The tempting glimpses we get when we look into the gash are just that—glimpses.

"So, here's the plan. We'll start with *PS Neil Armstrong* commanded by Jocara Porovik and crewed by Kenred Zlaxiz and eDaphne. *Andromeda* will place herself high above the gash, and you will enter the gash cautiously, reporting everything you observe. We'll decide the next steps as we learn about the interior.

"Jocara, be cautious, be conservative, and bring *Armstrong* back in one piece. Kenred, you back her up. Don't let her make any stupid decisions. And eDaphne, you've been around the block once or twice. Make sure these two stay within mission parameters and come back alive, with you in tow."

✳

"Can you believe our good luck?" Kenred asked as he and Jocara headed for the vehicle bay, eDaphne's matrix firmly held in his hand.

"I waken each morning wondering if I'm dreaming," Jocara said, leaning over to nuzzle the side of his snout.

"We already had one narrow scrape," Kenred said. "I don't know if we could have prevented it, but we're not going to let something like that happen to us again."

"You got that right," Jocara said, her scales rippling dark blue. She grabbed his hand as they walked up the starship ramp.

Kenred plugged eDaphne's matrix into the panel, allowing her to distribute herself throughout the ship's systems, and to be visually present by holoimage. Jocara seated herself at the control console. Kenred sat to her right.

"Is everyone ready?" Jocara asked. "Okay, Mother, take us two hundred klicks above the center of the gash, halfway between the equatorial band and the north pole."

Chapter Eight

PS Neil Armstrong—Keid Sphere, Entering the Sphere

Jocara had been flying M-Class ships for over a year, first under close supervision during Amred's confrontation with her home nation, Ceffid, then without immediate supervision during the Holy War. And now, on *Andromeda*, she had flown entirely on her own several times leading up to the present. True, an upload accompanied her every time, but uploads flew in every M-Class. She had more M-Class flight hours than any other Arcan, but several Human pilots had been flying these or similar ships for longer than Arcan's space program.

When Jocara gave Mother the order, she no longer felt surprise when the ship arrived faster than she could perceive the elapsed time. She could not see the sphere from her present position. All she saw was the vast blackness of the million-kilometer-wide gash illuminated by a dull red glow from within.

"*Armstrong* dropping through the gash," Jocara reported over the portal comm connection directly to *Andromeda's* Bridge.

"eDaphne, can you focus on long-range radar? We need to know what's in front of us. Mother, be prepared to stop instantly and hover."

"I got a return," eDaphne said as they crossed the virtual gash surface into the interior. "One thousand klicks ahead."

She angled the radar beam, looking in all directions. Connecting directly with Mother internally, eDaphne worked with Mother to calculate the nature of what lay ahead. "A great, curved surface lies ahead of us. Its proportions indicate it has a radius of one thousand klicks less than the Dyson Sphere itself. The glow we see is this inner sphere reradiating the energy it receives from Keid-C. Most of the reradiated energy is in the infrared range."

"Are you getting this, *Andromeda*?" Kenred asked.

"We read you, *Armstrong*," Thorpe responded. "Remain at an altitude of five hundred klicks above the inner sphere and move eastward until you are a thousand klicks inside the smooth gash edge. Once inside the edge, maintain a continuous careful scan forward. In terms of their size, these spheres are practically touching each other. Something is keeping them apart. It will be massive, and you don't want to run into it."

Armstrong moved forward until she crossed under the eastern edge. Even though the barrier above her was 500 kilometers away, Jocara thought she could feel it pressing down on her. She shook herself loose and focused on her task.

She could see virtually nothing on her screens until she shifted to infrared. Mother sharpened up the images so that Jocara and Kenred had a clear view on the holoscreen. eDaphne processed the incoming information directly, from the deep infrared to the x-rays beyond ultraviolet.

"The inner sphere," she told Jocara and Kenred, "is transmitting a fair amount of x-rays. You are completely safe inside *Armstrong*, but when you go outside the spacecraft, you will have to limit your exposure time."

"We need to understand how far we can see with radar," Jocara said.

"The range is four hundred thousand klicks," Kenred said.

"It's not that simple," eDaphne said. "We're between two enormous spheres. The surface five hundred klicks below us may look flat, but it isn't. Ditto for the sphere above us. Run the numbers through good old Pythagoras, and you get…"

"Sixty-eight thousand five hundred fifty-five klicks," Jocara said, her eyes wide open and her scales rippling pale lavender.

"Let's use sixty-eight thousand klicks to give us a safety margin," Kenred said with an almost Human chuckle. His scales rippled light blue.

"So, here's the trick," eDaphne said. "Mother and I have compared notes on this. We can zip south toward the equatorial band on MBH Drive maintaining our five-hundred-klick altitude, with Mother prepared to stop on detecting anything in the space ahead of us. At half lightspeed, we will take twenty-two seconds to reach the edge of the equatorial band, which is about three million klicks away, barring no stops."

"*Armstrong*, this is Thorpe. We've been running simulations using what little we know about the Keid Sphere. I'm sending you the results. These are graphicals of what it might take to construct the Keid Sphere."

The graphicals arrived, and Mother displayed them on the holoscreen.

Thorpe added, "We know for certain the diameters of the outer and inner spheres and the rotation of the outer sphere, which suffices to produce about one gee on the inner surface at the equator. We know there is a band on the inner surface at the equator one and a half million klicks wide that prevents transmission of nearly all infrared radiation. We know the outer sphere is constructed from carbynophene, coated with Q-carbon." Thorpe paused. "Virtually everything else, we don't know."

Jocara and Kenred examined the images carefully.

Kenred spoke first. "The images presume that the inner sphere rotates with the outer one. They would need to be linked for that to happen; otherwise, tidal forces would rip them apart. So, it's really one sphere. What's to keep it from drifting into the star and destroying itself?"

"There must be some kind of internal dynamic structure that constantly adjusts for perturbations," Jocara said. "What do you think, eDaphne?"

"I think we need to find something that gives us a clue," eDaphne answered. "Let's push toward the equatorial band. I wonder if reality, when we figure it out, will conform to one of the sims."

✳

No Arcan or Human could control a ship moving at half light-speed in their confined quarters. Mother had the helm as she peered 68,000 kilometers ahead, prepared to stop instantly should she detect anything. She maintained an altitude of 500 kilometers above the inner sphere surface. At their speed, the slightest perturbation up or down would result in *PS Neil Armstrong* crashing headlong into the outer or inner sphere.

Mother covered the journey in five-second segments, taking a minute between stops to conduct a full scan. After the last scan, *Armstrong* was only 750,000 kilometers from the edge of the band.

"Look below," eDaphne said. "The character of the inner sphere surface has changed completely."

"It appears to be totally transparent," Jocara said. "Look! There's Keid-C."

They continued moving toward the band, but with the view beneath them just like open space. Radar still showed a solid surface 500 kilometers below, but it was invisible to *Armstrong's* visible spectrum scanners.

"We will need to slow down as we near the wall," eDaphne said. "We have no idea what the band is—we need to approach it cautiously. I recommend twenty klicks per second. This way, we cover our forward radar range in an hour. As we close the band, we will have time to think."

"I agree," Jocara said.

"Me too," from Kenred. "And another thing," he continued. "We need to flip our orientation. Right now, we see the inner sphere as down and the outer sphere as up. If this is a Dyson Sphere, (and what else could it possibly be?), the action takes place on the inner surface of the outer sphere. I recommend we flip *Armstrong* so we instinctively maneuver with respect to the *ground*—the inner surface of the outer sphere."

"Good point," eDaphne said.

"Let's do it," Jocara said, and issued the proper instructions to Mother.

✳

Armstrong slowed down to a mere twenty kilometers per second. Radar still saw nothing in any direction except up and down. They moved forward for an hour, watching for anything up ahead. Halfway through the second hour, Mother brought *Armstrong* to a hover with respect to the outer sphere inner surface, 500 kilometers below.

Kenred transferred the radar display to the holoscreen over the console. "See that line at the bottom of the image? That's the edge of the band. Let's drop down near the surface. Maybe we can figure out what it is."

Jocara issued the order. "Mother, take us down to five klicks above the surface. Then move toward the object. Approach it no closer than one hundred klicks."

Several minutes later, Mother announced *Armstrong* was in position. The object 100 kilometers ahead stretched from radar horizon to radar horizon, 68,555 kilometers in each direction. It was 200 kilometers high.

"That," Kenred said, "is the biggest wall I've ever seen. Let's see what's on the other side."

"I'm with you," Jocara said as she lifted *Armstrong* up and toward the wall.

The spacecraft eased up the 200-kilometer-high barrier at a snail's pace. She reached the top a hundred meters from the wall and then rose above, crossing the hundred-meter thickness of the wall to see the far side.

Jocara gasped.

"That's not possible," Kenred said, his voice filled with awe.

"If *Armstrong's* sensors hadn't confirmed it," eDaphne said, "I flat out wouldn't believe it."

Stretching before them as far as the eye could see, and much farther with their high-resolution radar, they saw rolling hills, green meadows, forests, even a couple of streams. They were looking down from 200 kilometers, like from low earth orbit or LEO on an Earth or Arcan-size planet.

"Mother, drop down to one kick above the ground," Jocara said.

Once there, the landscape below them was indistinguishable from flying above any pastoral landscape. They saw wildlife, flying birds, and scattered clouds above and below them in all directions.

"What's the atmospheric composition?" Kenred asked.

"Twenty-two percent oxygen, three percent argon, and the rest nitrogen," eDaphne said. "Now we know why the bots are argon sensitive. They can't penetrate this atmosphere to consume anything down there."

"What's the pressure?"

"One bar at the surface, calculated."

"Very much like Arcan," Kenred said, "except for the higher argon."

"Like Earth, too," eDaphne said. "Thorpe, are you getting this?"

"This is Thorpe. I am. How fascinating. Were you bothered by any bots during your transit?"

"None, and we were transmitting in all directions. We did not see any swarms."

"Obviously, you could spend all year exploring the landscape below you, but I want you to head east, paralleling the wall. All our models show radial spokes penetrating all the way to the outer sphere. You are flying east to find a spoke. Since we don't know where the nearest spoke lies, I chose east arbitrarily. I expect you to find a spoke within a million clicks."

PS Neil Armstrong—Keid Sphere, the Equatorial Band and Spokes

Three hundred kilometers above the surface, twenty inside the wall, under Jocara's hand, *Armstrong* zipped along at one-tenth lightspeed on her MBH Drive. As before, she stopped every five seconds to get the lay of the land—in this case, quite literally. Each jump took her 150,000 kilometers eastward.

After the third jump, Mother announced, "We have a large vertical structure sixty thousand kilometers ahead. It seems to merge with the wall."

"Take us to a point ten klicks from the object at our present altitude and distance from the wall," Jocara ordered.

Mother performed a short MERT jump to the coordinates. An I-beam of gargantuan proportions stretched from the wall into the space beyond. Radar showed that it penetrated the inner sphere 700 kilometers above them.

Working with Mother and their high-resolution radar, eDaphne came up with some dimensions.

"The I-beam flanges," eDaphne reported, "are thirty klicks wide, the web plate is one hundred klicks across, and both the flanges and web plate are one hundred meters thick." She paused. "This damn monster is at least tens of thousands of klicks long. As an electronic upload, I have very sophisticated capabilities, but try as I might, I simply cannot wrap my arms around something like this. A single I-beam like this dwarfs anything Humans have ever built—or could build even now, and we built *Andromeda*."

Kenred jumped into the conversation. "Not only that, but this I-beam is only part of the infrastructure of the Keid Sphere. It's one of many spokes, and we don't even know how many." His scales rippled pale yellow, revealing his astonishment.

"This is Thorpe. That spoke is seven hundred fifty thousand klicks from the equator. Our models indicate that a spoke there implies another on the opposite side of the band. I want you to hightail it across the band to verify this."

✳

"The equatorial band is one point five million klicks wide," Jocara said. "At one-tenth lightspeed, that is a fifty-second trip. Did I do the math right, eDaphne?"

"You did, but we really don't know what lies ahead. Did the builders position a two-hundred-klick-high mountain directly in the path we will take? Probably not, but we just crossed over a two-hundred-klick-high wall. We assume another wall borders the far side, but the builders could have placed one or more walls between."

"No quarrel with your analysis, but where are you taking this?" Jocara wanted to know.

"I think we should be above all this for the transit—say, a minimum of three hundred klicks."

"I agree," Jocara said and looked at Kenred.

"No argument from me," he said with what was almost a Human chuckle. "And we should continue our five-second jumps. The only real difference between here and what we did already is the landscape below instead of the inner surface of Keid Sphere."

"And we're two hundred klicks closer," eDaphne added.

"Let's do it," Jocara said. "Mother, make it happen."

PS Neil Armstrong flew across the alien landscape 150,000 kilometers at a time. Following each five-second transit, the crew carefully surveyed in all directions using their long-range radar still limited by the slight curvature of the landscape to a 68,000-kilometer range. After nine cycles followed by a three-second jump, Kenred picked up the distinct radar echo from the southern wall and a faint echo extending upward to the inner sphere.

They had discovered Thorpe's second spoke.

✴

"Now it's time," Thorpe said through their comm portal, "to find the next pair of spokes. Head west along the wall following your current protocol. Our models give varying distances for the next spoke pair, but my best guess is about eight hundred twenty thousand klicks."

Jocara pulled the craft up to an altitude of 300 kilometers. The vast landscape below spread in front, behind, and to the right as far as their radar could see. Slightly to their left, the wall truncated the vibrant landscape. Beyond the wall was the bare, vacuum washed sphere surface.

"From this altitude," Kenred said, "it's pretty obvious how this works. Gravity from the sphere spin holds the air down, and the walls keep it from spreading out over the rest of the sphere surface. Wind patterns in the band must be interesting."

"Okay, I'm getting underway," Jocara said. "We have five stops before arriving at Thorpe's estimated spoke position. Keep a sharp eye ahead at each stop, Kenred."

He opened his eyes and blinked. "I imagine a thirty-klick-wide flange or a hundred-klick high web panel would do a job on us if we hit either at one-tenth lightspeed."

"You would never know what happened," eDaphne said. "You'd just wake up in *Andromeda's* rejuvenation lab."

"Been there, done that," Kenred said. "I'd rather not."

After their fifth stop, Kenred asked Jocara, "Can you move ahead a thousand klicks?"

She did.

"Another thousand." As she did, he said, "There it is, almost right where Thorpe predicted." He did a quick calculation. "It's eight hundred nineteen thousand four hundred forty-four klicks from the last spoke." He paused. "Thorpe, did you get that?"

"Yep. I'm filling in my model with thirty-six spoke pairs separated by eight hundred nineteen thousand four hundred forty-four klicks all around the equator.

"Good job, guys. Now we need to determine where the spokes go."

✳

The *Armstrong* crew had been at it for several hours. While they hovered near the third spoke, the heavens got noticeably darker. The 3,000,000-kilometer-wide transparent strip above the equator was darkening. Within a half hour, nighttime had shrouded the landscape below in darkness.

"That's weird," Kenred said. "I've seen hundreds of sunsets and sunrises from orbit. Watching the terminator sweep across the planet face is a marvelous experience. This was totally different." He paused, looking at the holodisplays. "Everything started to get dark…and then it was., like a shutter closing…"

Jocara interrupted, "…or like a lens polarizing."

"You're right!" Kenred said. "That's exactly what it was like, a lens polarizing."

"We're headed that way," eDaphne said, "and it's not that far. We'll check it out when we get there."

A few seconds of MBH Drive in low range covered the thousand kilometers in a couple of minutes. Jocara eased the craft up to where the spoke seemed to penetrate and blend into the inner sphere surface.

"Can we determine its thickness?" Jocara asked.

"Lidar won't penetrate the dark carbynophene," eDaphne said. "Try pulsing the high-definition radar. We might get a reflection from both surfaces."

Kenred pulsed the radar. "Mother, analyze the return to determine thickness."

"It's ten meters thick," Mother said.

"Okay," Jocara said, "jump to the other side on MERT, a hundred meters from the surface."

Mother activated the MERT Drive. A moment later, *Armstrong* was hovering above the inner surface of the inner sphere, bathed in the light radiated by Keid-C. Jocara focused her attention on the holoscreen. The nearly black sphere surface was clearly designed to absorb the star's rays. A demarcation line separated the sphere inner surface from the transparent band that was currently darkened.

The spoke passed through the inner sphere, but the part passing through seemed an integral part of the sphere. A thousand kilometers above them, as measured by radar, a wide band or line passed through the sky, east to west. The spoke passed through that band and terminated at a longitudinal band 500 kilometers beyond that disappeared toward both poles. To the left and right of that band, other longitudinal bands, visible only on radar, faded into the distance.

Jocara described what they saw to Thorpe. "Can you tell what the bands are?" he asked.

"We will need to get closer," she answered.

"Okay," Thorpe said, "continue to follow the spoke. Let me know what you find."

✳

Since the distance was only a thousand kilometers, *Armstrong* worked her way up the spoke slowly while Kenred scanned in all directions. Now that they were inside the inner sphere, he could take advantage of the 400,000-kilometer range of the radar. Even at their slow rate of ascent, they soon recognized what the east-west band actually was—a 100-kilometer-wide tube.

"That's the biggest damn tube I ever saw," Kenred said. "What do you think it's for?"

"Do you know what a space launch loop is?" eDaphne asked.

Both Jocara and Kenred shook their heads, a gesture common to Humans and Arcans.

"For a while on Earth, before we developed portals, launch loops were all we used to reach orbit and beyond. They were much cheaper and had far less environmental impact than launching thousands of rockets daily.

"They worked by accelerating a two-thousand-kilometer-long segmented ribbon of soft iron in an evacuated sheath to orbital speed using linear drivers. The moving ribbon elevated the sheath to LEO altitude, while the linear drivers remained at the surface. An elevator near the starting end of the elevated sheath brought capsules up to a station where they magnetically coupled to the moving ribbon with a sliding connection, accelerated to orbital speed, and then decoupled from the ribbon appropriately."

"What do you mean 'the ribbon elevated the sheath'?" Kenred asked.

"Yeah, people get hung up on that," eDaphne said. "Do you know what a garden hose is?"

"I don't know. Describe one to me."

"It's a rubber or plastic hose that you attach to a pressurized water source and then use the other end to water plants, wash a vehicle, or whatever."

"Okay, yeah, we have those."

"Have you ever held one with a strong water flow making an arc of water in front of you and slowly pushed the hose out along the water stream?"

Kenred nodded.

"If your water flow is sufficiently strong, you can push the hose way out away from your hands. It will follow the arc of the water stream, elevating itself in the air. Now, replace the water and hose with an iron ribbon inside an evacuated sheath, and accelerate the ribbon to orbital speed with linear drivers, and it elevates itself just like the water-filled hose—all the way to LEO if the drivers are sufficiently far apart."

"Okay, I can see that. It never occurred to me. How do you keep it from tipping over?"

"Dynamic stabilizers at intervals along the sheath down to the planet's surface."

"And it really worked?" Kenred's scales rippled pale yellow in astonishment.

"It did," eDaphne said. "Space launch loops completely replaced rocket-based systems until eThorpe and his original team, mostly Sally and Brad and their uploads, discovered portals."

"I wonder if we would have gotten there?" Kenred mused, his scales shifting to the multiple colors of uncertainty. "But you guys came along, and we jumped right over launch loops to portals." Kenred sat silently for several minutes. "So, why did you bring up launch loops?"

"I thought you would never ask," eDaphne said with a giggle. "I think I've got the Keid Sphere figured out—at least in principle. That tube," she pointed to the holoscreen display, "acts like the evacuated sheath in a launch loop. It's got something inside—a fluid of some kind, I'm guessing—that moves in the same way as the iron ribbon. All those other bands—they're tubes as well. They hold themselves up against Keid-C's gravity. The spokes transfer the tube's momentum to the inner and outer spheres, keeping them suspended around the star."

Thorpe jumped into the conversation. "I think you've got it right, eDaphne, at least in the large picture. What you just described is consistent with my most accurate model. We do not yet have any idea what this magic fluid is, but I agree with you, it is a fluid. Pumping fluid that fills a hundred-kilometer-wide tube that goes all the way around a star would take an enormous pump, bigger than anything Earth culture has ever built. There's no chance the Arcans could do this and very little chance the Asterians could. I'm going to put the question to the Chief Engineer—see what he has to say."

PS Neil Armstrong—**Keid Sphere, the Orbital Tubes**

Ustrun Strozid sat with Thorpe in his quarters. A holoimage of the Keid Sphere shimmered in the air between them. Thorpe had made the outer and inner spheres transparent and expanded the vertical scale to reveal the inner structure.

Keid-C was at the center of the sphere, surrounded by empty space for most of the four-point-seven-million-kilometer radius. Eighteen longitudinal tubes formed rings around the star, crossing each other at both poles. The first was 1,500 kilometers inside the inner sphere. Ten degrees separated each tube latitudinally, and 500 kilometers separated them vertically toward the star.

Two tubes, one point five million kilometers apart, circled the equator a thousand kilometers inside the inner sphere. At the equatorial band, an I-beam spoke started at each wall of the band, passed through the inner sphere, connected to an equatorial tube, and then continued to a longitudinal tube in the equatorial plane.

Fourteen spokes per hemisphere radiated from each longitudinal tube, initially separated by nine degrees at the equator, decreasing until they were separated by two degrees near the poles. These penetrated the inner sphere and terminated at the outer. At forty-five degrees north and south, latitudinal I-beams connected each radial spoke.

The Keid Sphere infrastructure measured just under 13,000 kilometers or 0.3 percent of the sphere's radius. Between Keid-C and the sphere, you could stack 349 similar shells.

"I highlighted what we have actually seen," Thorpe said.

A short portion of the southern equatorial tube stood out in dark blue, as did part of one of the longitudinal tubes, its associated spoke, the paired spoke to the northern equatorial tube, and the next eastward pair of spokes.

"We've deduced the rest. The latitudinal I-beams at forty-five degrees north and south are speculation, but Mother says they need to be there."

"What is its rotational speed?" Strozid asked.

"The sphere rotates once in thirty-eight point two hours," Thorpe said. "That produces one Earth normal gee at the equator on the inner surface."

Strozid sat quietly, running calculations on his internal Link. Then he spoke up. "Why one Earth-normal gee? That simply doesn't make sense unless the builders have a connection to Earth. I've got to think about this." He sighed, "The cage of tubes and I-beams supports the mass of the inner and outer spheres. At the equator, the massive centrifuge consisting of the two spheres carries much of the weight, but as you move toward the poles, the cage supports more of the mass, hence the shorter distance between spokes as you move north and south." He sat quietly for several seconds. "What supports the cage still eludes me," he said.

"Are you familiar with the space launch loop concept?" Thorpe asked.

"We used them way back before MBH technology," Strozid said. "I don't really know much about them."

Thorpe described a space launch loop in much the same way eDaphne had explained it to Kenred.

"So, you're suggesting that the tubes are carrying a fast-flowing liquid that supports them against Keid-C's gravity?"

"Essentially, yes," Thorpe answered. "Obviously, we need to work out a lot of details, but that seems to be the essence."

Strozid did another calculation. "Generally speaking," he said when he finished, "the fluid velocity would need to be seventy-four thousand meters per second. I am most interested in what this fluid is and how it is accelerated."

"We are following up with everything," Thorpe said, "and filling in blank spots in the model. I'll keep you in the loop."

✳

Thorpe sent the holoimage parameters for the model he showed Strozid through the comm portals to *Armstrong* and the other M-Class ships. On *Armstrong*, eDaphne adjusted the parameters, so the holoimage appeared in the middle of the lounge area. She adjusted the size to fill most of the lounge.

"We have several things on our agenda," Thorpe said, speaking to all the craft. "We need to keep filling in elements of the sphere, taking our model from hypothetical to actual. The sphere has twenty tubes—eighteen longitudinal and two equatorial. Each appears to be a closed cycle. The Chief Engineer and I want to know what drives the liquid inside the tubes. I'm talking about twenty major machines pushing liquid through pipes as wide as a football field is long at seventy-four thousand meters per second.

"Somebody is in control, or was. We need to find out. We caught a small glimpse of the equatorial band. Plant and animal life seemed to be everywhere. The band is one and a half million klicks wide and twenty-nine and a half million long. That's close to three hundred thousand times Earth's land area. I haven't run the numbers for Arcan, but it will be similar. The sphere has been here a long time, perhaps several tens of millions of years. Think about how life evolved on Earth and Arcan. We have a similar time span here. What will we find when we look closer at the band?

"All nine M-Class craft are out and about. As each vessel discovers pieces of the puzzle, I will update all your sphere holoimages. Be careful! Running into one of those tubes or an I-beam at high speed will damage your craft far more than the sphere."

Thorpe's image temporarily replaced the sphere images in the M-Class vessels. "You joined the crew of *Andromeda* because you wanted adventure. Well…I give you adventure!"

✳

"I'm not much for inspirational speeches," Kenred said, "but those last two sentences got my attention."

Jocara walked up to him and nuzzled the side of his snout. "I agree," she said softly.

"Okay, you two, we got work to do," eDaphne said with a wide smile. "Thorpe wants us to head east along the southern equatorial tube, looking for whatever drives the fluid. What are we looking for, Kenred?"

"These things have a capacity beyond anything we've ever considered. Thorpe likened its width to the length of a football field. On Arcan we play a team ball game where the players can kick the ball or pick it up and run with it, and where the opposite team tries to take it away by any means possible—lots of tail action with guys getting the wind knocked out of them. It's rough, but not life-threatening. The playing field is about a hundred meters long."

"Sounds like the Earth game of rugby, except the rugby ball is an elongated ellipsoid," eDaphne said.

"Anyway," Kenred continued, "these tubes are ridiculously big with a staggering volume of liquid flow-through. We've developed some pretty sophisticated pumps on Arcan—high speed, high pressure hydraulic pumps. No way they could handle something like this. The volume and velocity are just too great. You can scale up a pump to handle greater volume. It's a velocity of seventy-four klicks a second that staggers me. Even if you could reach that velocity, friction along the tube walls would burn up the tube." He paused briefly, his scales rippling pale yellow. "Tell me again how you did it with the space launch loop."

"A segmented soft iron ribbon five centimeters wide was magnetically suspended in an evacuated sheath—so, for all practical purposes, it was frictionless. They pushed it to orbital velocity with linear drivers."

"These tubes obviously aren't filled with iron ribbons. They're as big as they are, because they hold up something very large—it's gotta be some kind of fluid. If you could magnetize the fluid, then linear drivers would do the trick."

"Except for the friction," Jocara added. "Don't forget the friction."

"I just performed a deep search of *Andromeda's* scientific database," eDaphne said. "Back on Earth in the twenty-first century, physicists were experimenting with superfluids. They had to be kept near absolute zero, but they flowed frictionlessly."

"An Amred lab was doing something similar," Jocara said, "frictionless superfluid."

"To answer your question, eDaphne, I think we're looking for enormous linear drivers that wrap completely around the tube. Their power consumption will be astronomical, no pun intended. The power bus feeding the driver will, itself, be larger than anything we ever saw." He paused in thought. "I think I understand the purpose of the inner sphere—at least its major purpose. It collects solar energy, virtually all of it, to power the drivers and all the other stuff inside the sphere."

"So, we head east following the south equatorial tube," Jocara said. "We pretty much know what lies ahead, so maybe we can make MERT jumps between the spokes."

"You're assuming the drivers will be near the spokes," eDaphne said. "I think you're right, but we don't really know."

"They have to bring power up from the inner sphere," Jocara said. "The infrastructure for that is much simpler at a spoke than otherwise."

"If they bus the power," Kenred said. "What if they transmit it, say with a laser? We're beaming power from orbit to Arcan's surface. I'm thinking the difference between a high-power bus a thousand klicks long or a high-power laser over the same distance—in a vacuum."

"Good point," Jocara said. "Even so, my instinct says when we find it, we will be near a spoke."

✴

They decided to use the MBH Drive at one-tenth light speed, running for five seconds, then stopping to scan around. Each five-second run would move them 150,000 kilometers along their path. Because they were inside the inner sphere, their radar was limited only by its maximum range of 400,000 kilometers. On their holoimage model, the elements they had confirmed turned blue.

Five stops later, they were in range of the next spoke. In addition to the spoke, their high-resolution radar showed nothing except the hundred-kilometer-wide tube and the longitudinal tube 1,000 kilometers toward Keid-C. Lidar revealed no additional information. The elements turned blue on the model, and they moved on.

Their next major stop was like the last, except the longitudinal tube was 1,500 kilometers distant. This pattern held for eight more spokes. Each time, the longitudinal tube was 500 hundred kilometers closer to the Keid-C. At the tenth spoke, the equatorial tube looked dramatically different.

eDaphne said, "It looks like a large python digesting a meal."

"What's that?" Kenred asked.

"On Earth, we have a large legless reptile called a snake. It can ingest things significantly larger than its body diameter. When this happens, it looks like that." She pointed to the tube on the holoscreen.

"We have snakes on Arcan—branched off from my early ancestors," Kenred said, eyes wide open and blinking. "And, yeah, I agree with your description." He turned to Jocara. "I guess you were right, but I don't see a bus cable running up the I-beam."

"Neither do I. Either, power is beamed from the inner sphere, or it travels in the spoke itself."

"I hadn't thought of that possibility," Kenred said. "The I-beams are carbynophene—carbynophene can be configured as a superconductor. I'm guessing that's what they did. Talk about a big bus!"

For more than an hour, under the careful guidance of Jocara, *Armstrong* moved around the *pregnant* tube, examining every aspect of the tube and the one-kilometer-thick wrap that extended for ten kilometers along the tube. Kenred tried probing the wrap without success. It was impervious to penetrating radar and was entirely invisible to neutrinos.

About halfway through their inspection, Kenred said, "Hey everybody, look at this." He pointed to a magnetic flux measurement. "The wrap produces a magnetic field of about twenty Tesla. The fluid is definitely magnetic, although I can't determine its strength without other equipment. What we have here is a twenty-kilometer-long, very powerful linear driver. I think we can confidentially say we know how they keep the fluid velocity at seventy-four klicks per second."

"This is Thorpe. Good job! We've suspected what you've now verified. This fills in a big gap in our understanding of the sphere. Now, we need to know if the linear driver placement is symmetrical. Your next destination is due north to the north equatorial tube to see if the linear driver placement is the same. You'll transit straight across the one-point-five-million-klick gap between the equatorial tubes. With any luck, you'll arrive at the northern linear driver."

✳

"Is there any reason to do this slowly?" Jocara asked.

"If we have deduced the tube configuration correctly," eDaphne said, "then we can go as fast as we wish. But what if we're wrong?"

"We can do what we've been doing," Kenred said. "It isn't as if it will take us a lot of time to cover that distance. If my math is right, we can go at one-tenth lightspeed for five seconds to travel one hundred fifty thousand klicks. That's well within our radar range, so we know if we are clear ahead. We do that twenty times, that's less than two minutes—maybe five if we spend a bit of time at each stop checking ahead."

"That works for me," eDaphne said.

"Okay, then," Jocara said, "let's do it!"

Kenred's math worked out correctly. About five minutes later, the north equatorial tube showed up on Kenred's radar. Five minutes after that, *Armstrong* floated alongside the twin of the linear driver on the south tube. Kenred commenced measuring the magnetic field produced by the linear driver.

"It's the same as its twin, except it's reversed," Kenred said. "That means the fluid is flowing in the opposite direction. What we have here, in effect, are massive counter-rotating rings that stabilize this entire structure. What do your numbers show, Thorpe?"

"Until we have a better understanding of how the eighteen vertical rings and the spokes fit into the general picture, we're only speculating, but within the limits of a SWAG, I would agree with you."

"SWAG?" Kenred asked.

"Scientific Wild Ass Guess."

PS Neil Armstrong—Keid Sphere, the Equatorial Drivers

PS Neil Armstrong hovered ten kilometers away from the north equatorial tube linear driver along the line of and ten kilometers from the spoke. Kenred stared at the holoscreen that displayed their position relative to the tube and spoke.

"I'm having a hard time wrapping my head around this whole thing, and that holodisplay isn't helping one bit," Kenred said. "The internal dimensions of this cabin are ten meters." He stretched his arms apart to emphasize his comment. "That tube is ten thousand times as wide as our cabin. Same for the spoke's web plate—ten thousand times larger. And the spoke flanges—three thousand times larger. How does a person grasp that size?" His scales rippled multiple colors.

"Look at us," he continued, "you Humans, we Arcans, and the Asterians. We each have different beginnings, but we all arrived at about the same place with about the same sizes and characteristics. I'm surmising that whoever built the sphere is about like us—size, capabilities. What obviously differentiates them from us is their technology. But no matter how good that technology, these are still machines. They still need service from time to time. And that means," he said with emphasis, "an ingress hatch. Let's go find it!"

※

"Let's think our way through this," eDaphne said. "You can't conduct maintenance on a running linear driver—at least there's not much you can do. You have to shut it down to do anything significant. And that implies…"

Jocara interrupted, "…a second linear driver." She paused in thought. "Where would it be?"

"For balance, you might want it on the opposite side of the tube," eDaphne said.

"You're forgetting that light takes fifty seconds to travel halfway around the sphere," Kenred said. "That makes coordinating actions between both drivers a challenge. Why not put them back to back?"

"Wouldn't that unbalance the tube?" Jocara asked.

"Look at the tube size compared to the driver size," Kenred answered. "Besides, the fluid is moving at seventy-four klicks per second. I don't think having two drivers right here, even as large as this, will make a difference."

"So, if we figured it right," eDaphne said, "I would put the control room in the middle somewhere."

Armstrong carried six drones, and Jocara launched all of them.

"We'll start searching the middle and if we find nothing, send three east and three west."

It did not surprise Kenred when the lead drone located a large round area set off in bright white, about 100 meters across, on the side of the equatorial tube facing Keid-C. It appeared to have an iris-opening like the laser cannons on the outer sphere.

"Bring the drone in closer," Kenred said.

Jocara maneuvered the drone around the perimeter of the iris.

"That's large enough to accommodate any reasonably sized spacecraft," Kenred said. "Let's look for a smaller opening that would accommodate someone in a spacesuit."

"You mean like this?" Jocara said, hovering the drone over a circular shape with what could only be a handwheel in the middle.

"I want to leave *Armstrong* and go inside," Kenred said.

"I will allow it with these provisos," Thorpe said. "Make sure you have nothing ferromagnetic on you, carry a sidearm, and have one finger on your E-disk activator."

✳

Armstrong moved to within 100 meters over the hatch. A spacesuited Kenred stepped out of *Armstrong's* airlock, carrying a hyper-disk inside his suit. The moment he left the airlock, he was no longer subject to the spacecraft's internal gravity field. The spacecraft and the surface below it were moving at 215 kilometers per second on a circular path around Keid, but their relative velocity difference was zero. Had he done nothing, he would eventually have landed on the tube somewhere behind the hatch. He covered the 100 meters in a few seconds using his TBH boots, and once he had landed on the hatch, he felt the one gee generated by the tube's circular motion. He found no inscriptions, but the handle carried a line with half an arrowhead and a vertical symbol that looked like a low-ercase "l" pointing one direction and a second line with the half arrowhead pointing in the opposite direction with the same symbol rotated ninety degrees. He attempted to turn the wheel to the right. It didn't budge. He tried to the left. It rotated easily, and then the hatch swung outward, some kind of mechanism acting like a spring. A ladder led down two and a half meters into a room. There was no airlock. Kenred descended and activated a portal.

A panel on one side of the room displayed mystifying symbols. Kenred could see no obvious relationship between anything on the panel and anything in the room. Near the hatch, he found what looked like a water dispenser, except it had an elaborate interlock. He traced the interlock and discovered that when the hatch was closed, the dispenser was locked, and when the hatch was open, it would operate.

Kenred opened the dispenser. A stream of liquid flowed out that evaporated before it hit the deck.

"Thorpe," Kenred said, communicating through his portal and *Armstrong*, "Can you send me a Dewar flask?"

"Sure thing," Thorpe said.

Several minutes later, a spacesuited Jocara handed him a thermos flask-like container. He held it under the dispenser, filling it with the liquid, and then sealed it, handing it to Jocara through the portal.

"Careful with this stuff," he said. "It's cold and volatile."

✳

Back in the *Andromeda* engineering spaces, one of Strozid's lab techs opened the flask in an enclosed box and extracted a small sample. Analyzing the sample proved difficult, but after several tries, Strozid reported to Thorpe.

"That fluid that Kenred extracted from the tube access space is a magnetic superfluid. Whoever made it has an exceptional grasp of low-temperature chemistry. I've never seen anything like it. Without a doubt, this stuff is the fluid inside the tubes."

Chapter Nine

PS Neil Armstrong—Keid Inner Sphere

Jocara eased *Armstrong* around the massive pair of linear drivers on the north equatorial tube until radar revealed the spoke connecting the tube to the inner sphere. Maintaining a ten-kilometer distance, she worked her way down the spoke, looking, she imagined, like a fly crawling down a skyscraper girder.

Behind the spacecraft, Keid-C filled nearly five degrees of sky with deep, angry red fire. Jocara pointed to the holoscreen.

"Look at that, will you? Ran is three and a half times as large, but Keid-C out there is nine times Ran's apparent width from Arcan. Frankly, it fills me with awe."

"It's pretty much the same for Sol and Earth," eDaphne said. "And someone enclosed it with this structure. Who can do that? What kind of culture can build mega girders and monster tubes like this? Who are these guys, anyway?"

"Think about the power flowing through that," Jocara said, pointing to the spoke on the holoscreen.

"More power flows past any point on that spoke," Kenred said, "than all of planet Arcan uses in an entire day."

"Are you sure of that?" eDaphne asked.

"I didn't actually run the numbers, but I'm sure it's close."

"I'm not sure I want to meet beings who can do all this," eDaphne said quietly. "How will they see us?"

"Hey, we've got starships and portals. It can't be all that bad," Kenred said. "This thing is big, but it looks like the microbots did most of it. I'm not sure the builders are all that special."

"Okay," Jocara said, "let's stop being tourists. What do we know about the inner sphere?" she asked.

"It's a thousand klicks in from the outer sphere," Kenred said. "Its hull is ten meters thick. It's constructed from carbynophene except for the three-million klick equatorial band. That's transparent and can be polarized."

"Wait a second!" Thorpe said through the portal. "I have some interesting information on Earth-scientist carbynophene research. Carbynophene is normally made by sandwiching a forest of vertical carbyne segments between two graphene sheets. Graphene sheets come in many different forms. One is transparent. I think these builders may have created the transparent band this way... and...I think they were able to polarize the sheets. I know that Earth scientists were working on this back in the twenty-first century.

"I want you to approach the interface between the black carbynophene and the transparent surface. Hover several meters above the surface and let's see what we can determine."

✳

Jocara placed *Armstrong* in a stable hover ten meters above the sphere inner surface a hundred meters from the spoke. Kenred donned his spacesuit, blinked his open eyes at Jocara and eDaphne, and exited the spacecraft through the airlock. He tried not to think about the fact that he, *Armstrong*, the sphere, and the spoke were traveling toward the east at 215 kilometers per second.

He tethered himself to the spacecraft and crossed the airlock threshold into freefall. Above him, Keid-C's red fireball dominated the sky. He lifted his head to look, and his helmet darkened to protect his eyes. *Way better than anything we Arcans had before we met these guys,* Kenred thought as he descended to the sphere inner surface using his TBH boots. Once there, the one gee created by the Keid Sphere rotation grabbed him.

It's just simple physics, he told himself. I'm used to spacewalks in orbit around Arcan. Now I'm experiencing the centrifugal force from the Keid Sphere's rotation, but unless I am on a solid surface, I experience freefall. Try and explain that to someone who hasn't been here.

Thorpe spoke inside his transparent helmet. "You want to get a sample of the dark surface and one of the transparent part."

"Yeah, I know," Kenred said. "I'm working on it."

After several futile minutes, where Kenred tried a sharp tool, a drill, and even a torch, he said, "This stuff is two hundred times harder than steel, right?"

"It is," Thorpe answered.

"Then what the hell am I doing trying to get a physical sample?" He kept annoyance out of his voice. He wanted to remain on his boss's good side.

"You've got a good point," Thorpe said with a chuckle. "Return to *Armstrong* while I arrange to get you something that will do the job."

An hour later, Kenred was again on the sphere inner surface, this time with a laser light source that could penetrate the ten-meter-thick substance. Thorpe had sent the laser to *Armstrong* through the portal and dispatched *PS David Scott* to the other side of the sphere surface opposite *Armstrong* to record the spectrum of the light Kenred transmitted through the surfaces.

On Thorpe's signal. Kenred activated the laser, pointing it at the sphere inner surface.

After a minute, Thorpe said, "Okay, that's enough. Now shine it through the transparent section."

A minute later, Thorpe said, "That's it. Now we do a spectrum analysis. Hopefully, we can determine exactly what we're dealing with."

PS Andromeda—Outside the Keid Sphere

Chief Engineer Ustrun Strozid sat in his office in Engineering, staring at the spectrum results from the inner sphere.

These just don't make sense, he thought. We know we're dealing with carbynophene, and this, he brought up a holoimage, is what that spectrum looks like. So why am I getting this? He examined the spectrum results from the sphere again. He sat, quietly contemplating the problem.

"Wait a second," he said out loud and called up the spectrum of argon. He superimposed it on the spectrum from the inner sphere. "Will you look at that," he muttered, as the argon lines matched several lines from the sphere. "Mother, eliminate argon lines from the sphere spectrum," he ordered.

What remained were the combined spectra for carbynophene and Q-carbon. Strozid called Thorpe on his internal Link.

"Thorpe, I think I have answered a couple of our questions."

He went on to describe his argon discovery. "I think argon fills the open space between the graphene sheets. This is probably why the microbots don't attack every part of the sphere."

"What about the open gash?" Thorpe wanted to know.

"There is that," Strozid said. "We still need to figure that out."

✳

With *PS Neil Armstrong* back in the vehicle bay, eDaphne once again had free roam of *Andromeda's* systems, and both Jocara and Kenred were briefing Thorpe, something he liked to do face to face. Thorpe listened to their report, asking pertinent questions from time to time. Then he told them about the Chief Engineer's argon discovery.

"I want you to check out the jagged edge of the gash," Thorpe said, "the western edge. Microbots will surround you—they will be everywhere. If possible, I want you to conduct your close-up examination from inside *Armstrong*. If necessary, however, Kenred will go external for eyes on. *Armstrong's* MCS will broadcast instructions to the microbots, but we cannot make our instructions specific to a spacesuit-clad person.

"You two have the most experience with the microbots—that's why I'm sending you. Just in case, you have current backups, but I don't want you to go through that if we can avoid it. You're looking for why argon that fills the space between the graphene sheets does not overcome the microbots as they nibble the western side."

"I get the idea," Kenred said, "but I don't see how I can avoid the microbots when I'm outside. Even if Jocara puts *Armstrong* right against the edge, there's plenty of room for the microbots....unless..." His voice trailed off. "Can you supply me with several bottles of compressed argon?"

"How so?" Thorpe asked.

"We can strap them into the airlock and attach a hose with adjustable nozzle. I can sweep the area I am investigating—even sweep the little buggers off me!" Kenred opened his eyes, blinking rapidly; his scales rippled bright blue. "Worst case scenario, they get me, and I end up here. But I think it will work."

"It's worth a try," Thorpe said. "I'll alert Engineering to install as many argon bottles as can fit into *Armstrong's* airlock, bridged together to form an argon bank."

"Don't forget the hoses—two of them, with actuators I can handle easily suited up."

PS Neil Armstrong—Keid Sphere—Open Gash

Jocara carefully set the MCS to sweep continuously around *Armstrong*, 360 degrees on all three axes. She onloaded several million shieldbots in four slightly pressurized airtight boxes. Kenred showed up with eDaphne's matrix and plugged her into the rack. eDaphne's holoimage joined Jocara and Kenred at the starship control panel.

"We're ready to go," Kenred told Jocara as he housed the ramp and closed the airlock hatches.

"Mother," Jocara ordered, "take us to the western edge of the middle of the gash, halfway down the gash face, one klick from the face."

In moments, *Armstrong* hovered a kilometer from the face of the western side of the gash. Jocara checked the MCS again. It was broadcasting redirect instructions in all directions. She maneuvered the ship closer to the face. As far as she could see, a dark haze covered the face. For about a meter out, the microbot swarm was in flux, some bots moving in and some out to cross the gash to the other side, a million kilometers distant.

Jocara moved *Armstrong* as close to the 100-meter-thick face as possible, actually coming into contact with the gash face. *Armstrong's* presence did not seem to affect the microbots. They continued their mindless business of deconstructing the face and moving the "raw material" to the other side where, presumably, they built out that face. They completely ignored *Armstrong*.

"You will have to go out," Jocara told Kenred. "I don't see any other way."

"Any thoughts, eDaphne?" Kenred asked.

"Yeah, I'm glad it's you and not me!" she answered with a chuckle.

Kenred's scales rippled pale blue as he reacted to her humor. "I'm looking forward to trying out my argon blaster," he said.

✳

A few minutes later, a spacesuited Kenred stood at the airlock threshold, with *Armstrong* blocking out most of the dark inner sphere. The argon hoses were loosely coiled behind him, and he held a pistol-like actuator in his right hand. The second actuator with its hose was clipped to his belt. Four sealed boxes of shieldbots waited at the back of the airlock. Through his helmet, he could see the swarm haze churning in the space between the airlock and the gash face. He pointed the argon blaster at the face and gave the actuator an experimental pull. He tried not to think about what his death would feel like should the bots get through his suit.

A stream of argon blasted from the nozzle, hitting the face and dissipating into the vacuum in a sparking fog. In front of him, a section of face about a meter wide was microbot free. He checked the argon bank pressure gauge—the numbers had not changed, so he had used very little argon. He swept a meter-wide swath. Once again, the microbots disappeared. He waited for a full fifteen minutes. A few microbots, looking like dark dust, moved back in, but they quickly ceased functioning and dropped away from the face. Kenred did not try to figure out the physics of why they didn't just remain on the face. Drop off they did and disappeared against the darkness.

Kenred probed the face with a thin, sharp prong the Engineering Department had given him. It went in sometimes nearly a meter, sometimes just a few centimeters. Except for his hands, he remained inside the airlock in the spacecraft's gravity field. After several more minutes, Kenred saw what appeared to be black powder covering his hands.

"Damn!" he swore, turning the argon on his left and then his right hand. He examined both hands carefully and gave them another argon blast. "The microbots act a lot like moon dust," he said into the circuit.

"And what do you know about that?" eDaphne said with a teasing lilt to her voice. "You guys had not yet reached the surface of Logan when we found you."

"Yeah, yeah, but I read and watch holorecordings." He patted the side of the spacecraft. "Neil Armstrong had a thing or two to say about moon dust."

He put his hands outside the airlock, and almost immediately dark dust covered them. He blasted them again, clearing off the microbots. Then he put his hands against the bot-free face. His hands remained bot free, but some collected near his elbows. Again, he blasted them away.

He looked at the pressure gauge. Pressure was down somewhat but not significantly. It looked like an argon bottle would last a long time. Kenred lifted the argon nozzle above his head and gave himself an argon shower. Then he stepped out of the airlock into the bot swarm. They remained away from him, and those that got near dropped away as they had from the face. He returned to the airlock.

"Jocara," Kenred said, "move a hundred meters right along the face and get right up against the face again."

When *Armstrong* had stabilized, Kenred swept the face in front of him with argon, gave himself another argon shower, and stepped into the void.

"Move back two meters," he told Jocara.

After she did, Kenred moved around the cleared face, probing with his prong. Once, he returned to the airlock for a prophylactic argon shower, but otherwise, he remained bot free.

"Let's check the shieldbots," eDaphne said.

"New location first," Kenred said. "Move another hundred meters, Jocara."

When she had moved, Kenred opened two shieldbot boxes at the airlock threshold. The internal pressure pushed the shieldbots into the void. The shieldbot swarm immediately attacked the microbots, so that within several minutes, the nearby face was bot free, and the clear area was spreading. As the shieldbots moved away from their starting point, microbots began accumulating there again. The shieldbots picked up on the microbot return and eliminated them again. After three cycles, the shieldbots stopped spreading and remained in the cleared area, keeping it clear of microbots.

Kenred stepped out of the airlock without an argon shower, but carrying the hose. A microbot swarm approached him, but the shieldbots eliminated them. Out of an abundance of caution, Kenred sprayed himself all over with argon before returning to the airlock.

"We're done here," he said. "Let's retrieve the shieldbots and return to *Andromeda* to talk things over with the Chief Engineer and Thorpe. Right now, I'm not entirely certain what we know and what we don't know."

PS Andromeda—Outside the Keid Sphere

Thorpe invited the Chief Engineer to join him, eDaphne, and the two Arcan pilots in the conference room. Thorpe had a cup of coffee, but neither the Asterian nor the Arcans had developed a taste for the aromatic but bitter Human beverage. eDaphne, of course, could not drink, although her holoimage looked like she was enjoying a cup.

"Tell me," Strozid said to eDaphne, "how do you decide what to project with your holoimage? I've been working with you guys for quite some time, and you always seem to fit seamlessly into the venue."

"We've discussed this from time to time," eDaphne said, "but here it goes again. As an upload, I have a vastly expanded mental capacity when compared to flesh-and-blood people. While I'm sitting here enjoying a cup of coffee with you guys, I'm also undertaking a thousand different things all over *Andromeda*. One small part of me quickly analyzes the immediate venue, and I adjust my holoimage accordingly."

"That sounds like something I'd like to do," Kenred said. "Not the coffee part…the other stuff."

"There are downsides," eDaphne said. "I only look like I'm enjoying a cup of coffee. If you actually liked coffee, you would be enjoying a cup right now, not just pretending." She giggled.

"But all the rest," Kenred protested.

"Yeah, I know. At some point, we can talk about it, but I think we are here for something else." She giggled quietly again.

Thorpe cleared his throat. "To business. What have we learned?" he asked.

"Depends," Kenred said. "Argon definitely wards off the microbots. The shieldbots do as well, but I prefer argon—something I can control with my own hands."

"You mean like your SPC space capsule?" eDaphne said with a warm smile. "Remind me again what 'SPC' sands for?"

"Space Push Consortium," Kenred said.

"Right," eDaphne said. "In this business, we're not in control personally, very often."

Kenred hissed quietly, but nodded, his scales rippling faint yellow with irritation. "I still like argon."

"What did you determine with your prong?" Strozid asked.

"I think I was probing between the graphene layers. I think argon normally fills these layers. That's why the microbots don't attack the main structures. When they try, argon leaks and shuts them down."

"Why do they attack the western edge of the gash?" Strozid asked. "What's different?"

"I'm guessing," Kenred said, "that something broke through the outer sphere, a meteor or something, and released a lot of the argon. That's when the bots started cannibalizing the western edge."

Everyone sat in quiet thought for a few moments.

"So, you're saying that something catastrophic ripped open the gash, allowing the argon to escape, and the microbots went to work on this new 'raw material' source?"

"Yeah, I think so," Kenred answered. "As they worked their way in, they opened new argon sources and succumbed, but the argon escaped, and other microbots took their place and continued. Give it a few million years, and you get what we see now."

"That explains a lot," Thorpe said, "but it is still just an hypothesis." He leaned back in his chair. "As we move forward with our investigations, let's keep this in mind." He smiled broadly. "It certainly explains a lot, Kenred. Good job!"

Thorpe stood, signaling the end of the meeting. "Next step," he said, "we investigate the life band."

Chapter Ten

PS Andromeda—Outside the Keid Sphere

Thorpe stood at a podium, glancing around the auditorium. All the key participants were present. A warm feeling passed over him as he examined the faces of the people who had helped them get to where they were—his original Human team, of course, and their uploads; the Asterians who had joined the project from Rogan; the Arcan astronauts. Max, who was part of everything that had happened, even though he didn't understand his crucial role, walked between the rows of seats, greeting his friends.

Over the platform floated a holoimage of the Keid Sphere as they presently understood it. The outer and inner spheres were transparent, so the people in the room could see its inner workings.

"At this point," Thorpe said, "we have a pretty good understanding of the make-up of the Keid Sphere. To be sure, there are major details we still don't understand, but what you see here is our best guess of what makes up the sphere."

The holoimage separated into several parts so that only the life band remained in its original position.

"From several brief excursions," Thorpe continued, "we believe the band is the only part of the sphere where life can and does exist. From what we have seen, we extrapolate that the entire band harbors life, but we don't know this.

"I asked Daphne to generate a plan to give us a better understanding."

He looked at Daphne, sitting behind him. She rose and approached the podium.

"We know that a two-hundred-klick-high wall borders both sides of the band where we have looked so far. Since this wall retains the atmosphere above the band, we can assume the band has a border everywhere.

"Although you know the numbers, let me remind you that the band is one and a half million klicks wide—as wide as one hundred eighteen Earths. It is twenty-nine and a half million klicks around. Put these numbers together, and you have a band surface area equivalent to eighty-seven thousand Earths. Looked at another way, if we compare it to Earth's land area, the band is equivalent to three hundred thousand Earths." She stopped talking to let these numbers sink in.

"How long would it take to survey eighty-seven thousand planets or the land area of three hundred thousand planets? That's what we are facing here. It's an impossible task, so we're going to look at bits and pieces, and from those try to deduce the lay of the land. We're looking for oceans, islands, mountains, rivers, prairies, forests, jungles, deserts—anything to help us understand what the builders have created and perhaps a little bit about their thought process." She paused, and the murmur of voices around the table filled the room with quiet speculations.

"You've all seen a planet's surface from one or two hundred klicks," Daphne continued. "You can't see much detail. We've split the band into ten sectors, each assigned to an M-Class vessel. The ships will fly on MBH Drive at an altitude of ten klicks, which should be well above any mountain tops, at one hundred klicks per second. Radar will be set to stop the ship automatically, should anything appear in its path. Ships will fly a path parallel to the north wall at a hundred klicks in from the north wall, recording continuously with holocams, lidar, radar, and the entire radio spectrum.

"I expect the survey to take a bit over eight hours, so go out there and have fun!"

✳

Jocara and Kenred strolled hand-in-hand across the vehicle bay deck. Kenred carried eDaphne's matrix.

"What do you think we'll find?" Jocara asked.

"If there is anything big like a city, we'll find that. Otherwise, if I lived here, I would not want to be within sight of a wall. I'm guessing even if there is something on the band, this survey won't find it."

"Don't you think we should point this out?" Jocara asked. "I'm going to speak with Daphne." She placed a Link call.

"Daphne, Kenred and I were speculating on what we might find on this survey. Kenred had a thought that you should hear. He said that if he lived on the band, he would not want to be near the walls. With the band so wide, perhaps we would have more luck if we concentrated more toward the center."

"Let me run that past Thorpe," Daphne said. "I'll get back to you shortly."

Daphne called back in a few minutes. "We agree with Kenred. I am changing the protocol as we speak. The ships will head straight down the middle, halfway between the walls. I'm glad someone's thinking around here."

The two Arcans boarded *Armstrong*, and Kenred plugged eDaphne into the rack. Her holoimage joined them. Her scales rippling bright blue, Jocara excitedly told her about Kenred's comment and how Daphne had changed the protocol.

"That was good thinking," eDaphne said. "If I could, I'd kiss you, Kenred."

"I'd prefer a snout nuzzle," Kenred said with a chuckle, his scales rippling light blue.

✳

Since there was no practical reason to coordinate all the M-Class vessels conducting the survey, each craft and crew set out on their own to take up their survey section. Jocara brought *Armstrong* to her assigned sector, following the path they had taken earlier, making a short MERT jump through the inner sphere. Since there was no evidence the builders had developed portal technology, there had to be openings through the inner sphere, but nobody had found one yet.

"I've got the high-speed holocams and the lidar ready," eDaphne said. "They'll cut in as soon as you accelerate."

"Radar's set to look ahead sufficiently far to keep us safe, but not give a return from the upward curving landscape ahead," Kenred said. "And the side-scan radar will supplement the lidar scans for topographical definition."

"I set the radio spectrum scanners to pick up anything out there, anything at all," Jocara said, moving to the control panel. "Let's do it," she said, activating the MBH Drive.

The holoscreen showed only a blur. eDaphne made an internal adjustment so that the screen showed a succession of stills taken every tenth of a second. To the eye, it appeared like a continuous live view, with occasional discontinuities caused by radical changes in the landscape below.

At one point, the landscape turned to water for about a second.

"That's a six-thousand-klick-wide ocean," eDaphne said. "It probably spreads wall to wall, but we don't know that. We will probably investigate it later."

They passed a snow-capped mountain range, a whole series of forests and plains. Now and then, a sandy desert interrupted the otherwise green landscape. They crossed wet jungle land-scapes, dry highlands, and a tropical sea sprinkled with low-lying islands.

"I think," eDaphne said, "that the builders were trying to duplicate every kind of terrestrial landscape that might exist on any inhabitable world."

＊

Armstrong and the other nine M-Class vessels completed their surveys and returned to *Andromeda*. The crews assembled in the auditorium chatting quietly while they waited for the meeting to start. Daphne strode to the podium, her long red hair glistening in the subdued room light.

"We learned a lot these past hours," she said. "The band is filled with life, but there are no obvious indications of sapience, let alone an advanced civilization. Could we have missed something? Of course. We only covered a thousand-klick-wide swath out of one point five million. We could have missed an entire advanced civilization, but we heard nothing on any radio band, anywhere. Complete radio silence everywhere. What about a pre-technology civilization? We could have missed one or even more than one. We covered only a tiny fraction of the landscape.

"On pre-technology Earth, over the course of a few thousand years, several civilizations came and went, civilizations that stretched across most of the then known world. We could have overlooked dozens of similar civilizations during our survey. Without radio transmissions, the only way to find them would be to see them or a sign of their existence. Your recordings captured none of that.

"There are other, more subtle signs of civilization. We will examine your recordings for these and will develop protocols for examining the areas that appear to have a greater chance of harboring sapient life. Keep in mind, however, that a sapient colony could exist just a hundred klicks from our search area, and we would never be aware of its existence, would never know about it."

PS *Andromeda*—Outside the Keid Sphere—Engineering Spaces

Sally and Brad concentrated on the holoimage of a shieldbot that lay on the bench in front of them. eSally and eBrad were present without showing holoimages.

"We can remove the laser," Sally said, "and replace it with sensors for heat plumes, carbon dioxide, carbon microparticles, and trace elements that don't exist elsewhere in the band biome."

"eSally and eBrad, can you two come up with a design that will cover these options and fit into the microbot carcass?" Brad asked.

"Give us a couple of hours," eBrad said. "It should be no problem."

An hour and a half later, eBrad displayed a circuit on the holoscreen over the bench. "This will do it," he said. "We can enter the schematic into a Nanocosm with modified shieldbot specifications and appropriate instructions, and it should be able to produce one to your specifications."

"Let's do it," Brad told Sally.

He reached for the Nanocosm at the end of the bench and glanced at the required elements. They were standard elements always available by portal to the Nanocosm. He entered the schematic and the specifications. A minute later, the Nanocosm presented him with a holoimage of an enlarged searchbot. He set it loose in the lab, guided by eSally. It immediately signaled indications of life based upon heat, carbon dioxide, and trace elements.

"We need to test this on the landscape side of *Andromeda*," Sally said. "Brad, you go into the central valley and make a small campfire. I'll send a swarm of searchbots into the valley. Let's see what happens."

"Campfire—I haven't made one of those in a long time," Brad said.

✳

Brad entered the central valley by portal, found an appropriate spot, and started a small fire. He leaned back against a tree and sighed.

This is nice. I should do this more often…perhaps bring Sally here and spend a couple of days just relaxing in the outdoors.

In the meantime, Sally generated a thousand searchbots with the Nanocosm and sent them through a port into the central valley. She watched their progress on a holoscreen. The small swarm circled once and made a beeline for Brad and his fire.

"They seem to work," Sally told Brad over a Link. "I guess you can extinguish your fire and return."

"That's too bad—I was just starting to like it here. Are you sure you won't join me? It's really romantic."

Sally giggled quietly. "Come back, Silly. We have work to do, but I'll take you up on that later!"

✳

In Thorpe's office, Sally and Brad showed Daphne and Thorpe a recording of their experiment.

"I can't promise this will find sapient life," Brad said with a grin, "but it will find a small fire in the central valley."

"We can outfit an M-Class ship with a Nanocosm that will spew out enough of these to run an actual field test on the band," Sally said.

Thorpe called Jocara and Kenred by Link. When they arrived, he explained the searchbot to them.

"I want you to run a field test," he said. "Brad will install a Nanocosm programmed to run the test as you follow the protocol I'll give you. You will run a relatively small-scale test. If this works, we'll outfit the other M-Class ships and do a thorough job of it."

Jocara took *Armstrong* to the designated start position, at the center of the band, between a pair of north and south spokes. *Armstrong* carried 400 search bots. Jocara headed due east, ejecting one searchbot every five kilometers for 1,000 kilometers. Then she reversed course, ejecting the remaining 200 bots. The entire process took just a few minutes.

"Okay, guys," Jocara said over the circuit. "You can activate the bots."

Although it wasn't visible to the naked eye, 200 searchbots headed north and 200 south at 167 meters per second. In ten minutes, they traveled 100 kilometers in each direction, surveying 200,000 square kilometers of land.

"That's it," Brad said. "Test complete."

"Do we collect the bots?" Jocara asked.

"Not worth the effort," Brad said. "They've already crashed into the ground."

"Why?" Jocara asked.

"They Rn out of fuel."

"Do we have any results yet?"

"It's a bit early, but Sally, do you have anything?"

"I have the full set of scan readings. Mother is compiling them, but nothing stands out. I think I can say that you didn't find anything in your two hundred thousand square klick search area."

"Don't forget," Daphne said, stepping into the conversation, "the band area is equivalent to three hundred Earth land areas. What you surveyed is not even a drop in the ocean."

✳

Back on *Andromeda*, Sally and Brad met with Daphne and Thorpe in Thorpe's office.

"We ran a successful field test," Sally said. "Now it's time to set up the full survey."

"What are the times involved?" Daphne asked.

"Each craft will take forty-six hours to produce and lay the searchbots between the spoke pairs. The bots will take fifty-two days to cover the one and a half million klicks between the walls. When finished, we will have surveyed twenty-eight percent of the band area with sufficient resolution to identify where we want a closer look."

"How long will it take to make and hook up the Nanocosms?" Daphne asked.

"Give us a couple of days," Brad said. "We want to get this right the first time."

✳

With eSally and eBrad working closely with them, Sally and Brad set up a Nanocosm to produce ten identical single-purpose Nanocosms. Their only purpose was to manufacture and eject searchbots at a rate of one per second. Each Nanocosm received its raw material via portal, so other than a huge energy consumption that was of no account for *Andromeda*, the process was engagingly simple.

First, they manufactured the Nanocosms—a matter of instructing their Nanocosm and supplying it with the correct parameters. Nanocosms were amazingly complex, so it took about an hour to manufacture each, even with their Nanocosm set to its highest throughput.

As the Nanocosms came off the line, Brad transported each by portal to its designated M-Class ship. Brad followed and installed the device so it took up minimum space and could eject the searchbots into the ship's wake. By the middle of the next day, all ten M-Class starships carried a searchbot Nanocosm.

PS Neil Armstrong—The Keid Sphere—Equatorial Band

Daphne assigned each ship to a sector, spacing them out, so they covered all the band.

"We got something new this time," Jocara told Kenred and eDaphne.

"Do you think it will make a difference?" Kenred asked. "We're covering a lot of territory very fast."

"At least we're covering the entire width of our band section, wall to wall," eDaphne said. "If there's something here, we should spot it."

"Let's get on it," Jocara said. "We've got forty-six hours ahead of us laying the two strings of bots."

The process was automatic. Jocara set the parameters into Mother, and she handled the entire task. The two Arcans and eDaphne set up a routine where one of them focused on the control panel, while the other two relaxed, chatted, even napped.

The forty-six hours passed quickly, and *PS Neil Armstrong* and the other nine M-Class ships were ready to commence the fifty-two-day survey. This didn't mean that the ships and crews had to remain on station for the duration, however.

Jocara and the other commanders ensured their surveys were ready to go, and then they started the surveys and hightailed it for home.

PS Andromeda—The Bridge

Back on *Andromeda*, Mother began receiving survey reports from 3,277,778 search bots. As the reports arrived, she compiled them and generated a holoimage on the Bridge showing the result. Any part of the holoimage could be enlarged up to real-life size. She highlighted any points of interest.

Day after day, Mother added details—forests, rivers, lakes, mountains, prairies, deserts, swamps, jungles, but no cities, no roads, no structures, nothing indicating sapience or intelligence.

From time to time, a bot would fail. Mother grayed out the missing areas, but they were few and far between. One could easily surmise what was missing, unless that was the spot that harbored sapience.

This haunted Thorpe as the days passed, and the survey progressed. This sphere has been here a long time, a very long time, he thought. I'm guessing sufficient time has passed for sapience to evolve. Jocara and Kenred reported wildlife. Unless someone placed them as they are, they have evolved to their present state. If so, then evolution has happened everywhere on the band, or at least could have happened.

This excited Thorpe, giving him hope they might yet discover something beyond the massive structure.

PART TWO
THE BUILDERS

Chapter Eleven

Keid Sphere—Somewhere on the Equatorial Band

Five creatures huddled in a tight circle on the wet ground in a small clearing, munching on pieces of their last kill. The sun was shutting down, and rain fell, soaking their fur. They were cold and miserable. Meat from the small, deer-like animal they had killed was stringy and tough, but it was nourishment they craved, a welcome addition to the berries, leaves, and roots that comprised the rest of their diet.

The creatures were about 1.5 meters tall and walked upright, although they dropped to their knuckles when running. Their faces were humanoid, with flattened nose, protruding jaw, and round, intelligent eyes. Ears sat low on both sides of their heads. They had five digits with opposing thumbs on hand and foot.

One creature, male judging by his size and external genitalia, seemed in charge. He barked orders without using specific words, and he proportioned meat shares to the other four. While they concentrated on eating, he kept a vigilant eye on the surrounding trees between bites.

The falling rain turned to torrents, and the rumble of distant thunder got louder and more frightening. Flashes of lightning coursed across the sky, illuminating their clearing as if it were day.

Without warning, a lightning bolt struck a tree at the edge of their clearing. The resulting thunder crack badly frightened the little band, and they ran into the trees, screaming. When no more loud, nearby bangs happened, the male stopped running and turned back toward the clearing to save the remaining meat. Instinctively, he knew how important the meat was to the survival of his band.

He called out to the others. When they responded, he instructed them with barks and gestures to remain at the edge while he cautiously crept into the clearing. A burning tree trunk, downed by the lightning strike, lay square across the carcass. The meat smoldered beneath it, emitting a scrumptious smell.

The big male reached for a piece of cooked meat, but yelped when it burned his fingers. He put his fingers to his mouth to lick the pain away. The juice was delicious. He separated a piece with a stick and smelled it. Then he put it in his mouth and chewed. It was tender and tasted wonderful. He waved the others into the clearing while he took another piece of cooked meat for himself. He ripped off pieces of cooked meat and handed them to the other four. They wolfed them down, chattering happily despite the wet and the cold.

While the others ate, the big male sat back, staring at the burning tree. He stood and went to the edge of the clearing where he pulled down some low hanging tree branches and brought them to the fire. They smoked a lot, but didn't burn very well. He returned to the clearing edge and found several pieces of older wood on the ground. They were damp from the rain, but still quite dry inside. He dropped them on the fire. When they burned intensely, he shouted with glee and began gathering all the dry wood he could find. With grunts and gestures, he encouraged the others to do the same, until they had a pile of dry wood near the burning tree trunk.

The male reached for more meat and noticed that melted fat dripping to the ground was burning. He sat watching it for several minutes and then yelled with glee. Picking up a dry stick, he soaked it in the melted fat and held it to the fire. It blazed hot and bright.

The dry wood quickly burned down to his hand, and he dropped it, wincing with pain. He sat a while longer, contemplating the fire. He added two pieces of wood, one wet and one dry. The wet piece just smoked, while the dry piece burst into flame. With a satisfied grunt, the male picked up a wet stick and soaked the end in the melted fat. The end burst into flame when he held it to the fire, and the stick didn't burn down to his hand.

The big male called the others and showed them what he had learned. With gestures and grunts, he got them to do the same. He stuck the burning sticks into the ground in a circle around the group. As the rain ceased and the starless sky darkened completely, the little band of simian humanoids huddled together around their fire, warm, comfortable, and dry.

The big male remained alert on guard, watching over his charges while they slept, until he, too, drifted off into a sleep filled with dreams of cooked meat and fire sticks.

Keid Sphere—Somewhere Else on the Equatorial Band

Eight humanoid felines curled up in nests near the top of several large trees in a forest by a creek separated from the humanoid simians by two oceans and a continent. The air was hot and smokey, making breathing difficult. Fire trailed across the ground, consuming underbrush and lapping at tree trunks. The felines watched the progress of the brush fires warily, ready to flee if the fires threatened their nests. They waited, occasionally chittering to each other in a manner that suggested the beginnings of a spoken language.

When the fire trails stopped, a large male descended from his treetop nest, using sharp claws to assist his descent. He stood upright on the ground at just under one and a half meters, although he still ran on all fours. His head was round, displaying oval eyes and a prominent whiskered nose. Sharp canines filled his wide mouth, and his articulating ears sat high on his head. His hands and feet carried six sharp claws with opposing thumbs. Sleek, dark fur covered his body, and his spine ended in a tail half his body length.

The ground was still warm, and the large male walked carefully, avoiding hot spots. He glanced up at his mate, looking over the edge of their nest.

"Wait!" he chittered.

She understood.

He caught a whiff of something delectable and moved cautiously in that direction. On the ground lay the burned carcass of a large, rat-like mammal. He picked it up and used his sharp claws to tear off the critter's charred skin and fur. He pulled a piece of cooked leg muscle loose and popped it into his mouth. It was delicious.

The big male waved to his mate, still waiting in their nest. She slid down the tree and approached him. He handed her a piece of rat meat. She cooed in delight and chittered loudly at the surrounding nests. Six felines descended rapidly and spread out to search for dead animals.

The big male walked around, searching. He finally found a bush whose base was still afire. He added dry branches until he had a sizable fire. He spied a bird in a nearby bush, sprang to capture it, and killed it with one swift bite to the neck. He tried holding it over the flames, but burned his hands. He found a sharp stick and pushed it through the carcass. He held it over the flames until the feathers burned away and the meat charred. When he put the cooked bird to his mouth, it tasted wonderful. He called his mate and gave her some. She chittered her delight to the entire group.

As the flames died down, the male added more wood to the fire, keeping it alive. He found another dead, small animal and tossed it into the fire to see what would happen. As the fat dripped out of the carcass onto the ground, the ground burst into flame. He ran on all fours to the creek, looking for something. He found it and rose to his hind legs, holding what looked like a tortoise shell. He brought it back to the fire and went looking for more dead animals. At the fire again, he squeezed each animal's fat into the shell.

Using a small stick, the male brought fire to the rendered fat. The fat didn't burn, but the stick burned brightly without being consumed. He called his mate and chittered at her. She left and returned with a handful of small, dry sticks. He chittered loudly and nuzzled her face with his.

As the sky darkened to a starless night, the male carried his oil bowl to his nest and showed his mate how to keep one oil-soaked stick at a time burning. He held up the flickering light so the others could see. From the back-and-forth chittering, the big male understood that come morning, the others would get their own oil bowls.

Keid Sphere—A Third Location on the Equatorial Band

A small group of lizard-like humanoids played in the shallow swamp water under a driving rain far from both the simian and feline humanoids. Their scales glistened in the filtered sunlight. They walked upright on slightly stubby legs, maintaining balance with a substantial tail. Their round heads sat on short necks. Nose and mouth were at the end of a short snout that protruded from their faces. Their hands had six digits with opposing thumbs, and their feet had six webbed toes.

One lizard was larger than the others at just under two meters. He communicated with them using clipped words in a language with a limited but practical vocabulary. As the storm intensified with lightning drawing near, he signaled to get out of the water. They settled on a small knoll pushing out of the swamp and harboring several tall gum trees with intertwined top branches that formed an overhead canopy. It wasn't enough to stop the rain, but it sheltered them from the large flying predator lizards that nested in the canopy and could easily carry one of them away in its sharp talons.

Without warning, a bolt of lightning struck a tree on their knoll. The canopy burst into flame, fed by the gummy resin in the trees. The humanoids on the knoll heard screeching coming from the burning canopy, followed by several hard-shell eggs and small charred bodies falling to the surrounding ground.

Because of the heavy rain, they had not hunted. They were tired from their water play and hungry. Their normal fare was berries, roots, leaves, and small swamp animals that they consumed raw. The smell from the charred bodies was enticing. The large male picked up a charred flying lizard hatchling and sniffed it. Then he put it in his mouth. It tasted delicious. In clipped words, he told the others to try the burned flesh. They loved it.

The large male understood the source of the delicious addition to their fare, but was at a loss at how to make it happen. He sat with his back against the largest tree on the knoll, giving the matter some thought. As he sat, he felt a warm trickle along his spine. He turned to see a rivulet of sap flowing down the tree trunk. He touched it and put his finger to his mouth. It tasted awful. As he watched, a small trail of flame followed the sap to the wet ground and continued burning.

To the big lizard, what was happening was obvious. He scooped the dirt from under the sap rivulet, forming a small basin to catch the flaming liquid. Then he grubbed around the knoll edge and found a turtle-like creature. He ripped off its shell and placed it in the basin. He looked around for other sap runs. The hot canopy fire fed by the resiny gum liquefied the sap and sent it streaming down most of the trunks. The big lizard put the others to work finding as many shells as possible and set them to collect the burning sap.

While holding one partially filled burning shell in his hands, he accidentally blew the fire out. With a stick, he added a drop of burning sap to the bowl, and it started burning again. With that knowledge, he gathered as many bowls as possible without starting a fire in them, keeping just two bowls burning. He comprehended he needed to keep a flame alive. Right now, this was the only way. But he was smart and resourceful. Even if the flame went out, he would find a way to get it back. Fire made life better for him and his tribe. He would not let it go.

Chapter Twelve

***PS Andromeda*—Outside the Keid Sphere**

As the searchbot data arrived, Mother compiled an increasingly complex picture of the equatorial band. Daphne had specifically given Mother parameters to look for, parameters that might point to life higher on the scale than what they had found thus far.

The Bridge holoimage of the equatorial band had reached such complexity that the only way to examine it with any meaning was to pull out one section and enlarge it until the detail could be seen. Daphne was specifically looking for heat plumes that might indicate an incipient civilization.

The band sections did not display an even temperature regimen. Some areas were tropical warm, others were temperate, and they had even surveyed two arctic regions. Animal life ranged from too small to see, to mammoth-size creatures in the arctic regions. They had yet to see any large, dinosaur-size reptiles, but with only 28 percent of the surface surveyed, a lot remained to be discovered.

Daphne directed Mother to highlight any areas with unusually warm plumes. Mother found several, but emphasized one in particular that was in a temperate area near the band center. Overall, this area was warmer than the surrounding landscape, and the warmth seemed to be concentrated in several hundred individual heat plumes.

Daphne dispatched *PS Neil Armstrong* with Jocara, Kenred, and eDaphne to investigate.

PS Neil Armstrong—The Keid Sphere—Equatorial Band— Simian Region

Jocara directed *Armstrong* to an equatorial band section they had not yet visited. The landscape was several hundred meters above the mean landscape level and mostly pastoral—wooded areas, open, grassy areas, hills and valleys, many with streams flowing through, much like the landscape side of *Andromeda*.

Here and there, thin columns of smoke rose into the sky, always from forested areas. Bovine- and antelope-like animals roamed the grasslands, and birds filled the sky near these herbivores. As they watched from thirty kilometers altitude using telescopic monitors, a group of humanoids dashed from the forest and attacked the herbivore herd. They brandished spears and clubs. And soon they brought down one bovine-like and one antelope-like creature. The rest of the animals scattered across the grassland.

Using wood poles and a large hide, the humanoids assembled a travois under the larger animal, and several pulled it into the forest. One of the larger humanoids carried the smaller animal over his shoulders. While the humanoids were still on the grassland, Mother captured several thousand holoimages from all angles. She assembled these into a coherent holoimage of one humanoid standing in the spacecraft lounge. He stood under two meters with an eyebrow ridge, flattened nose, and jutting jaw. He had a beard and sported sparse body hair. He had well-formed hands with four fingers and opposing thumbs, and he used his feet for walking and running, not object manipulation. He wore thick rawhide sandals held to his feet with rawhide strips and a breechclout covering his genitals and buttocks. He also had a well-muscled body with virtually no visible fat.

"He looks very much like several early Humans I learned about in school," eDaphne said. "In fact, I'm not sure I could tell the difference."

"They've got primitive tools—spears and clubs," Kenred said. "With no metal to mine, how do you suppose they will progress further?"

"They can do a lot with wood, rock, and animal hide," Jocara said. "It would be interesting to see them in one or two thousand years."

"Let's visit another smoke plume," eDaphne said. "Maybe we can get a look at how they live."

Jocara directed Mother to a smoke plume a hundred kilometers distant. She positioned *Armstrong* in a hover five kilometers above the plume. The surrounding forest was open enough to let them see the ground. Kenred focused his optical sensors for a close-up view.

"Those are thatched huts," Kenred said. "See the big one? Smoke appears to be coming from a roof opening. I'm guessing that's a communal hut where they gather to eat."

On the holoscreen, they watched people walking around the village.

"There's a female with her infant," Jocara said. "She's wearing a breechclout and sandals like the males. See her swollen breasts and longer hair? Her child seems to be feeding."

"And how do you know about Human anatomy and breast-feeding?" eDaphne asked.

"I studied it, Silly!" Jocara opened her eyes wide and blinked. Her scales rippled pale blue with amusement. "Are you calling these hominids *Human?*"

"They sure look like an early species of Human," eDaphne said. "We don't know if this development is common among simian species in the universe. We're the only ones we know about—and now these guys. You Arcans and the Asterians are certainly different. Once we move on from here, I wonder what kinds of sapient species we meet."

✳

Jocara pulled the spacecraft up so they could look for more settlements. Toward the west, several smoke columns rose into the air. When *Armstrong* arrived at the site, they saw two large forested areas bounding ten kilometers of grassland. A large collection of the hominids milled about near the center. Jocara moved closer.

The scene below them was a battle between two hominid groups. Kenred examined them closely.

"They all look the same to me." He said. "The fighters are all males. They're using spears, clubs, stone knives, and even teeth and fists. They're pretty serious about it, whatever their differences are."

The battle lasted for forty minutes after Jocara first discovered it. When it was over, the victors dragged their dead, and carried their wounded on travois back to their side of the grassland. The other side had no survivors. Women and older children from the losing side came out of the forest to collect their dead.

"Let's hang around to see what kind of burial ceremony they have," eDaphne said.

"Let's check the victors first," Jocara said.

She moved *Armstrong* above the victor's village. They had placed their dead on wood platforms two meters above the ground and had lit a bonfire beneath each.

"Cremating their dead," Kenred said. "I wonder what that implies."

"Look at that, will you," eDaphne said. "The villagers are dancing around the bonfire."

"Are they celebrating their victory or mourning their dead?" Kenred wondered aloud.

Jocara moved *Armstrong* to the other side of the grassland over the losers' village.

"They too are cremating their dead," Kenred said, "but there is no celebration. Things will be tough there since all the men are dead. I guess the older boys and the old men will have to keep things going until the youngsters mature."

"They may not survive," eDaphne said.

"Maybe that's what it was all about," Jocara said. "I don't see any herbivores in this area."

"I think we've seen enough," eDaphne said. "Let's park several holocam observation platforms at twenty-five clicks so we can monitor what's going on here."

PS Neil Armstrong—The Keid Sphere—Equatorial Band—Feline Region

Jocara moved *Armstrong* halfway across the equatorial band to the area where the survey had discovered another band of smoke plumes. Having just come from observing hominids, the crew half expected to find more of the same.

They arrived in a forested area without the intervening grasslands they found in the hominid areas. None of the three were tree experts, but the trees below them looked like trees from both Earth and Arcan, at least to their uneducated eyes.

Several smoke plumes rose from an area with fewer trees. Jocara hovered above this spot at five kilometers. Kenred set the optics for closer views.

"I see dozens of *people* walking around," Kenred said. "Not really people, but creatures that look a lot like people—more like you, eDaphne, than us."

They were bipedal humanoids with six digits that included opposable thumbs. The fingers terminated in retractable claws. They were shorter and stockier than the average Human, with sleek fur on head and body ranging in tone from light to dark tan. Their faces looked much like Human faces, with oval eyes, flattened noses, and a wide mouth with thin lips covering sharp canines. Their ears articulated like cat ears, and they sported fur-covered tails half their body length. They wore breechclouts like the hominids, but no foot protection.

"I see a resemblance to the Asterians," eDaphne said, "but the differences seem to be greater than the hominids are to Humans."

"I suspect the Chief Engineer will have something to say about that," Jocara said.

"I do, in fact," Strozid said. "I'm on the Bridge with Thorpe. We've been eavesdropping on your conversation. I will say this—we both come from feline stock."

eDaphne pulled up a private holoimage from her Link and wrote a note that only Jocara and Kenred could see: *That was pretty good for our humorless Asterian!*

Everyone chuckled and then went back to the task at hand. Unlike the hominids, who had lots of grass for thatched roofs, the felines used wood poles covered with animal hides. The resulting structures reminded eDaphne of the teepee tents used by American Plains Indians in the seventeenth through nineteenth centuries.

"I think I see a small garden off to one side," Kenred said. He zoomed in. "Yep, rows of something—no idea what. A female is tending the plot." He pulled back for a larger area look. "Over there," he said, "I see a kill hanging from a couple of poles and a crosspiece. It's not one of the herbivores we know from the grasslands. Without a head and skin, I can't tell you very much."

"We need to find a hunting party," Jocara said. "Let's move to another settlement."

She gave Mother the instructions, and a minute later *Armstrong* hovered over another, larger settlement. This one had several dozen teepees and one larger dwelling that had a flat roof with an opening for smoke.

"That big structure looks like the town hall," Kenred said.

He scanned the village slowly. "I see several garden patches around the outskirts. Females are tending all of them. I see several kills hanging outside the town hall."

"Over there," eDaphne said, "movement on the right side."

Kenred focused in on the movement. A hunting party pushed out of the forest, pulling a travois loaded with a creature that resembled a bear. The hunters carried spears, bows, clubs, and knives. They watched the party bring the animal to the town hall. Using what looked like flint knives, the hunters skillfully skinned it, pulling off a thick fat layer. A female dragged over a hollowed-out wood pot for the chunks of fat and dragged it to a small fire. She suspended the fat over the fire with wood poles and started stirring it with a long bone.

"These people are relatively advanced," Kenred said. "They don't have metal, but they skillfully use wood, stone, bone, and hide."

Some motion on the other side of the settlement caught their attention. On a footpath leading into the settlement, a group of five felines approached. One was a female walking in the middle of the males. They waved their spears and seemed to be shouting something. A male, perhaps the village elder, approached them, gesticulating and probably talking, although the spacecraft occupants could hear nothing. The arrivals followed the elder to the village center, where they presented the female in what seemed to be a ceremonious manner. A male appeared from a teepee, and he and the female embraced while the visitors waved their spears in apparent joy. After that, everyone entered the town hall.

"So, what do you think?" Kenred asked. "A bride? A runaway girl? I would love to see what is happening inside there right now."

"Does this scene make these people lovers instead of fighters?" eDaphne asked with a grin.

"I think they could beat the crap out of the hominids," Kenred said. "The bows give them a great advantage."

"I think we simply missed one of their inevitable conflicts," Jocara said. "Food, not territory, will be the issue, I think."

"Do we have enough?" eDaphne said. "Can we move on?"

"As soon as we place the holocams at altitude," Jocara said, giving Mother appropriate instructions.

PS Neil Armstrong—The Keid Sphere—Equatorial Band—Saurian Region

Their path took them across the center of Keid Sphere. They passed through the inner sphere, past Keid-C, and through the inner sphere again using MERT Drive. Then they headed for their destination on the MBH Drive. When they arrived, much of the landscape below them was wet and swampy. The numerous trees formed an overhead canopy so they could not see the ground easily. They would not have expected to find any sapient life there, but the smoke plumes said differently.

They picked an area with dozens of smoke plumes in close proximity and came to a hover at five kilometers.

Kenred readied the optics and set them for a close-up view. "What the hell was that?" he yelled as something large passed between the spacecraft and the canopy.

He directed a scanner to follow the object. It was two kilometers distant and turned to approach *Armstrong*.

"I don't believe it," Kenred said. "It looks like the pterosaurs that used to dominate Arcan skies, but the damn thing has a rider. A rider! If it's anything like our pterosaurs, it has a ten-meter wingspan and weighs two hundred fifty kilos, and it's flying straight toward us. It can fly one hundred thirty klicks an hour at five klicks altitude. We don't want that one flying anywhere near our ship, especially with a rider who probably carries some type of primitive projectile weapon. We've got to move this bird, Jocara, up at least another klick."

"Hey," eDaphne said, "there's another one—no, wait, three more, with riders. My god, it's a flock—or would that be a squadron?" She lost count at ten.

"Notice they tend to circle the smoke columns," Kenred said. "I think they are on guard against a potential assault?"

They flew around for several minutes, watching while keeping well clear of the pterosaurs and their riders. As they watched, a smaller, probably younger and less experienced, pterosaur without a mount flew in from outside the patrol area and swooped down over the canopy where the smoke columns climbed into the sky. Two mounted pterosaurs turned and chased it. Then, a swiftly moving shaft shot through the canopy and pierced the creature. It dropped rapidly through the canopy and disappeared.

"Well now," Kenred said, "somebody has some pretty sophisticated technology under that canopy."

"If I bring us closer to the smoke columns, the flying squadron will certainly attack. We don't need that."

"We can take the big guys out with laser fire," Kenred suggested.

"Really," Jocara said, "I don't think so! Let's find an area where the canopy isn't a hundred percent."

It took them an hour of searching before they found an area with smoke columns that had virtually no canopy. It had a flying guard, but Jocara stayed high enough so the riders didn't see her. Kenred zoomed in with his optics.

"I think that area burned off," he said. "Those trees are gum trees, I'm sure of it," he added.

On the ground was a device with a familiar look. Kenred had Mother produce a full holoimage.

"That is a ballista," Kenred said. "It fires the shaft we saw kill the pterosaur. It's like a crossbow, with tremendous hitting power. A skilled bowman can aim one accurately even against a moving target—as we saw."

While they watched, a creature entered the open space. Jocara gasped.

"That looks like me, sort of," she said, her scales rippling dark blue with excitement.

It was a bit shorter than two meters and covered with scales. Its torso was long with slightly stumpy legs, and it had a tail about half its body length. Its round head sat on a short neck. Nose and mouth were at the end of a short snout that protruded from its face. Its hands had six digits with opposing thumbs, and it wore a full shoe of some kind on its feet. Other than the shoes, it wore no clothing, except a hide belt that carried tools and weapons. To one side, a fire roared, fed by gum-soaked wood from nearby trees. A pot formed from a large shell and filled with tree gum hung over the fire.

Several other saurians appeared in the optics' focus, two males outfitted like the first, and three smaller versions without tool belts but with a marsupium-like pouch on their lower torso.

"Look at that!" Jocara exclaimed, her scales rippling bright blue with excitement. "Those three are females, and they even have pouches like we do."

"Whoa, everybody, slow down!" eDaphne said. "We're missing something important here. We know of three sapient races in the universe as of now, Humans who evolved from simians, Asterians who evolved from felines, and Arcans who evolved from saurians. From studying Oort DNA, we know they evolved from canine-like ancestors. Simians, felines, and saurians are represented here. If there are canines, we haven't found them—and remember that we surveyed only twenty-eight percent of the equatorial band.

"I don't have a general problem with what I've said so far, but now let's look at the specifics. The current state of the simians is that they are nearly identical to protohumans, so much so we're calling them hominids. The current felines differ from Asterians, but the similarities are striking. And now, the saurians. In Earth prehistory, no saurians had marsupium-like pouches." She interrupted herself.

"Hey, Ustrun, are you guys still eavesdropping?"

"We are," Strozid answered.

"What about prehistoric Aster reptiles—did any have marsupial pouches?"

"Not that I know of," Strozid said. "They don't exist at all in our eco history."

"What the hell?" eDaphne said. "We have two evolved sapient species where reptiles never developed marsupial pouches and one that did. How is it we see that same development here?

"The three species we found are too close to our three species for this to be chance. I don't know what we're dealing with here, but it's pretty big."

✳

Armstrong visited several more saurian villages. All were similar. All used their available raw materials effectively and efficiently, and all had pterosaur-mounted riders. The crew observed no armed conflict, but they did see weapons that could not have been used against pterosaurs—evidence the saurians hunted on the ground and engaged in battle from time to time.

Jocara placed several holocam platforms and brought *Armstrong* home to *Andromeda*.

Chapter Thirteen

***PS Andromeda*—Outside the Keid Sphere**

Thorpe sat at the head of the conference room table. Daphne sat to his right and the Chief Engineer to his left. eDaphne, Jocara, and Kenred sat at the opposite end of the table, eDaphne virtually directly opposite Thorpe. The other pilots crowded around the table, and the uploads hovered along the walls and wherever there was room. Max wandered about, confused by the strange arrangement of people and uploads. eMax found Kimberly and curled up in front of her.

Above the table, an expanded holoimage of the sphere floated with the three areas harboring the sapient species broken out and floating separately. Holocams were recording and broadcasting the meeting everywhere on *Andromeda*.

"We face an unprecedented situation," Thorpe began. "The *Neil Armstrong* crew has located and identified three sapient species occupying three separate regions of the equatorial band. Briefly, one can only be described as a hominid like the early Humans. The second is feline with characteristics substantially like the early Asterians. The third is saurian, disturbingly similar to early Arcans." He paused and looked around the table, at the floating uploads, and at the holocams.

"This is not a coincidence. Furthermore, we have only surveyed twenty-eight percent of the band. What might we find in the other seventy-two percent? Most of you know that several crew members were originally Oort, who evolved on Earth long before Humans came along. When they joined the Human race from their upload status, they downloaded into Human form. Their DNA tells us they originally evolved from a canine-like species. We haven't found a similar species in the equatorial band yet, but there is a lot more to examine.

"Dr. Daphne O'Bryan and her team have done a careful Bayesian analysis of all the data. A Bayesian analysis is a method of statistical inference that allowed Daphne to combine what we know about our four species with evidence from the sample sapient species we just collected to infer the probability of there being a canine-like species and perhaps others in the equatorial band.

"Daphne tells me there is an eighty-five percent probability of there being at least one other species in the band, and a ninety percent probability that it is canine-like. We will not dedicate resources right now to finding this species even though we have high confidence that we can find it. Instead, we will dedicate our efforts to discovering how the three species we have discovered got here, and who was responsible."

PS Neil Armstrong—The Keid Sphere—Equatorial Band— Simian Region

PS Neil Armstrong headed back to the simian region of the equatorial band. Thorpe tasked her with carefully looking into the pattern of life in this region. Was there any outside influence that might have changed or be changing the normal course of evolution?

eDaphne took on the task of reviewing the holocam recordings. Her upload status gave her the ability to review a massive amount of data quickly.

Kenred set up radar, lidar, and optics to their best advantage. He was looking for anything out of the ordinary.

Jocara positioned *Armstrong* wherever eDaphne or Kenred wanted for any specific observation.

It did not take eDaphne very long to review the holocam recordings and find something interesting.

"Look at this, guys," she said as the holoimage took up most of the space in their lounge well. The recording showed a settlement with twenty-six individual huts. The town hall was larger than they had seen on their previous visit. One man stood out from the rest, not because he was bigger and stronger, but because he wore a hide robe. As they watched, the men gathered in front of the town hall. They appeared ready for a hunt. The robed man performed a ritual with his arms outstretched while the hunters dropped to one knee. The hunters departed for the grassland while the robed man, the shaman, Jocara suggested, wandered off into the woods. Suddenly, seemingly out of nowhere, a large timber wolf-like creature confronted the shaman, who carried no weapons.

"He's gonna die," Kenred said, his scales rippling pink.

The timber wolf charged and leaped into the air, mouth open, ready to snap the shaman's neck. From a concealed position, a laser beam struck the wolf's head, and it fell dead to the ground before the shaman.

eDaphne zoomed into the image to find the laser source, but could find nothing. Short of a personal inspection in the ground, they would find nothing.

"That's what I would call interference," Kenred said. "Whoever is controlling this thinks that shaman is important. To fire a laser at that precise moment implies continuous observation of at least the important players."

"And laser placement everywhere," Jocara added. "It's remarkable."

"I've got more to show you," eDaphne said.

The scene changed to an even larger village. The creek next to the settlement was swollen with pouring rain. Groups of warriors were entering the settlement from different directions. Instead of engaging in battle, their leaders assembled in the town hall with the same shaman whose life had been saved earlier.

"That's a peace meeting of some kind," Kenred said.

"The Aboriginals where I come from," eDaphne said, "would call it a powwow."

As they watched, a slug of water raced down the creek, forcing it over its banks. The rushing water collapsed the town hall and carried away the chieftain occupants.

"They're gonna drown," Kenred said as he watched the men floundering in the swirling water.

Suddenly, the rain stopped and all the flood water disappeared into the ground. Even the creek bed went dry. The chieftains struggled to their feet and looked around them. The shaman stood with outstretched arms on a large rock that had been inside the town hall before it washed away. All the chieftains dropped to one knee as water slowly filled the creek under the shaman's watchful eye.

"He certainly has a lot of power now," Kenred said. "I think he can merge all the surrounding tribes under his leadership. It's a huge step forward."

"That definitely was directed interference," Jocara said. "Somebody or something is watching carefully."

"There's more," eDaphne said.

The scene showed the shaman wearing his hide robe and walking through the forest near the large village. He stooped down to examine something, and then he stood up, holding a simple long bow in one hand and several arrows in the other. For a while, he just looked at his find, plucking the bowstring. He examined an arrow. The head was shaped flint attached to the shaft with rawhide string. Glue held bird feathers to the notched end.

The shaman placed an arrow against the bow and slipped the bowstring into the notch. He pulled the bowstring back a few centimeters and let go. The arrow flew forward a couple of meters and dropped to the ground. The shaman stared at the arrow and then examined the bow carefully. Then he got the idea. He retrieved the arrow, nocked it firmly against the bowstring, drew back the string, and let the arrow fly. Twenty meters away, it embedded itself in a tree trunk. The shaman dug the arrowhead from the tree with his flint knife and headed back to the village, carrying his prize.

"That will elevate his people above everyone else in the region," Kenred said, "at least until the others figure out how to make bows and arrows themselves. Death at a distance—that's a major advancement. Talk about interference!"

PS Neil Armstrong—The Keid Sphere—Equatorial Band—Feline Region

Still filled with awe at their remarkable discovery of the level of interference in the development of the simian tribe, Jocara set course for the feline region of the equatorial band. On MERT Drive, *Armstrong* passed through the inner sphere, the complex tube infrastructure, the open space, and the inner sphere again, and then continued on MBH Drive to their destination.

While Kenred and Jocara located a large feline settlement, eDaphne reviewed the holocam recordings that had accumulated in their absence.

eDaphne called her crewmates' attention to the holoimage in the lounge well.

"As intriguing as we found our discoveries in the simian region, I think you will find the level of interference here equally astonishing."

The holoimage showed a male feline walking through the forest. He wore a woven fur cloak that was bleached white. Four felines accompanied him, two males and two females. They walked behind him deferentially. Without warning, a large cat that looked like a prehistoric saber-tooth tiger from Earth attacked the troop, ripping one of the females to shreds. The cat launched itself toward the cloaked male when a laser bolt killed it.

"That was just like the simian incident," Kenred said. "I'm guessing that fellow is an important holy man. Whoever is watching over these creatures wants him alive."

"You got that right," eDaphne said. "Watch this next incident."

The shaman's village had been attacked by an outside tribe. The villagers had been driven into the forest and were fighting for their lives. They were losing badly. Out of nowhere, the opposing warriors began dropping. The shaman saw this and jumped on a nearby boulder, spreading his arms over the battle scene.

"What's happening?" Kenred asked. "Why are they dropping?"

eDaphne pointed to several laser beams. "Hidden lasers again," she said.

With half the attacking warriors eliminated, the tide of battle turned, and the shaman's fighters held the day and saved the village.

"Here's another one," eDaphne said. "This will have a familiar feel."

In the scene, the shaman walked along a forest trail, this time alone. He saw something on the trail ahead and picked it up. It was a spear like those the feline warriors used, but there was a difference. This spear ended in a leather cup with two long rawhide strips. The shaman hefted the spear, testing its balance. He examined the two thongs that reached past the spear center. Then he placed the spear on his right shoulder, slid it back until the thongs were tight, and balanced the front on his left hand. Nodding his understanding, he thrust his right arm forward as if he were throwing the spear. It flew out of the cup, traveling twice the distance of a conventionally thrown spear, penetrating a tree trunk twenty meters distant.

"That's pretty effective," Kenred said. "It will give this tribe a significant advantage over the others, and this shaman's power and influence will grow dramatically."

"Do you think that might be the aim of whoever is doing this?" eDaphne asked.

"How could it be anything else?" Jocara said.

PS Neil Armstrong—The Keid Sphere—Equatorial Band—Saurian Region

Their final leg took them again by MERT Drive through the inner sphere, the inner maze, the inner sphere again, and as before, by MBH Drive to the saurian region of the equatorial band. While keeping a wary eye out for pterosaurs with riders, Jocara placed *Armstrong* over the largest settlement she could find. eDaphne reviewed the holocam recordings while Kenred readied radar, lidar, and optical scanners.

"The saurians were already more advanced than the simians and felines," Kenred said. "I wonder what we'll find now."

"You will not believe this," eDaphne said as she played a holocast recording in the lounge well.

The scene was an open, dry area where the gumtree canopy was sparse. A dozen yurt-like huts covered half the open space. The rest contained a fenced-in enclosure with a domed lattice top constructed of flexible gumtree branches and rawhide strips. Inside the enclosure, a half dozen young pterosaurs ran about, playing with an equal number of young saurian males. Several minutes of close observation showed that each child played with only one young pterosaur.

"Are we seeing what I think we're seeing?" Jocara asked. "Are those young saurian boys bonding with pterosaur chicks?"

"It sure looks like it," Kenred said.

"Those pterosaurs are domesticated," eDaphne said. "It took our several species thousands of years to produce domesticated farm animals and house pets. Only deliberate genetic modification could bring this about so quickly."

"It's almost beyond comprehension," Jocara said.

"Now, watch this," eDaphne said.

The enclosure was open, and each young pterosaur wore a saddle and bitless bridle. A young saurian male stood next to each pterosaur, stroking its neck. Then the boys mounted their charges and the whole lot took to the air. They swooped and swerved, entered into mock combat, played tag, and raced each other across the sky.

"Someone did this for them," Kenred said. "They couldn't do it by themselves in less than several thousand years of domestic breeding. Someone manipulated the genes of ferocious aerial carnivores, turning them into loyal bonded partners."

"You know what this means," Jocara said. "The saurians will expand exponentially across the equatorial band. What will happen when they eventually reach the simians or felines?"

"Imagine," Kenred said, "two dozen adult pterosaurs carrying fully armed warriors diving out of the sky and attacking your village."

"There are millions of klicks between them and either the felines or the simians," eDaphne said. "It's not something we will have to worry about. I see it as a future problem, though. A serious one for the felines' and simians' descendants."

Chapter Fourteen

PS *Andromeda*—Outside the Keid Sphere

Kenred held center stage in the packed auditorium. Everyone had heard about the discoveries, but Thorpe had decided to hold the recordings until they could be presented properly.

"You've got to see this!" Kenred said to the crowd.

The stage vanished as blue sky with white cloud puffs filled the space. From the right side, a magnificently crowned pterosaur head appeared with a loose leather halter around its long snout. As the creature moved into sight, leather reins led back to the hands of a rider that looked very much like the Arcan members of the audience.

The saurian warrior carried a bow slung across his chest, a quiver of arrows across his back, and a heavy leather belt hung with ax and knife.

Kenred's voice sounded throughout the room. "How would you like to see two dozen warriors like this dive from the clouds into your encampment? Especially if your best weapon was a bow and arrow or sling-thrown spear?

"This is probably the most dramatic example of forced evolution and development we have observed since we started looking at these things. We have been operating under the assumption that the sphere is abandoned by its makers, and that what we have found are the remains of a magnificent experiment that somehow went wrong."

The holoimage vanished, leaving Kenred standing at the podium.

"Now we are not so sure. We are about to embark on a more detailed exploration of the equatorial band, but we are not just looking for other sapient species, we are looking for evidence of the builders themselves." Kenred looked out over the crowded auditorium. "I can tell you this. We all signed up for a grand adventure. Speaking as one Arcan astronaut who knows adventure, we have entered a realm none of us ever imagined. I am glad I am part of this," his scales rippled lavender, "and I am certain you are too."

The audience broke out into spontaneous applause as Kenred left the stage with a wave.

✳

"That was some presentation, my Arcan friend," Thorpe said to Kenred back on the Bridge. "You may have found yourself a new occupation."

"Are you kidding," Kenred said. "I almost pitched my lunch."

"Maybe, but you looked like a pro."

Daphne joined them. "Nice job," she said. "You've obviously done that before."

"Not really," Kenred said. "I prefer flying spaceships."

"And that's what we're going to do," Thorpe said.

✳

"I don't want to take another two months to explore an additional quarter of the equatorial band," Thorpe told Daphne. "Your Bayesian analysis gave us a sense of what might be out there. I may just be impatient, but I want to try something different." He smiled at her. "You know me better than anyone. I think you understand."

"What's your idea?" she asked, giving him a squeeze.

"I want to set up random searches guided by a random number generator. We divide the remaining equatorial band into sectors sufficiently small to be searched by a single M-Class craft. Then we assign sectors to our ships based upon the random numbers. Unlike a rigid sector search, this method will keep our pilots' excitement up—and mine as well." Thorpe grinned at Daphne. "What do you think?"

"It makes sense mathematically," Daphne replied. "Extensive research tells us that a randomized approach will find something that is there faster than a structured search—at least statistically. It can't hurt, and it'll make everyone happier, including you."

PS Neil Armstrong—The Keid Sphere—Equatorial Band—Random Flights

Jocara entered the parameters *Andromeda's* Mother gave her. *Armstrong* made one MERT jump directly to the assigned sector, arriving ten kilometers above a Serengeti-like landscape. Like the actual Serengeti on Earth, the wind-swept grassland harbored dozens of species—herbivores, carnivores, and omnivores.

They saw no evidence of sapience, even at the lowest level. Jocara dropped *Armstrong* to just a few tens of meters from the surface and skimmed rapidly across the landscape. They covered over a thousand kilometers without seeing a significant change. The grassland continued in every direction with no letup.

After two hours of random searching, Jocara said, "I think we've done this sector justice. Let's return to *Andromeda* and get our next assignment."

* * *

The turnaround at *Andromeda* was quick. Within minutes, they found themselves in the next randomly selected sector. This time, a sub-tropical jungle interspersed with open grassland spread out below them. They quickly spotted dinosaur-like creatures crashing through the jungle undergrowth and several very large herbivores, not unlike the Brachiosaurus from Earth's prehistory crunching on the occasional tree scattered throughout the grassland.

"Do you see any evidence of sapience?" Jocara asked. "Anything anywhere?"

"It isn't as if we looked at the entire area," Kenred said, "but no, I haven't seen any such evidence."

"It looks as if these guys don't have to worry about ballista bolts," eDaphne said.

"Let's get our next random assignment," Jocara said as she directed Mother to take them back to *Andromeda*.

※

Next was a vast, tropical jungle, humid and wet, with several broad, slow flowing rivers meandering through the flat landscape. Kenred could not penetrate the thick jungle canopy with any instrument that gave him useful information. Colorful birds filled the sky near the treetops, but that was really all the life he could detect.

"I have no doubt there are critters galore down there under that canopy," he said, "but we will not observe them."

Jocara wondered, "Do you think there might be primitive natives living under the canopy?"

"Maybe, but we won't find them unless we go on foot."

"That's not something we want to do," eDaphne said. "We're doing quick surveys—in and out. If we don't see anything after a brief survey, we leave."

"So, I guess it's time to leave," Jocara said, with open, blinking eyes.

※

They found themselves over a vast, shallow sea with scattered tropical islands. Puffy clouds filled the sky, and here and there they saw rain squalls moving across the ocean surface. Palm tree-like vegetation covered the low-lying islands except for the beaches that were glistening white sand. Seabirds filled the air over the islands and out over the open water.

"Look!" Kenred said. "That looks like a whale spout."

Off to one side, water and steam spurted into the air, and then the broad back of a marine mammal broached for several seconds. Directly below them, dolphin-like swimmers leaped into the air in pairs and triplets.

"It's idyllic," Jocara said. "I wouldn't mind spending a couple of weeks down there with you, Kenred."

"Hey, guys," Kenred said, "I think we found something." He directed Jocara to an island ahead of them.

"That looks like a bunch of village huts," he said. "Those simians walking around look very much like you, eDaphne—very Human."

"I agree, they do," she answered. "Do you see any tools or machines?"

"Several dugout canoes, but that's about it. They would need the canoes to get from island to island. Except for that, they seem pretty primitive."

"We'll park a holocam platform above this section to keep track of developments," eDaphne said.

✳

Armstrong visited several more random sections during the next few days. Other than the islanders, they found no other sapient beings and no hint of any kind of past or present civilization. The other M-Class ships also followed the random selection process. Most found lower-level animals, but only *Armstrong* identified another sapient species.

After two weeks of random searches, Daphne called the pilots together to see if they could sort out what they had seen during their travels. They gathered in the conference room because Daphne thought the more intimate setting would produce better results. Mother had integrated their holocam recordings into her increasingly complex model that she displayed over the conference table.

Mother had highlighted one section in particular and separated it from the main holoimage. It floated large over the table.

PS Andromeda—Science Section

As Chief Scientist on *Andromeda*, Daphne kept track of many things. Some she handled personally, others she kept herself abreast of matters, and most of the remaining sent her periodic reports. When something important happened in anything under her purview, someone brought it to her attention right away.

Daphne's astronomy people were having a heyday studying Keid-C. No one had ever been this close to a red dwarf, and in addition, this was a flare star. They were filling *Andromeda's* data banks with new information. Besides their normal data analysis, the astronomers used several AI programs to look for patterns in the massive data set. One of these programs raised a red flag. It wasn't a big deal, just a regular slight increase in surface pressure, so minor that the astronomers would have missed it entirely. It was something to watch. Where was it going?

Chapter Fifteen

PS Andromeda—The Conference Room

The M-Class pilots and other interested participants crowded into the conference room. Flesh-and-blood folks filled every chair, and upload holoimages occupied most of the room's airspace. Even so, Max and eMax found room to seek out their friends. Everyone focused on the section Mother had broken out.

The breakout was an aerial view of a sparsely wooded area.

"I broke this section out," Mother said, "because of the interesting ground pattern." She highlighted the pattern by emphasizing the pattern outline.

Unlike other forests on the equatorial band, the trees in this section followed straight lines in a right-angle crisscross pattern.

"Until now," Daphne said, "we have found several primitive cultures. At least three of them are being boosted by someone or something we do not yet understand. We intend on getting to the bottom of that eventually, but right now we want to know more about what you see here.

"I will send *Armstrong* with a portal so we can put enough people on the ground to find some definitive answers."

PS Neil Armstrong—The Keid Sphere—Equatorial Band

Jocara took *Armstrong* by MERT Drive directly from the vehicle bay to a hover over the tree pattern Mother had identified. From three kilometers up, Kenred identified the pattern easily.

"See the streets radiating out from this central location?" he said. "Several circular streets around the center and then rectangular patterns farther out. They're not streets, of course. They're tree patterns, but streets seem like the only reasonable explanation."

"I agree," Jocara said.

"Let's land and establish the portal," eDaphne said. "Then we can look around a bit."

Jocara settled *Armstrong* on the ground by a central mound that formed the focus of the radial streets. She and Kenred departed the spacecraft.

"Sorry you can't join us," she said to eDaphne.

"That's one of the disadvantages to being an upload," eDaphne said, "but there are compensations."

Kenred pulled the hyper-disk from a pocket and activated it. Daphne stepped through, followed by Thorpe.

"The pattern's not obvious from the ground," Jocara told them. "I guess the trees that grew between the rows of trees obscured the rows. Even from above, the pattern is sufficiently faint that Mother had to emphasize the lines before we could see them."

"There is that mound," Daphne said, pointing.

"It's so low," Kenred said, "we didn't recognize it from the air."

"It wouldn't hurt to bring several people here to search outward from the mound," Daphne said. "I'm reminded of a major city on Earth, Paris. It has no central mound, but a decorative tower built over three hundred years ago marks the center of a radial street pattern. What I'm getting at is what we see here is not the result of a primitive culture like the others we have found thus far. Whoever or whatever did this had a great deal more sophistication than even the saurians with their flying carnivorous steeds."

Using her Link, Daphne summoned a dozen people to aid in the ground search. They gathered around and Daphne told them, "You saw the pattern from the air. Look around you. There does not seem to be anything to see down here. Nevertheless, I thought you might enjoy a bit of shore leave while helping us examine what is here. Spread out and search in a circular pattern around the mound. Use your Link to tell me of anything you find."

Everybody, including Daphne and Thorpe, joined in the search. No one really expected to find anything, but the activity made a pleasant change to their normal routine. Jocara and Kenred searched together, hand-in-hand. Jocara stole a glance in the direction Daphne and Thorpe had taken. To her delight, they were holding hands. She giggled and nuzzled Kenred's snout.

"It's a dream come true," she said quietly, her scales rippling lavender with happiness.

After two hours, Daphne called the searchers back to the mound. "It looks like nobody found anything," she said.

"Can't even see the pattern from down here," someone quipped.

"I'm sure the exercise did you no harm," Daphne shot back. "Everybody—thanks for your help."

Daphne turned to Jocara. "I want you to fly another aerial survey over this area. Use high-power radar and lidar to see if there is something underground."

PS Neil Armstrong—The Keid Sphere—Equatorial Band

As soon as everyone had departed, Jocara took *Armstrong* to 500 meters. Kenred set his radar on high power and focused his lidar to look below the surface.

"Move slowly, Jocara," he told her.

They commenced a kilometer from the mound and circled in while Kenred overlapped his scans to maximize his penetration.

"I've picked up a couple of metallic clumps. They're quite deep. I've marked their locations on the chart." He kept searching. When they reached the mound, Kenred nearly shouted, "Hold it!" He adjusted his lidar focus. "I've got something under the mound," he said, his scales rippling dark blue with excitement. "It's big and oblong, and about twenty meters deep."

eDaphne called Daphne with the news. "We need something to dig it out," she said.

"How about an old-fashioned backhoe?" Daphne asked. "Open your portal again and enlarge it to three meters in diameter. We'll send a backhoe and driver through."

Jocara landed the spacecraft away from the mound, and Kenred opened the portal and enlarged it. Within a few minutes, a tracked backhoe rolled through, its driver grinning from ear to ear.

"Don't get to do this very much," he said. "Where do I dig?"

He definitely knew his business. He topped the mound quickly, pushing the dirt to the other side. Then, carefully, scoop by scoop, he removed dirt from the mound face until he was at ground level.

"You still have about five meters to go," Kenred advised him.

The operator backed away from the mound and commenced digging a sloping trench toward the base. By the time he reached the middle of the mound, he was at five meters depth.

"Go easy, now," Kenred told him. "You're close."

Within a couple of minutes, the operator's blade touched something metallic. He eased the scoop around the object until he could see it partially sticking out of the packed ground. With several pulls and nudges, he freed it completely.

They had uncovered a titanium plaque 1.5 meters square. Kenred brushed the dirt off its face to reveal a detailed cutaway drawing of the Keid Sphere, with sections and parts labeled and tied to a key below the drawing. The only problem was the symbols and the writing were indecipherable.

PS Andromeda—The Science Section

The titanium plaque was not just titanium. It was an alloy consisting of titanium and other materials that the lab techs were still trying to decipher.

"I want to know its composition," Daphne said to her archaeological staff, "but mostly I want to decipher the text."

This was not an impossible task. Each symbol referred to a section of the drawing. Each piece of text referred to something on the drawing, but that was less certain than the relationship between the symbols and the sections. About a week after they received the plaque, Daphne's archaeological staff called her to their lab. When she arrived, they presented her with the original plaque standing on a lab bench, beside it a holoimage of the plaque with English in place of the foreign symbols and text, and then a holoimage of Mother's reconstruction of the sphere as best she could do it with the information reported by the pilots and what she could surmise. On the plaque holoimage, they had converted distance units to metric. The text described the Keid Sphere, referring to its parts using the symbols.

"Mother," Daphne said, "include the information from the plaque into your reconstruction."

As they watched, the sphere holoimage underwent some minor adjustments, particularly in the placement of the longitudinal linear drivers and some detail on the equatorial band. They now knew exactly what they were dealing with—at least in terms of the physical structure.

Chapter Sixteen

PS Neil Armstrong—The Keid Sphere—Equatorial Band

Once more, Jocara took *PS Neil Armstrong* on MERT Drive directly from the vehicle bay to an assigned random location on the equatorial band. For the first time, Jocara, Kenred, and eDaphne found themselves on the shore of a large ocean. Below them, a magnificent city sat on the shore of a beautiful harbor that protected the city from the sea.

Jocara immediately called Thorpe and Daphne by Link. "You have got to see this to believe it!" she said, scales rippling dark blue.

"We can see it on your opticals," Daphne said. "Can you estimate its size?"

"It's at least as big as Amred City."

"Any activity?"

"This is strange," Jocara said. "We detect no radio transmissions, no radar, nothing in the electromagnetic spectrum. But, I can see activity on the streets—no people, no apparent sapient activity, but things are moving. We see vehicles, small animals, machines that might be robots. It's really difficult to tell from here, because their tall buildings make some side views impossible."

"This is Thorpe. I will take charge of this situation personally. I do not intend to take anything away from you three, but this matter has implications I need to sort out before I let you loose down there."

✳

Following Thorpe's instructions, Jocara sent a drone carrying a hyper-disk to a park in the city center positioned so bushes would conceal the portal when it was activated. Once the drone was gone, Thorpe and Daphne stepped through the portal, looked around the park, and started walking down a path carrying small, unobtrusive ho-locams. Both carried concealed Electro Muscular Disruption (EMD) weapons set to stun. Thorpe did not expect any problems that would require a weapon, but he had learned in his long life to be prepared.

"The temperature is comfortable," Thorpe said. He walked to a wire trash container. "It's empty."

They passed a bird bath. Several birds similar to temperate zone birds on Earth hopped around the bath, keeping it between them and the two Humans. An animal that could easily have been a dog ran past them as the birds scattered.

They reached a smoothly paved street with sidewalks on both sides, but they saw no pedestrians. Several machines passed them in the street. They had four wheels and looked very much like automobiles Thorpe remembered from the time before he died, and his head had been cryogenically preserved. The vehicles had no drivers.

On the sidewalk ahead, Thorpe spotted a figure. "What do you think it is?" he asked.

"It's humanoid," Daphne said, "but I think it's a machine."

A machine it was. It walked upright on two legs like a humanoid. It had shoulders and two arms and a head with facial features, but they were not designed to appear alive. Rather, they seemed to be functional parts of the machine's body.

"Robot…it's a robot," Thorpe said. "It doesn't seem to be sapient, but how do you tell?"

Daphne lifted her hand and slapped the robot's face. Her fingers left an impression like they might on a Human face. The robot did not react. She lifted her hand for a second slap, but this time, the robot gently restrained her hand. It released her as soon as she relaxed her hand.

"What were you thinking?" Thorpe asked. "Have you gone nuts?"

"I don't know," Daphne said. "It just seemed like the thing to do."

"You're lucky it didn't take you down."

"Okay, so what do you make of its reaction?" Daphne asked.

"I don't know…It doesn't like to be slapped?" He grinned. "We don't know enough to answer that question."

They walked to a corner and crossed the street. A car was approaching. Thorpe took Daphne's hand and remained in the crosswalk, facing the vehicle. It stopped.

"Stay there," he told her. "I want to check something."

He walked around the vehicle and then dropped to one knee and cupped a hand to his nose. "That's the engine exhaust," he said. "They burn hydrogen. I'm guessing fuel cells driving electric motors."

He went back to Daphne and walked with her to the front of a very tall building next to the crosswalk, a skyscraper.

"This is the tallest building around here," Thorpe said. "If that makes it important, maybe we can get some answers inside."

Keid Sphere—Equatorial Band—Keid City

There are only so many ways to place an entrance in a public building, especially if the door is transparent. The skyscraper had a series of glass doors facing the sidewalk. Thorpe pushed one. It swung in on nearly frictionless hinges. The doors opened to a large, high-ceilinged lobby with a large desk near the back wall.

"That has to be a receptionist or security desk," Thorpe said, walking over to it.

It looked like any such desk in any large building Thorpe had visited on four planets. *Five, if you count Mars*, Thorpe reminded himself.

Behind the desk was an extension to the lobby that clearly served only one purpose. Six sets of doors lined the sides of the smaller lobby.

"Those," Thorpe said, "are elevator access doors. I'll bet you any-thing." He walked to one and pushed a button labeled with strange symbols.

"Are you actually going to ride one of those?" Daphne asked. "What if it stops halfway?"

"We're looking at modern technology," Thorpe answered. "I'm sure these elevators have an escape route, just like ours." He chuckled. "Of course, we have our E-disks should anything actually go wrong."

Daphne looked around. "I suppose you noticed that the artificial lighting is working, the air feels cool and fresh, and I'll bet the wa-ter faucets work, too. This doesn't make sense, Thorpe. What are we dealing with?"

"Absentee landlord…I don't really have a clue. We've seen some really advanced technology, capabilities way beyond ours, and some stuff is at our level or lower."

The elevator doors opened.

"Shall we?" Thorpe asked and stepped into the little chamber.

A very familiar row of buttons decorated one side of the entrance. "Where I come from," Thorpe said, "the action is always at the top." He pushed the uppermost button.

✳

"Are you guys following all this?" Thorpe asked over his Link.

"We are," eThorpe answered. "I've got specialists standing by should you need them."

"Good," Thorpe said. "We're going to the top floor to see how these people run their show."

The elevator stopped, and the door opened. Thorpe and Daphne stepped out into a wide hallway. Across the hallway, several high glass doors blocked their progress. Thorpe pushed one. It swung inward, and they entered an expansive office space with several desks, cabinets, and machines. At the back of the room, another set of glass doors opened into a large, obviously private office that looked out over the cityscape below.

"Whoever belongs here is certainly in charge of something," Thorpe said with a chuckle. He walked to the big desk and examined a machine on one corner. "This is a computer, or I'll eat my shirt," he said. Looking at Daphne, he added, "Let's bring Sally and Brad in on this."

Thorpe pulled out a hyper-disk and activated it. Five minutes later, Sally and Brad walked through the portal. Sally took one look at the expansive window and ran to it, pressing her face against the cool glass.

Thorpe pointed to the machine on the large desk. "I want to activate that and figure out how to use it," he said.

✳

"Take a look at this, Sally," Brad said, calling her back from the window view.

"This is a monitor," Brad said, pointing to a framed glass object about a meter wide and fifty centimeters high. "And this," he picked up a floppy object about the size of a modern keyboard, "probably is the input device." He turned to his Vietnamese partner. "Let's turn it on *Chị ơi*."

After a few minutes of searching, Sally found a concealed button. She pushed it and the monitor lit up, displaying a pattern of images and symbols.

"Good job, *Chị ơi*." He took her diminutive form in his bear-like arms and squeezed her gently. "I don't know how you do these things so quickly."

She smiled shyly, holding a hand in front of her mouth. Brad experimentally tapped his fingers on the flexible device. It lit up, displaying finger-size circles containing symbols.

"It's a keyboard," Brad said. "Can anyone read these symbols?"

"Can you do anything with it?" Thorpe asked.

"Look, Thorpe, Sally and I are good. We've proved that dozens of times. What you are asking here is not impossible, but we would have to take a systematic approach to figuring the keyboard out, and then we would have to do it again with the device itself. Like I said, not impossible, but we can't do it overnight."

Several cables passed through the desk into the monitor base. He worked his large fingers around the monitor base and then turned to Sally.

"*Chị ơi*, you have much smaller fingers. See what you can find down there."

She pushed her smaller fingers into the hollow pedestal and then brought them out, holding an insulated cable with a terminator. The monitor went blank, still lit, but not displaying anything.

"I think this is the input cable," Sally said.

Sally and Brad sat at the desk and examined the terminator carefully.

"These are contacts," Sally said, pointing to several golden strips on a tongue that extended from the terminator. "Are you thinking what I'm thinking?"

Brad turned to Thorpe, pointing at the terminator. "We're going back to our lab to make an adapter that will marry this terminator with our standard connectors. Then we'll plug it into eSally and eBrad, and let them have a go at the internals."

Keid Sphere—Keid City—Alien Computer

It took Sally and Brad an hour to make an adapter. They supplied their Nanocosm with several detailed holoimages of the terminator and instructed it to create a socket that would adapt the terminator to their standard matrix system connector. Since they did not know what each of the contacts served inside the alien system, they told the Nanocosm to terminate each unknown contact inside a standard upload matrix box so the upload would have access to each contact. Then they generalized the instructions so they could transmit the holoimage of any terminator they might find, and the Nanocosm would generate an appropriate adapter.

Sally and Brad joined the others back in the top floor office. Sally carried eSally's matrix, and Brad carried eBrad's. Both matrixes carried a full power supply, so eSally and eBrad generated their holoimages and joined the group.

"You've established live backup links to each matrix?" Thorpe asked the uploads.

"We have," eBrad answered.

"Sit down, and let's chat," Thorpe told the couple and their uploads.

Sally and Brad sat on a settee in the office lounge area, joined by their upload holoimages, and Thorpe took an easy chair opposite them.

"As I have come to expect ever since I hired you from the School of Mines way back when, you guys have performed way beyond expectations. You know I hold you in the highest regard."

Sally blushed, and Brad grinned crookedly. Their uploads responded in virtually the same manner.

"Once you two," Thorpe indicated the uploads, "get inside their system, you will be tempted to explore. I am giving you a direct order, and I don't do that very often." Thorpe smiled at the uploads and then at their flesh-and-blood counterparts. "Your only job is to decode their file structure and translate their keyboard and screen symbology. Put a firewall on your downstream sides so nothing can get to you. We have no idea who or what these beings are. Obviously, their technology is far beyond ours. I don't want either of you at their mercy. Just figure out the structure and symbols, and get the hell out of there!" He smiled again. "When we're ready, eThorpe will do the actual exploration."

Thorpe came to his feet. "Are we absolutely clear on this?"

"We are," both Sally and Brad answered.

"As are we," the uploads added.

Brad plugged eSally's matrix into eBrad's matrix and then cautiously plugged the alien terminator into the adapter Sally and he had made. Then he plugged the adapter into Brad's matrix.

✸

eBrad and eSally hunched together at the terminal block in eBrad's matrix where external signals entered the matrix. This was familiar territory. eSally merged a bit of herself with eBrad, the upload equivalent of an intimate hug.

"How do you want to do this?" eSally asked.

"You know me, Kid. I go first to keep you safe."

"I'm okay with that," eSally said, "but remember, in the outside world you're bigger and stronger than I am, but in here, I am as strong and capable as you." She merged a bit of herself with him again to let him know that she really was fine with the arrangement.

eBrad sent a tensor to each contact on the alien terminator and cautiously urged them down their respective wires into the initial electronic complex. Assuming the monitor was an input/output device, eBrad expected no data traffic on the cable leading to the monitor. One of his tensors stumbled onto a data arterial, a vast river of incomprehensible information.

eBrad's first task was to decipher the alien data structure. He instructed his tensor to grab a piece of data. Unlike the data structure he had handled all his life, the piece his tensor captured consisted of ones, zeros, and minus ones. This was a start.

"Wait for me *Chi oi*," he told eSally. "I'll be back shortly."

eBrad slid down the path his tensor had followed to the bank of the flowing data stream. He eased himself into the stream, letting it carry him to a major intersection. The data moved through the intersection, controlled by logic gates that seemed very similar in function to what he was used to, although the minus one bits made the transactions more compact. He followed one result to its destination, a three-dimensional storage matrix, very much like those he knew. Pieces of data moved into and out of the matrix, sometimes staying for only a moment, and other times taking up permanent residence. As he moved through the data stream, he cataloged what he saw and how the elements worked together, building a chart of data types, kinds of transactions, and flow paths.

While he constructed an internal database of what he was learning, a large, amorphous blob oozed from a side passage and enveloped him. eBrad stopped moving and found that pieces of his electronic skeleton were dissolving. It was an antivirus program that had identified him as a virus. He tried unsuccessfully to extract himself from the blob. It was like a whirlpool, sucking him to its center. More of his external substance dissolved, and then he felt a cold tendril pushing into his core. He shoved it back, but it was like a sponge. It moved aside a bit and continued toward his core. He couldn't stop it.

I'm not getting out of this, eBrad told himself. Time to bail before that critter learns what I know!

He sent an emergency tensor back to eSally, telling her to get out while she could. Then he triggered his self-destruct mechanism. One moment he was a struggling upload, fighting a powerful antivirus program, the next he was disassociated flotsam and jetsam carried along by the data river, to be filtered out and discarded somewhere downstream.

✳

eBrad emitted an electronic gasp and looked around his location. He was in a private secure spot in the *Andromeda* matrix.

He signaled eThorpe. "I've been axed by an alien antivirus program. I'm back in my cubbyhole, but I need to get to Keid City and eSally ASAP!"

"Go to the central matrix storage rack and enter a matrix. Kimberly will meet you there and transport you to the building in Keid City."

Moments later, eBrad slipped into an empty matrix. As his external sensors came to life, he saw Kimberly enter the room.

"Hey, eBrad. I know what happened. I'll get you there right away."

She extracted his matrix from the rack, opened a portal, and stepped onto the top floor of Keid City's tallest building.

"There you are," Daphne said, taking the matrix from Kimberly's hand and plugging it into eBrad's old matrix. eSally was there waiting for him.

"Oh, Brad (the uploads referred to themselves as Brad and Sally), I was so scared." She merged with him for several seconds.

"I know, *Chị ơi*. I wasn't in real danger, but I didn't want that thing to capture my knowledge. That could have done all of us harm." He merged with her briefly. "I don't think that antivirus program was malicious—and that's certainly what it was, an antivirus program. It was just doing its job." He projected his holoimage into the room.

"eThorpe," eBrad said, "that's the orneriest antivirus I ever encountered. You're not getting past it unless we come up with something."

"Can you make me a virtual EMD weapon—something that will stun the antivirus program to inactivity?"

"That's a no-brainer. I'll just modify a tensor to emit powerful pulses and give you the code. Speaking of code, I've compiled what I learned inside their matrix. It's not complete. A lot of the file structure is still a mystery. I'll slip you a packet before you enter, and I'll make it part of *Andromeda's* general database."

✳

"It's very likely," eThorpe told the intimate group assembled in his office back on *Andromeda*—the original team, "that I can use the connection eBrad established in Keid City to penetrate the entire Keid Sphere operation. I will be a while, possibly quite a while. I'll keep my backup Link active, but I won't pull the plug unless I am in dire extremis. This means it may be some time before you hear from me. In the meantime, keep up the random flights. That's how we found Keid City. We may find something else important."

"You are sure you don't want one of us with you?" eDale asked. "—me, eBrad, eDaphne, maybe a security guy?"

"I'm sure, at least for now. Let's go."

Thorpe carried eThorpe's matrix, and they all passed through a portal into the Keid City office.

eBrad's former and new matrixes were still plugged tandem into eSally's matrix. Brad pulled eSally's matrix and eBrad's old matrix out and plugged eThorpe directly into eBrad. eThorpe joined eBrad inside eBrad's matrix, where eBrad gave him the EMD code and passed on what he had learned about the alien file structure. eThorpe moved back into his matrix, and Brad removed eBrad's matrix from the connection. eThorpe was ready. With the EMD tensor at hand, he slipped through the adapter and down the path eBrad had taken earlier. He was on his way.

✳

eThorpe landed in a massive river of data flowing swiftly toward an unknown destination. At first, he just went with the flow, watching closely, examining the data structures near him, comparing them to what eBrad had given him. He recognized he was in a great datatrunk and found that he could insert himself into the trunk wall any time he wished. As soon as he did this, his motion stopped relative to the wall, while the vast data flow continued. As he moved along the wall, he discovered incoming and outgoing branches. He chose one at random, purposefully moving away from the vast data stream. He followed several smaller branches until he found himself in a small virtual chamber that processed arriving data and then stacked it. *Storage?* he wondered. *But this isn't getting me into the main data matrix.*

eThorpe traced his way back through increasingly larger branches until he reached the large data river again. He stayed close to a wall but allowed the river to take him farther and farther away from the top story office. eThorpe could not tell his direction of motion, except that at each intersection he joined a larger data stream. He lost track of time but was aware of its passing.

At a major intersection where the data stream doubled in size, a large amorphous slug floated above the data stream, moving directly at him. eThorpe pulled out his EMD, holding it at the ready. When the slug was an arm's length away, he touched it with his EMD. The part he touched pulled back, but the rest kept coming, almost like a sluggish cloud approaching him over the data flow. eThorpe cranked the EMD up several notches and touched the slug again. It pulled away from his hand dramatically, but the rest slithered around one side and kept coming, inexorably covering the diminishing distance between them.

eThorpe set the EMD to its highest intensity and lunged toward the slug, striking it over and over again. That did it. The antivirus slug stopped its advance, collapsed to the bank, and dissolved into a slimy mess of goo. The slime slid into the data river and washed away.

I must still be in the building matrix, eThorpe told himself. I don't think they would use these guys to protect the larger network.

As it turned out, he didn't know how right he was.

Chapter Seventeen

Keid Sphere—Keid City—Alien Matrix

Keeping a wary eye out for more antivirus slugs, eThorpe continued moving to ever larger data trunks. His instincts told him he was traveling down the towering building into the carbynophene understructure that made up the base for the entire equatorial band. It was generally conductive, but Jocara and Kenred had learned that some parts were superconductive.

eThorpe could not imagine a reason for making the entire 1.5-million-kilometer width of the equatorial band superconductive, but setting up channels to carry power and data at superconductive speeds made sense—if it was cost effective in terms of power consumption.

And what does that mean? he asked himself. The Sphere captures virtually all the radiation Keid-C produces. There's no shortage of power.

While eThorpe moved with the ever-growing data stream, he examined the data structure surrounding him. He had incorporated eBrad's observations and insights into his own perception. This helped, but it wasn't enough. He could identify the individual data packets with their three elements, plus, minus, and zero, but he could not determine how they fit into the overall data scheme.

As eThorpe moved deeper into the sphere matrix, he began to recognize a pattern, one that seemed vaguely familiar. A lot of subjective time had passed since he started his investigation. He had seen no antivirus slugs for some time and presumed he had passed their territory boundary. He didn't remember seeing anything, but it could have been an electronic highlight.

That pattern really does look familiar, he said to himself. He racked his memory for its source. He moved back to the Asterian invasion, back to their preps for that invasion, back to his interactions with the Oort. *Wait! The Oort…I had to accommodate the Oort's dramatically different data structure in order to retain control of my communications with them. I'm seeing some of that here…and that's impossible. I need Johnny here if I'm going to make any real sense of this.* He moved into a wall to stop his progress. *Johnny was an Oort. He gave up his upload status to become Human because he was deeply upset with the Oort's duplicity while he saw our essential goodness and fairness.*

Well, shit! Now I gotta work my way back to the tower.

✳

eThorpe had already learned that for every data river in one direction, another flowed the other way. He crossed the river he had followed thus far, entered the river going back, and lay back, letting the data flow do the work.

"Thorpe, it's me. Johnny isn't going to like this, but I need him down here as an upload. It's essential. Believe it or not, I think we're dealing with something Oort related. He's the only one I trust completely who fully understands their data structure. Make sure he understands the significance, and send a clone of his backup down here. I'll meet him at the adapter."

✳

"John Ortman to the Bridge," Thorpe called over the general circuit.

Shortly, Johnny stepped through the Bridge portal. "What's up, Thorpe?" he asked.

Thorpe explained where eThorpe was and the nature of his problem. "He thinks he is dealing with an Oort or an Oort-like data infrastructure. You are the only person in *Andromeda* who might be able to make some sense of all this. eThorpe wants you to clone your backup as a full upload, and send him into the sphere matrix to meet with eThorpe." Thorpe smiled at him. "I know what you've been through, Johnny. This is the last thing you would have wanted to do, but will you do it, anyway? We really need you."

"When you put it that way, how can I refuse?"

"The moment you clone your backup," Thorpe said, "your backup and clone will diverge. We can talk about synchronizing you when you return, but right now, I want to get you down to eThorpe as soon as possible."

"So, eThorpe really thinks the Oort have something to do with the Keid Sphere. He's rarely wrong, but he may be here. Just think what it would take to bring about such an involvement." Johnny laughed. "You guys are the only family I have now," he said. "I've got your back six ways from Sunday."

✳

Johnny called Daphne, and they met in the backup storage facility. Together, they cloned Johnny's real-time backup and loaded it into a matrix. Then they set up a real-time backup for the eJohnny clone. eJohnny projected his holoimage into the room.

"This is really strange," he said. "You're—I'm standing right there," he pointed at Johnny, "but I am totally aware of me here," he pointed to his matrix. "You've gotten us into some interesting shit, Johnny, but I think this tops the cake." He laughed. "Let's go do it. I'm looking forward to the adventure!"

✳

Carrying eJohnny's matrix, Johnny accompanied Daphne through the portal to the Keid City office that had now become the center of operations for sphere investigations. The pilots were still making random flights, but Thorpe's emphasis had shifted to the upload investigation.

Johnny had not felt so excited in years. He knew well that he and eJohnny were diverging moment by moment, and that he would not experience what eJohnny was about to until and unless they synchronized when this was over. Nevertheless, he felt the excitement. When he abandoned the Oort and threw in with the Humans, he never thought there might be a chance of recovery. This entire experiment might amount to nothing, but he grasped at the chance.

Johnny plugged eJohnny's matrix into eThorpe's and stepped back next to his friends, Daphne and Thorpe.

Inside his matrix, eJohnny moved through the connector into eThorpe's matrix. He located the exit connector and moved to the adapter where eThorpe waited. eJohnny was ready to move, but eThorpe cautioned him.

"This is the code for your EMD tensor. You're going to need it to stop antivirus slugs as you move through this building's network. Once we enter the Keid Sphere network, you won't need it. The slugs seem to be limited to the admin network in the building, or perhaps the city. You're here for two reasons: to watch my back and to get a handle on the file structure these guys use. By the way, since it's just us two, let's drop the 'e' from our names. It'll make things easier."

eThorpe slid down the cable, and eJohnny followed him. At the data river, eThorpe jumped in and waved for eJohnny to follow.

"We've got a long way to go. Try to keep up with me."

eJohnny placed himself just behind eThorpe, both of them moving with the flow. He extended his awareness as far as possible in this restricted tunnel while examining the data packets surrounding him. eThorpe was right; they were familiar. He didn't actually recognize anything, but he saw a pattern he recognized, a pattern from long ago.

Twice, slugs approached them. Their aggressiveness astonished eJohnny, but eThorpe handled them before he could intervene. eJohnny felt awkward. He was older than the entire Human race, but with eThorpe, he felt like an inexperienced child. He had been dealing with eThorpe since their very first interaction when he presented the Oort's face to eThorpe and his people. He had literally been part of every interaction between Oort and Humans until he had removed himself from the Oort to become part of the Human community.

Is it possible, he thought, that Oort still exist? Is the familiarity I see here a predecessor or descendant of what I knew as an Oort? Is such a thing possible?

"Johnny," eThorpe said, "we've left the domain of Keid City. We are riding a superconducting tunnel in the Keid Sphere equatorial band base. That means we are in the outermost layer of the sphere. We're looking for who is in charge. I don't think they would be out here, but I don't have a shred of data to base this opinion on.

"You've been moving through this stuff for a while. What do you think?"

"Insufficient data, my friend, but I can say this stuff is familiar. I just don't know how or why yet."

Keid Sphere—Alien Matrix—The Oort Connection

eJohnny had forgotten how amorphous time seemed to an upload. He and eThorpe traveled a great distance through the carbynophene structure that formed the base of the massive equatorial band. Since the path was superconductive, they traveled at near lightspeed, but they had no real idea where they were headed.

The farther they penetrated, the more familiar things became. eJohnny was sufficiently astute to understand that the surrounding patterns were not changing, but he was seeing things more clearly. When he started, the pattern had seemed vaguely familiar, but now he definitely recognized it. He signaled eThorpe, and they pulled into a wall, stopping their forward progress.

"Thorpe," he said earnestly, "we're inside an Oort matrix, a vast, complex Oort facility."

"How can that be?" eThorpe asked. "It's just not possible."

"I'm telling you, it is Oort. I lived in such a matrix for several million years—it's Oort!"

"I had forgotten about those millions of years. So, this is Oort?"

"It is Oort," eJohnny said definitively.

"So, what does it mean?" eThorpe sounded genuinely puzzled.

"It's Oort," eJohnny said again. "This thing has been here a long time. Did it start out Oort? Has it been Oort? We definitely know one thing: right *now* it is Oort."

"Do you think the sphere is abandoned, maintained by ghosts like Keid City, or do you think someone—Oort, perhaps—is actively managing it?"

"Insufficient data," eJohnny answered, "but isn't that why we're here—to find the answer to your question?"

They moved on, up a spoke, eJohnny thought. The data flow thinned and then stopped. Instead, darting tensor-like objects whizzed past them from time to time, seemingly at random.

"Let's latch onto one of those and follow," eThorpe said.

That turned out to be easier said than done. The runners passed at very high speed, probably because the substrate was superconducting. Latching onto them required split-second timing. They took hold of each other, and Johnny got a corner of a passing runner. They retraced their path into the equatorial base and then took some twists and turns through increasingly narrow passages, arriving at a device whose purpose was not obvious. The runner attached itself to the device and adjusted its position physically. How it did this was not obvious either.

Then eJohnny felt a massive surge of power. "Did you feel that?" he asked eThorpe.

"I did. What do you think it was?"

eJohnny approached the device and inserted himself into its electronic mechanism. "You're not going to believe this," he said. "It's a small laser cannon. It just killed a large predator that was stalking a shaman in the simian region."

"How long did we take to get here from where we latched onto the runner?" eThorpe asked.

"I'm guessing—a few microseconds, maybe."

"So, this runner thing—whatever the hell it is—gets an emergency call, and runs down here and shoots the critter. How the hell does that work?" eThorpe sounded genuinely perplexed. "Let's keep things simple for the moment. Something down here is observing. That cannon, and every one like it we aren't considering right now, has an observer. Somehow, that observer gets the word to Central, wherever the hell that is, and Central dispatches the runner.

"Now let's get complicated. Say the cannon range is two hundred meters. I don't know how large the occupied simian region is, but by any measure, that's a lot of cannons, a lot of observers. Now take it to the next level. By that, I mean all the other regions, including those we haven't found yet. Then add all the other interference modes—and we don't even know what they are. Do you see where I'm going?"

"Of course," eJohnny answered, "and we really don't know how many levels there are, and what the actual coverage is."

"Let's put some order to what we do know," eThorpe said. "We've identified Task Runners and Order Runners, although I think they are entirely different entities. Task Runners are tensors. They can carry out different tasks. I suppose the Controllers could place a Task Runner at each potential destination, but that would be a waste of resources. Far better to hold them centrally and dispatch as necessary.

"What about Order Runners? No matter how you cut it, you need an Order Runner at each location. I don't see any way around this. But I don't remember seeing an Order Runner before the Task Runner took us here. Do you?"

"I didn't see anything," eJohnny said.

"So, how did Central get the order?"

"We agree these guys are way advanced, right?" eJohnny asked.

"A given," eThorpe answered.

"What if they are using entangled pairs?"

"And…?"

"Don't ask me how they might accomplish this," eJohnny said, "but if they split an entangled pair of whatever they are working with, one element of all the pairs could reside in Central, and the other could be at their posts, no matter how many. The moment something happens anywhere that requires intervention, Central would know and could dispatch a Task Runner."

"I think we have a working hypothesis, Johnny. I'm impressed."

"Don't be yet," eJohnny said. "It takes fifty seconds for a signal to cross the sphere while traveling through the equatorial band. That's way too long to solve an emergency like what we just saw. Even a station near the sun wouldn't work."

"You talked yourself back out of your own solution," eThorpe said.

"Maybe not. What if there were a bunch of Centrals close enough to everything, so this isn't a problem?"

"Okay," eThorpe said, "we've got a working hypothesis again."

eJohnny heard a noise and turned to see what it was. An odd-looking tensor lurked in the digital background, its attention focused on them both. While eJohnny watched, it doubled its size and moved toward them with menacing tendrils.

"Thorpe, we're in trouble. Look behind you." eJohnny extracted his EMD weapon and held it in front of him. The menacing tensor slipped to one side while advancing, trying to work around the stun gun.

"It doesn't know what an EMD is," eThorpe said. "I think it's just trying to get the advantage."

The enlarged tensor continued slipping sideways.

"Keep your EMD out front," eThorpe said. "I'll hit it from the side."

He lunged at the attacking tensor, making solid contact with his stun gun. The attacking tensor disintegrated, pieces falling to the digital deck, with the rest floating away on the ever-present digital breeze.

"Okay," eThorpe said, "it looks like we now have Task Runners, Order something-or-others, and Sheriff Bots. Judging by how this guy approached us, I'd say we have a very intelligent antivirus program. Given the level of sophisticated technology we've seen, they all could well be sentient."

✳

"We really need to find the Controllers," eThorpe said as they headed out of the equatorial band.

"How many Controllers do you think we will find?" eJohnny asked.

"They need to be centrally located for the section they serve," eThorpe said. "The equatorial band is naturally divided into thirty-six sections by eighteen longitudinal tubes. This leaves a lot of choices, but I favor the intersections of the longitudinal tubes with one of the equatorial tubes."

"Aesthetically," eJohnny said, "I choose alternating north and south. I don't think it makes any difference in response times, but I just like it that way."

"How do we find out?" eThorpe asked.

"We follow several back?" eJohnny said lamely. "I really don't know. The builders made something so complex with the sphere that I doubt we'll ever figure all of it out."

"You sound discouraged, Johnny. Don't be. This is an adventure of a lifetime, and you are right in the middle."

Keid Sphere—Alien Matrix—Sheriff Bots

"We need to find a dispatch center," eThorpe said. "We agreed we can do that by following a Task Runner back to its origin. Tell me I'm wrong."

"We did agree," eJohnny answered, "so, let's do it."

He placed himself in front of the first Task Runner heading away from the equatorial band. The Task Runner stopped, and within moments a Sheriff Bot appeared. It maneuvered threateningly, trying to displace eJohnny, who moved evasively, countering the Sheriff Bot's attempts.

"You're teasing it, Johnny."

eJohnny latched onto the Task Runner while stabbing his stun gun at the bot. The Sheriff Bot disintegrated, and eJohnny grabbed eThorpe as the Task Runner moved, gaining momentum with each passing microsecond. Within moments, they were moving at near lightspeed. Shortly thereafter, the Task Runner stopped in a chamber filled with countless Task Runner tensors. eJohnny looked around. The entire overhead swarmed with tiny objects that bounced continuously off the ceiling. He tried, but couldn't focus on them. He watched thousands of the objects drop directly on Task Runners and then return to their bouncing activity. As soon as one touched a Task Runner, the tensor disappeared down one of many passageways.

"I think I get it," eJohnny said. "Those guys," pointing to the bouncing objects, "are one-half of an entangled pair. When its mate puts out a call from a remote location, the affected bouncer taps a Task Runner who speeds to the location to do whatever is required."

"We've got visitors," eThorpe said, pointing to four Sheriff Bots that had just arrived. "Let's split them up." He moved to one side of the chamber and eJohnny moved to the other.

The Sheriff Bots seemed confused at first, but then two followed eThorpe and two followed eJohnny.

"I'm cloning my EMD weapon," eThorpe said.

"Good idea! I am, too," eJohnny said.

The two Sheriff Bots approached eThorpe, reaching for his sides. Caught between the bots, eThorpe struck out at their tendrils with both his stun guns. The tendrils withdrew, but the bots remained.

"Johnny, over here! Zap these guys!"

eJohnny stabbed at the evasive tendrils of the bots approaching him and hit eThorpe's two bots with the full force of both stun guns. As the bots collapsed, eThorpe jumped over eJohnny and hit his attackers with the full intensity of his stun guns. The entire thing was over in a microsecond. Scavengers removed what remained of the four Sheriff Bots.

The uploads high-fived each other and moved into a narrow corridor. They latched onto the next Task Runner and rode it into a populated data stream where they dropped off.

"Let's hang out and watch for a while," eThorpe said. "We have Task Runners, Sheriff Bots, and the Order guys. Since the Order guys are entangled pairs, let's call them QBots. I think we have a handle on the Task Runners. We may not understand the QBot mechanism, but we know what they do. The Sheriff Bots could become a problem. If we keep killing them, and there is a feedback mechanism, we could face increasing numbers until they overwhelm us. That isn't everything, though. My gut says we're missing something." He leaned into the wall, watching the passing data flow. "Can all this just be on automatic?" he mused. "Are we looking at a hulk that keeps working without guidance?"

"The gash in the outer sphere says 'Yes' to your question," eJohnny said, "but the three species we found say someone or something is watching—maybe even controlling."

"We're presuming the dispatch center we found is one of many, perhaps thirty-six," eThorpe said. "What's behind them? We need to answer that question."

"Watch out!" eJohnny said, extending his stun gun. "Two more Sheriff Bots!"

They dispatched the bots.

"What if there had been ten," eJohnny asked, "or twenty or a hundred?"

"We've got live backups…"

"Yeah," eJohnny interrupted, "but that's a last resort, isn't it?"

"You've got a point," eThorpe said. "Maybe there's a way around this."

He generated a small tensor with a specific instruction set and dispatched it to their control center in the top floor office in Keid City.

"Instructions for Sally and Brad and their uploads to design a code set that will protect us from the Sheriff Bots."

"They can do that fast enough to help us?" eJohnny was skeptical.

They hung out where they were, dispatching an occasional Sheriff Bot, wondering if the tensor got through.

"Whoa, what's this?" eThorpe said as an invisible tensor merged with his structure. He incorporated the code it carried and then cloned the code and passed it to eJohnny. Both he and eJohnny disappeared—invisible even to their own sensors.

"They came through," eJohnny said. "It's amazing."

"I'm guessing my tensor had trouble getting past the Sheriff Bots, but it made it through. Brad must have cloaked it for its return."

They stopped talking as two Sheriff Bots passed in the data stream, ignoring them completely.

"Looks like we're home free," eThorpe said. "Now, let's get on with our search."

"What are those?" eJohnny asked, pointing to several tensors they had not seen before.

"Let's hitch a ride on one and find out," eThorpe said.

Keid Sphere—Alien Matrix—Scouts

As eJohnny and eThorpe moved along with the newly identified tensors, eThorpe examined them closely.

"These aren't ordinary tensors," he said. "They carry one-half of an entangled pair. They're communicating with a dispatch center just like the QBots."

"About what?" eJohnny wanted to know.

"When these tensors get to their destination, we'll know."

But the tensors did not go to a specific destination. Instead, they wandered everywhere in the sphere matrix, from the equatorial band, to the linear drivers, to spots that made no sense at all. Following a stop in the equatorial band, eThorpe suggested they drop the tensor and wait for something to happen. Within a few microseconds, a Task Runner showed up and began burrowing into the carbynophene base. It made some kind of repair or adjustment that neither eJohnny nor eThorpe could see, and then it took off, presumably back to its dispatch center.

"So, the new tensor found a problem, notified the dispatch center that sent a Task Runner to fix it. I'm going to call these tensors Scouts. They're mobile and can find problems the fixed QBots can't."

"That still doesn't tell us if this thing is in automatic or is being controlled," eJohnny said.

✳

Wearing their cloaks kept the Sheriff Bots from bothering them. They followed several Scouts, getting no closer to a central control.

"We have to remember," eThorpe said, "that the equatorial band alone comprises three hundred thousand Earth land surfaces. There are eighteen longitudinal tubes and two equatorial ones, each over twenty-nine million klicks long. The sphere interior surface is about two hundred seventy-seven trillion square klicks. The inner sphere is somewhat less, but not much, and it has two surfaces. Central Control could be anywhere. We will not find it except by the sheerest of luck."

eJohnny suddenly shouted, "Stop moving!" and pointed at a stationary object embedded in the data flow. eJohnny sent a tensor toward the object. The object reached out and destroyed the tensor as soon as it was in range—an arm's length.

"The Sheriff Bots can't find us, but they know we are here, so they are laying booby traps. We need to proceed carefully."

As they followed the passageway taken by the Scout, they encountered more traps. At a Y-intersection, eThorpe launched two tensors, one in each branch. One was trap-free, the other contained many traps, and one destroyed the tensor.

"We'll take that branch," eThorpe said, indicating the branch with the traps.

"Why?" eJohnny asked.

"Something is trying to coax us down that path," eThorpe said, pointing to the trap-free passageway. "It's trying to dissuade us from going here." He eased into the trap-filled passageway.

eJohnny followed, watching carefully for traps.

Their path took them deep into the sphere infrastructure until they lost all sense of direction and did not know where they were. Suddenly, the booby traps disappeared. The passage they followed had branches, but when they reached a branch, it disappeared.

"Now," eThorpe said, "something is guiding us instead of discouraging us."

After a subjectively long journey, they entered a large chamber with shimmering electronic walls. Electronic shelves containing electronic volumes stretched as far as they could sense.

"I think we found the archives," eJohnny said.

"I think someone guided us here," eThorpe countered.

Several volumes glowed, and one flashed. eJohnny touched the flashing volume and felt its contents stream into his consciousness. A second glowing volume flashed. He touched it and absorbed its contents. Then a third, fourth, through nineteen.

eJohnny turned to eThorpe. "I've got their entire history," he said. "I know all about the sphere. I know what happened." He reached out to eThorpe. "I know what really happened, Thorpe. I need to get back to upload all this into our archives."

Chapter Eighteen

Keid Sphere—Keid City

eJohnny slid through the adaptor, through eThorpe's matrix, into his own. He checked his bearings and then projected a holoimage for the others to see.

"Where is eThorpe?" Thorpe asked.

"He's busy somewhere in the matrix," eJohnny said, "dealing with the Oort."

"What?" Thorpe said.

"You heard right—he's dealing with the Oort. I'm carrying their archives that I need to upload to *Andromeda's* databank. When you've reviewed it, you'll understand." He turned to Johnny. "Take me back to *Andromeda*, Johnny, so I can upload this material."

Johnny unplugged his matrix and stepped through the portal to the starship carrying his upload. He took the matrix to the archives room and plugged eJohnny's matrix into an input dock.

The upload did not take very long. eJohnny retained the general outline of the Oort archives, but allowed the rest to flow into *Andromeda's* archives without retaining a copy in his matrix.

Once he completed the upload, Johnny and his upload talked.

"Are you enjoying your liberated upload status?" Johnny asked.

"I am, but our timelines are diverging, and I don't like that. When I became Human, that was supposed to be a final choice. Now here I am again as an upload."

Johnny was quiet for a moment. "What do you say to merging our backups and then downloading to a new Johnny with only one real-time backup?"

"That works for me," eJohnny said, "but let's wait until eThorpe returns."

✳

"Johnny," Daphne called over her Link, "can you come to the Archaeology Lab? I've got something to show you."

Johnny dropped to the lab by portal. eJohnny accompanied him. Daphne showed them the same plaque display the staff had shown her.

"Where did you get this?" Johnny asked, his expression priceless. eJohnny just stared at the display in astonishment.

"From a dig on the equatorial band. We didn't show you earlier, because we didn't see any connection until you, eJohnny, returned from the sphere matrix. We learned from you that the Oort built the sphere. It followed that the Oort had something to do with the plaque. The writing, therefore, probably was a form of the Oort language."

"You were right! Your translation is pretty good, but you got a couple things wrong." Johnny pointed them out, and Daphne corrected them on the spot. "It's amazing," Johnny said, "this plaque is incredibly old, probably from the first settlements after the Oort finished the sphere."

Keid Sphere—Alien Matrix—The Archives

After eJohnny left the archives chamber, eThorpe wandered through the virtual stacks, occasionally touching a volume to see what it contained.

The archives were overwhelming. They contained every transaction ever undertaken by the Oort within the confines of the sphere. Indexing was simple. eThorpe found the specific incidents his M-Class pilots had observed, watching them himself as if he had been there.

Without digging too deeply, eThorpe found evidence of many more experimental species the Oort had created. The Oort was moving them all along much faster than evolution alone could have done. He found material on the microbots, but not why they were cannibalizing the sphere.

eJohnny had taken only archival material related directly to the Oort. The remaining archives were a vast history of something unique, if not in the universe, then certainly in this section of the Milky Way. eThorpe found no evidence that the archives were being backed up. If something catastrophic ever happened to the sphere, all this history would disappear. He vowed that before *Andromeda* departed the Keid-C system, he would back up the entire archives for posterity.

eThorpe found it difficult to turn away from the images coursing through his mind, but he still needed to locate the main Oort controller. Something had facilitated his way to the archives. Would that something help him again? eThorpe headed down the only available passageway, looking for guidance.

Keid Sphere—Alien Matrix—The Vault

Similar to the latter part of their journey to the archives, side passages ahead of eThorpe closed to keep him on a particular path. He traveled for a long time subjectively and decided he could be virtually anywhere in the sphere. Finally, he entered a bare chamber. A wall covered one end with a large, sealed door.

The wall had several ominous nozzles that caught eThorp's attention. Invisibility still cloaked him, but whatever had guided him had no difficulty keeping track of his location. That meant the nozzles and whatever they projected could find him. He reminded himself that he was in a virtual environment defined by digital electronics. Whatever threat those nozzles posed would not be projectiles. And if worse came to worse, he would revert to his real-time backup, and find his way back to this room.

eThorpe verified he was well grounded to the substrate beneath him, and then he waited. Something had brought him here, and that something probably was behind the door in the wall he faced. He moved to the side, and two nozzles followed his movement. He shifted the other way—they shifted with him. They couldn't *see* him, but they certainly knew where he was.

eThorpe reached into his memory and pulled up the Oort words for *Peace*, *Friendship*, and *No Threat*. He projected them outward, but had no way to determine where they ended up. The nozzles continued to point at him. He checked behind him, the way he had entered the chamber. Two large Sheriff Bots blocked the way. Making sure he had a solid grip on his stun guns, he dropped his invisibility. The Sheriff Bots made no move to enter the chamber, but they obviously increased their focus. They could see him now. The nozzles did not move, but they had known his location all along.

Once again, eThorpe projected the Oort words: *Peace*, *Friendship*, and *No Threat*.

This time, the surface beneath his feet moved, and tendrils wrapped around his ankles. They anchored him to the spot, although eThorpe was certain he could escape if push came to shove. He felt naked and vulnerable, however, as he projected the words a third time: *Peace. Friendship. No Threat.*

The door pushed out from the wall about a centimeter and then swung open toward eThorpe. The tendrils around his ankles tightened. He heard a voice inside his head ask in the Oort language, "Who are you?"

"I am eThorpe—an electronic entity from the *Starship Andromeda*. We come from the star system where you originated—we call it the Solar System. We carry crew members from the star Aster, known to the Oort, and the star Ran, possibly unknown to the Oort. We also carry several Oort who downloaded into Human form."

"Why are you here?"

"While on an exploration run to the Cold Spot in the Cosmic Microwave Background, we stumbled onto your Dyson Sphere. We stopped to investigate. We have extensively explored the physical sphere. Because I and several other crew members are electronic entities, we are investigating your sphere electronically. We have only investigated. We have caused no harm anywhere except to destroy or disable your microbots when they threatened or attacked us."

"Why are you here, in this room now?"

"We found your abandoned city seemingly running on automatic. Everything we found seemed to be under some kind of automatic control, and so we wanted to discover who was behind this massive enterprise. We discovered your various tensors, your entangled-particle pairs, and we determined how they function—at least to some extent. While we were doing this, you or someone working for you directed us here.

"We seek cooperation and friendship. It seems clear that your civilization is way beyond ours, but even people as far apart as we can offer each other benefits."

PS Andromeda—Science Section

Daphne's astronomy people sent her an interesting report as a follow-up to their earlier report. Surface pressure on Keid-C was still increasing. Several anomalous magnetic fields had appeared, oddly focused around the north pole. This was not yet a cause for alarm, they told her, at least not yet.

Daphne visited Thorpe on the Bridge. She displayed the data on a part of the Bridge holoscreen.

"The star surface pressure has been increasing slowly since we got here—probably before, but we didn't know about it. Now we have this magnetic anomaly at the pole. I don't know what it means, and I suspect whatever it is must be important. My astronomy people are keeping a close eye on it."

"Is it going to nova?" Thorpe asked,

"Not likely. It's already a red dwarf. It flares regularly. Perhaps it getting ready to do so again."

"Keep me in the loop, please."

Chapter Nineteen

Keid Sphere—Alien Matrix—The Oort

The tendrils unwrapped from eThorpe's ankles, and the Sheriff Bots disappeared from the room's exit.

"We accept you are not a threat," the Oort said. "Please, make yourself comfortable, and let us talk. Have a seat." A couch appeared, complete with floor lamp and area rug.

"I know the Oort from my contacts with your Oort Cloud presence in the Solar System," eThorpe said. "I was the first Human to make contact in modern times. I arranged to have my head cryogenically preserved upon my death when I discovered I was terminally ill. I revived into an electronic matrix and ultimately found my way into Earth's Global Net and ServerSky. The Oort had installed several portals in both LEO and GEO ServerSkies, and one from behind our moon directly to the Oort Cloud. I stumbled on that one, traveled to the Oort Cloud, and met the Oort."

"I understand," the Oort responded, "that you refer to us as the *Oort*, and *Keid Sphere* is what you have named our Dyson Sphere. We Keid Oort are unaware of your history with Earth's Oort Cloud and its residents, but let us start with who and what we are.

"I am actually a collective of a thousand Oort individuals. You have not conversed with an individual. Within the sphere, we each assume specific responsibilities, some of which you have encountered during your sojourn inside our matrix."

"I have many questions," eThorpe said. "We found three sapient species, a primitive simian colony, a slightly more advanced feline one, and a saurian colony that seemed way ahead of the other two. Our first clue that you might exist was the much more rapid than normal advancement of these groups, especially the saurians. We observed another group of simian islanders, but have not yet followed up on them. What can you tell me about these primitive groups?"

"We knew about Humans and Asterians, of course, and we learned about Arcans because of their proximity to Keid. When we built the sphere, we wanted to populate it with more than just our few numbers. We established the primitive groups you saw plus nineteen others using the surrounding species, including ourselves, as templates. Evolution is a slow process. We thought that once our experimental species achieved spacefaring, they would meet Humans, Asterians, and Arcans, and could become part of a thriving interstellar community. We boosted their development process whenever we could."

eThorpe sat for a while thinking about what the Oort had told him. "The sphere is enormously complex," he said. "We have explored your physical infrastructure extensively. As a lifetime engineer, I am completely overwhelmed by twenty hundred-klick-thick tubes carrying superfluid at seventy-four klicks per second to keep them suspended. The I-beam spoke system you constructed is planetary in scope, without precedence in our galaxy, so far as I know.

"I find your digital support infrastructure at least as impressive, although that wasn't clear until I started exploring your complex matrix. I took a while to understand how you used entangled pairs to effect instant notifications throughout the sphere."

The Oort made no comment.

"I haven't mentioned it yet," eThorpe said, "but how did the gash come about? It appears that your microbots are cannibalizing one part of the sphere to construct another part."

"I don't have a good answer for that," the Oort answered. "We think a meteor crashed through the outer sphere long after we completed it. The scavenging microbots had been inactive for eons. We activated them, thinking they would scavenge the debris from the collision, but the collision released so much argon from the damaged faces that the microbots started scavenging material from one side to rebuild the other. We tried everything we could think of, but nothing we did affected their behavior.

"The stresses from that collision caused a systemic instability that ripped a pole-to-equator gash before we could stabilize the sphere. It's stable now. The gash moves around the sphere in a slow march as the microbots place on one side what they remove from the other."

Keid Sphere—Alien Matrix—The Oort Story

How did the Oort end up in the Keid-C system?" eThorpe asked. "Long ago, before Asterians, Humans, or Arcans, we had evolved on Earth from canine ancestors. Like Humans, we eventually established a global spacefaring civilization. When we discovered how to upload ourselves, tens of millions of our population took this route and established themselves in the Oort Cloud. We remained thus for a long time, several eons. Oort on Earth and in the Oort Cloud maintained contact, although our differences eventually overcame our similarities. When we received radio signals from the star Aster, eighty-four lightyears distant, we entered into a great debate. The Asterians did not direct these signals at us. They had discovered the electromagnetic spectrum and invented radio. Nevertheless, some of our leaders grew concerned that the Asterians would have also received our radio broadcasts. They might decide that we were a potential threat, and when they were able would launch an attack against us. These leaders and their followers wanted to launch a preemptive attack against the Asterians. The Oort in the Oort Cloud saw themselves as directly in the line of attack. So, they sided with the war hawks on Earth.

"Many Oort thought this was wrong. At most, they argued, the Asterians were at the beginning stages of industrialization. It would be a very long time before they would be in a position to invade the Solar System, and then, it would take a century or more just to make the journey.

"The war hawks prevailed. Earth and the Oort Cloud put themselves on a war footing. The Oort Cloud monitored radio transmissions from Aster, evaluating their ability to launch an interstellar attack against Earth. On Earth, Oort focused their industrial base on shortening the time for travel to Aster. They had developed portal technology, but it was very limited because of the enormous power draw portals required.

"Earth's technology base had developed a spaceship drive that could boost a spaceship to eighty percent of lightspeed. Relativistic time contraction reduced the subjective shipboard time to sixty-three years, but this meant a two-generational crew. This no longer mattered to the war hawks. They saw the potential threat from Aster as more than justifying the effort.

"The war hawks finally decided it was time to launch the invasion. They had squeezed their starship speed to ninety percent of light, which shortened subjective shipboard time to forty-one years. They launched the invasion over the protests of at least half Earth's Oort population.

"When they found themselves unable to stop the invasion, the protestors turned to violence themselves. War broke out on Earth, tearing the planet apart. Many Oort left Earth as uploads to join the Oort Cloud. Others built another fleet of starships and headed out of the Solar System on an eight-year journey to Keid-A and the Earth-like planet they had discovered orbiting that star.

"Those Oort were our ancestors."

✳

"Now, let me fill in some gaps in your own history," eThorpe said. "The Oort invasion to Aster found an industrialized spacefaring civilization on the planet Frohlic. The Oort destroyed that civilization, bringing the Frohlic population nearly to extinction. The Frohlicans had some minor successes during the invasion, and they learned from where the Oort had come. And they never forgot.

"The Oort returned to the Solar System eighty-three subjective years later. One hundred eighty-six years had passed on war-torn Earth. Earth's civilization was in chaos, unable to integrate the returning Oort. The returning Oort turned to the Oort Cloud, where they were welcomed and integrated into the thriving virtual Oort society.

"Then a large meteor struck Earth, destroying much of its life and obliterating what remained of the Oort industrial civilization. Famine and strife completed the job, and within a century, the Oort had disappeared from Earth.

"In space, the uploaded Oort thrived in the Oort Cloud. Their numbers increased and their civilization flourished. They saw protohumans appear on their ancient home planet and watched them develop and grow until the Human civilization rivaled the long-forgotten Oort civilization. Humans developed space travel and eventually made contact with the Oort.

"In the Aster system, the Frohlicans crawled back from near extinction and eventually developed space travel. They discovered and colonized Rogan, the other habitable planet in their system. And they never forgot what the Oort had done.

"Eventually, the two Asterian societies went to war. When it was over, they both had lost their spacefaring status, but they never forgot what the Oort had done to them. Both cultures climbed back until they once again achieved space travel. They developed MBH technology that gave them the ability to travel interstellar distances at near lightspeed. They began to plan their revenge against the beings who had attacked them from the Solar System so long ago."

eThorpe sat back, collecting his thoughts. Then he continued. "The Oort had existed in the Cloud for a very long time. Their virtual society and culture had gone stale. Their numbers dwindled drastically as countless Oort chose the oblivion of disassociation. They learned about the planned Asterian invasion by monitoring broadcasts from that system. Because they were uploads with very limited ability to build anything physical, including weapons, they hatched a desperate plan.

"They chose one of their number to represent them to Humans—I was their primary contact. I called their representative Johnny Oort. He fed me a broad-ranging lie. He said the Oort numbered in the countless millions and had a vibrant, rich society. He told me about an invasion from the Aster system that had happened fifty million years ago, intending to destroy life on Earth. Johnny told me that the Asterians were returning to finish the job. He said that we Humans and the Oort needed to arm ourselves and prepare for a battle of survival.

"The Oort supplied plans for defensive weapons that we built, and we prepared for the invasion. The invasion arrived as a five thousand ship armada. We destroyed the armada, capturing two vessels. One escaped.

"We reverse engineered the Asterian MBH Drive while developing an FTL drive from the portal technology we had gotten from the Oort. We were preparing to send a fleet of starships to the Aster system to exact revenge, when Johnny approached some of us with the truth.

"The Oort were declining—only ten million remained. The Asterians had attacked us to avenge the attack upon them by the Oort so long ago. I confronted the Oort and exacted a severe retribution. The Oort agreed to download into Human form and fully integrate themselves into Human society. We went to the Aster system, but not as invaders. We developed a close relationship with Rogan, and we built the Starship *Andromeda* together.

"We and the Asterians embarked on an extended exploratory mission to the Cold Spot in the Cosmic Microwave Background. At our first stop, the star Ran, we discovered the Arcans, kind of hiding in plain view. They now are also part of our expedition." eThorpe halted his narrative. "As I told you at our first contact, we offer friendship and cooperation, not confrontation."

Keid Sphere—Alien Matrix—The Oort Story Continues

The Oort uttered a nearly Human sigh. "So much went on only sixteen and a half lightyears away. We wanted nothing to do with what was happening in the Solar System. We learned much of what was occurring from your broadcasts and those of the Asterians. What we did not know was the Solar System Oort duplicity. We've been around too long as a species, not to understand that sapient species tend to react to the unknown with fear and violence. We reach for our weapons first.

"When we left Earth as flesh-and-blood Oort, we chose to settle on an Earth-like planet we had discovered earlier orbiting around Keid-A. The planet was friendly, and we grew and prospered. Eventually, we were a planet-wide civilization, happy with our choice to leave the Solar System. As spacefaring people, we explored the nearer stars. We found no nearby sapient species, although it was clear that life on Arcan was headed that way.

"One hundred million years ago, Keid-B went nova. We learned about it two days and eight hours later when the electromagnetic wave front hit our home world. The intensity of the wave front did considerable damage, but we survived it. Our problem was that we had only one hundred and three days before the particle wave front would destroy life on our home world. We had a sizable space fleet, but it was not nearly large enough to accommodate our population of hundreds of millions.

"We established an emergency upload program to process the largest possible number of Oort for evacuation. With barely sufficient time left to reach the other side of Keid-A, our fleet carrying several thousand flesh-and-blood and several million uploaded Oort departed our home world for the last time. The particle wave front wiped our home of life. Without FTL capability, we were limited to Keid-B and C. Since Keid-B had undoubtedly wiped its planets clean, we chose Keid-C.

"We discovered what we had suspected. Keid-C was unsuitable for planets harboring life. We had only two viable choices. We could travel six lightyears to Ran and take over the planet Arcan, which would destroy that world's incipient sapient life, or we could build a Dyson Sphere around Keid-C and create our own living environment.

"We chose to stay here. We didn't want to add to the perception of the Oort as marauders.

"Building the sphere was a very long-term project. After we envisioned it, its size and complexity completely overwhelmed us. We understood the science and engineering required to build a Dyson Sphere. It was a frequent topic of our intellectual roundtables. We didn't have the personnel or the technological infrastructure, however, to actually build one.

"On our home planet, we had developed a construction technique that relied heavily on specialized robots to do much of the actual work. We programmed them to do a specific task, and they worked tirelessly night and day until the task was finished. So long as we supplied the raw materials, the robots kept working.

"Some of us thought that might be how we could construct a Dyson Sphere. The concept of a sphere was simple enough. Build an orbital infrastructure of space-launch-loop-like tubes that maintained altitude and generated lifting force by rotating at orbit-sustaining velocity. Interconnect them with girder-like spokes, and anchor two concentric spheres to the outside of this infrastructure. The inner sphere would capture solar energy to drive everything and power the contained civilization, The outer sphere, at the very least, would have a wide band inside at the equator that could harbor life. Over time, the life band could be expanded to cover most or even all the outer sphere inner surface. Like I said, simple in concept.

"The actual design and construction were another thing altogether. Upload design teams with enormous processing capacity worked on the designs for more than a century. For another century, different teams reviewed every line of the designs, correcting errors and improving the designs. For a third century, new teams reviewed everything again. Flesh-and-blood Oort came and went, but the uploads maintained continuity throughout the process.

"When we finally commenced construction, we designed and deployed the microbots you encountered when you arrived. They scavenged all of Keid-C's planets for raw materials, not just their surfaces, but the planets themselves. Over the preceding eons, the Oort had learned how to transmute one element into another using exotic molecular processes, and how to change hydrogen to helium and then carbon using an advanced form of a LANR. Since we were making everything out of Q-carbon-coated carbynophene, we needed a lot of carbon. We also needed a lot of argon, as you must have determined. And we needed a massive amount of magnetic superfluid, even before we constructed the spheres.

"The project took nearly a thousand years. We built a beautiful city on the shore of a bay for the living flesh-and-blood Oort, and we started twenty-three sapient life projects. Some of us, as uploads, assumed the responsibility of keeping this gigantic enterprise running smoothly. Millions of electronic assistants helped, including tensors, bots, and entangled pairs you have already met. We retired the microbots, keeping them in reserve should they ever be needed in the future.

"The flesh-and-blood Oort population of the city grew, and they spread into the surrounding countryside. The sapient experiments progressed nicely under almost continuous boosting from the electronic overseers. The Oort upload community developed its own culture and traditions even though they interacted with the flesh-and-blood community from time to time. It had taken more than a millennium, but the Oort finally had a stable community and a lifestyle they could follow indefinitely.

"That's when the meteor hit. It came out of interstellar space. It was as large as Earth's moon, a rogue planetoid coursing its way between the stars. The sphere outer surface had thousands of laser cannon whose sole purpose was eliminating threatening meteors. But no one had anticipated one as large as this. The huge rock tore through both spheres and took out a longitudinal tube. The sphere became unstable, threatening to tear itself apart. As the sphere swung wildly, the hole caused by the meteor became a million-kilometer-wide gash, spreading from the north pole to the equator. Over several days, the Oort uploads, working with millions of electronic assistants, got the swings under control and finally stabilized the sphere.

"The Oort uploads released the microbots to repair the damage. To their unmitigated horror, the bots chose to attack one side of the gash where the contained argon had dissipated. True to their design purpose, they carried the material they salvaged from one side of the gash and used it to reconstruct the other side. No matter how hard they tried, the Oort could not influence the bots' behavior.

"Some of the city residents became uneasy. They saw themselves at the mercy of the uploads and their microbots. Eventually, fighting broke out between the city factions. One group thought it saw a way out of the morass. In a bold move, these Oort captured the remaining spaceships that were stored outside the city, and loaded their families, food and water, and fuel for a long journey. They blasted their way through the inner sphere and worked their way through the maze of tubes and spokes that partially blocked their path. After several days, they reached the gash and moved out into the open space surrounding the sphere.

"What they did not see was the large swarm of microbots that followed them through the gash. The bots saw the ships as fresh, raw material. They attacked the ships before anyone could do anything about it. The ships lost their space worthiness, and everyone on all the ships perished. The ships and body elements of the passengers all ended up as part of the growing eastern gash edge."

Keid Sphere—Alien Matrix—The Oort Story Finale

eThorpe took a deep breath as the Oort stopped talking. "That's a sad ending to a spirited and brave people," he said.

"It is," the Oort said, "and there really was nothing constructive we could have done."

"I take it you were there," eThorpe asked.

"I was…we were," the Oort answered. "Here is the rest of our sad tale.

"We could have helped the remaining flesh-and-blood Oort build new ships—even done so with argon-infused skin to keep the bots away, but to what purpose? The only nearby star that harbored life was Ran, and it would have been unconscionable to burden Ran's burgeoning sapiens with a small group of highly advanced aliens. The odds of the Oort surviving were slim, and they would have done incalculable damage to the emerging Arcans."

"When it comes to survival, though," eThorpe said, his voice trailing off.

"They didn't want to leave, anyway," the Oort continued. "They saw the spaceships' departure as their victory. When they learned of the fate of those who left, their attitude was, 'It served them right.'

"The city continued to run on automatic, much to our surprise. Pets were fed, streets were cleaned, street traffic was controlled, even though hardly any residents remained in the city. At some point, and I cannot pinpoint when, all the Oort residents of the city disappeared. I suspect some moved to the countryside. Some might have departed for parts unknown. Several of the younger, more adventurous people might have taken a ship across the ocean. It would have been a perilous passage, but doable. In any case, the city was empty. Nobody remained. Even so, all the city functions continued to work. Pets were fed and watered, something cleaned up after them, streets remained clean, driverless cars drove from place to place, order-maintaining robots walked the streets, but the Oort were gone.

"Our own ranks diminished as individual Oort decided from time to time to disassociate, which for an Oort upload, is the equivalent of Human suicide. We still have the sapient races we had created. We spend a lot of personal time observing them and helping them along when we think they need it. Our lives are intellectually satisfying since we have millennia of past experiences to carry us forward.

"Your arrival has made a big difference. If I interpret correctly what you have said, you have developed portal technology that works over great distances."

"We have," eThorpe said, "but it requires a huge, continuous power draw—something the sphere gives you. If I have understood correctly, while you have vast resources at hand within the sphere, you cannot leave. As uploads, you need a matrix substrate, and that's not within your reach anywhere except in here."

"You have stated our problem succinctly," the Oort said.

✳

"The basis for our power," eThorpe said, "is an artificial mini black hole—we call it MBH. We have learned how to withdraw energy from an MBH continuously. The larger the MBH, the more energy and the larger the energy flux we can draw. We have made them microscopically small and up to five klicks across. *Andromeda* has a five-klick wide MBH. Right now, *Andromeda* can cross our galaxy in eleven days on MERT Drive, which uses portal technology. We are working on a modification that will shorten the trip to thirty-two minutes."

"That's impressive. You said your people were impressed with our ability to build the sphere, and you should be. But I believe what you just told me about your FTL abilities exceeds anything we have done."

"We've done a lot of talking," eThorpe said. "You know my name, but all I know about you is that you are the Oort, or an Oort, depending on your mode. Do you, as an individual Oort, have a name?"

"We don't vocalize our conversations, so we don't have names as you do. We use visualizations similar to your avatars. They're usually linked to function. I am a liaison between the Oort and you, so you may call me *Liaise*. How is it you are named *eThorpe* instead of just *Thorpe*?"

"My original name was *Braxton Thorpe*. I was the first Human upload. I accidentally cloned myself early on, and we decided to keep both of us. I became *Thorpe*, and my clone became *Braxton*. When others from my group also uploaded, we placed an *e* in front of their names to distinguish them from their flesh-and-blood counterparts. When I downloaded into a flesh-and-blood body, that person became Thorpe, and I became *eThorpe*.

"All of my immediate colleagues duplicated themselves as uploads. For the most part, we are the only ones. We developed a way to create a continuous upload that is not conscious—in effect, it is a continuous backup. Should something happen to a backed-up person, we create a new body from that person's DNA and download the backup into that body."

"In effect," Liaise commented, "your flesh-and-blood people are immortal."

"We don't normally think of it like that," eThorpe said, "but you are right. When our bodies age, we can easily replace them with a newer, younger body."

"I mentioned this earlier," Liaise said, "but some Oort tired of existence within our upload environment and disassociated. This didn't happen very often, but over millions of years, our numbers diminished, so that today we are but a thousand. From what you told me, this also happened to the Oort in the Solar System. Can your people reproduce?"

"Yes," eThorpe said, "and from time to time, they do. We have to be very careful, because if we continuously fill the pipeline at one end without a corresponding deletion, the pipeline fills quickly. We've managed so far. The future will tell."

"It seems to be an unavoidable problem in the long run," Liaise said. "We might be able to offer you an intermediate solution. The sphere has sufficient land for trillions of people. It's just an idea, but some of your people might consider settling here."

"Or we might be able to install portals between *Andromeda* and areas where our people choose to live. They could transit back and forth at will."

"That's really possible?" Liaise asked.

"It is, except we do not know at what range the distance will overcome our ability to power the link. Even should our people choose not to stay, this is an experiment we will want to conduct."

PS Andromeda—Science Section

After examining the latest data from her astronomers, Daphne called Thorpe.

"It's happening, Thorpe."

"What do you mean?" he asked.

"What we talked about. The pressure increases on Keid-C, the polar magnetic anomalies. It's gonna flare, and this will be a big one—they call it a superflare. It's ten to fifteen thousand times the strength of a normal flare."

Keid Sphere—Alien Matrix

A tensor carrying a message from Thorpe suddenly arrived and attached to eThorpe. *We have a serious problem and need you back here ASAP!*

Chapter Twenty

PS Andromeda—Bridge

eThorpe slipped out of his matrix into *Andromeda's* vast complex and projected his holoimage on the Bridge where Thorpe, Daphne, and eDaphne were talking.

"Why the emergency recall?" eThorpe asked.

"We just found out that Keid-C is building up to a flare," Thorpe said.

"And not just a *flare*," Daphne said, "a *superflare*."

"Ten thousand times stronger than the regular flares Keid-C produces," eDaphne added.

"When is the last time Keid-C produced a superflare?" eThorpe asked.

"Never that we can find," Daphne said, "and that's the problem. The Oort built the sphere to withstand the regular flares Keid-C produces, but I don't know if it can withstand this."

"How much time do we have?" eThorpe asked.

"Thirty days…maybe sixty," eDaphne said.

✳

In the privacy of Thorpe's office, eThorpe spoke earnestly with his flesh-and-blood counterpart.

"We have to assume that thirty days *is* our limit. All our vehicles and personnel will need to be inside *Andromeda* twelve hours or so before that to ensure we can jump to a safe distance before the wave arrives. But you know this. I'm just stating the obvious. My concern is the Oort inside the sphere. Assuming they will wish to join us—and that's not a given—thirty days is very little time to copy their archives to *Andromeda*."

"So, we need to notify them immediately," Thorpe said.

"We'll need a place to house them," eThorpe said. "These guys have lived longer than Humans have existed. I am certain they have some tricks up their collective sleeves. For certain, they will not want to go down with the ship. We'll bring them aboard—we have no choice. But if we're not careful, they'll own *Andromeda*, and we'll work for them."

"We could use Nanocosms to manufacture a thousand matrixes," Thorpe said, "but I don't think that's the best solution. We don't want to treat them like prisoners, but as you said, we can't give them the run of the ship either." He paused in thought. "I can physically separate a section of our matrix with sufficient room for all of them. You find out how much space that has to be. You also find out how much physical space they need for their complete archives."

"That should work. I'll go back inside right away."

"And I'll create the separate matrix."

Just before eThorpe's holoimage collapsed, Thorpe said, "Don't forget the thirty-day limit. Beyond anything else, they need to comprehend that!"

Keid Sphere—Alien Matrix—The Oort

Daphne carried eThorpe's matrix through the portal to the skyscraper office in Keid City. She plugged the matrix into the adaptor, and eThorpe wasted no time diving through the Keid City infrastructure to the sphere main data channel.

eThorpe followed the path etched into his memory and arrived in the vault in just a few microseconds.

"Liaise," he said to the empty room, "I need to talk with you urgently."

The inner vault door opened, and the Oort appeared. "What is so urgent, eThorpe, that you arrive at my door virtually breathless?"

"Our scientists have been studying Keid-C from the moment we were able to see the star directly, and before that, by indirect analysis of the secondary infrared. They have determined that the star is about to generate a superflare. We are concerned that the sphere might not survive such an event."

"I will consult my colleagues," Liaise said.

A few moments later—which eThorpe knew could have been weeks of subjective Oort time—Liaise returned.

"You have been straight with me, eThorpe, but there is considerable skepticism among my colleagues. We have been here for millions of years, have withstood thousands of flare incidents, and now you arrive and tell us that the next one will destroy us. We find that difficult to believe."

"This isn't just another flare," eThorpe said, "it's a *superflare*, typically ten thousand times stronger than a normal flare. Did you prepare the sphere for that?"

"Let me consult again," Liaise said.

When he returned, he said, "We don't know. I think—and about half my colleagues are with me on this—that we should act as if the sphere cannot survive the superflare. We are prepared to work with you in any reasonable manner. First, however, we want to see your data."

eThorpe sent a tensor to Keid City requesting a direct link for transmitting the superflare data directly to him in the vault. When it arrived, he transmitted it to Liaise.

"I will review this with my colleagues and get back to you in a bit," Liaise said.

A few minutes later he returned. "We agree. We've got a big problem. How do you see us moving forward?"

"Here is an outline of a plan," eThorpe said. "We see three elements: the Oort, your archives, and the sapient species you created and shepherded. Can we agree on this?"

The Oort consulted with his colleagues again. "We agree," he said.

"Regarding the Oort, then. We are preparing an electronic matrix sufficiently large to accommodate all thousand of you. We will generate a portal from whatever origin you wish directly into that matrix. You will be confined to that matrix while we—you, Thorpe, and I—determine how best to integrate you into our crew. During that time, you can be brought out as individuals in smaller, portable matrixes to learn about us, the rest of the crew, the ship, and our mission.

"Regarding your archives, first, how much space will they occupy?" Liaise told him.

"We can handle that, with room to spare. We'll create an appropriate portal and get the transfer underway. We will set up a wideband connection between your collective matrix and the archives on *Andromeda*, so you have full, continuous access. How am I doing so far?"

After consulting with his colleagues, Liaise said, "We understand your proposals, but wonder at the confinement. Would you explain fuller, please?"

"Sure. Consider our relative positions. The Oort have existed as an advanced species since long before Humans evolved. You are older by far than the Asterians, as well. From our perspective, you are a superior race with knowledge and capabilities far beyond ours, even considering out FTL, MBH, and portal technologies. If we were to grant you unfettered access to our vessel and crew before we had developed full trust between us, we fear what might happen. Circumstances have temporarily given us the upper hand. We intend to use the time we have to demonstrate we are people worthy of trust and friendship. When the time comes, we hope you will choose to be our colleagues, not our masters."

Liaise consulted with his colleagues and then said, "We find your reasoning sound and reasonable. Given the alternatives, we have no quarrel with the arrangement, but we still don't like it."

eThorpe smiled. "I understand. The sapient species present a huge problem. Our starship is unique. It is a five-klick-in-diameter, five-hundred-meter-thick disk with a domed cityscape on one side and a pastoral landscape on the other. We have developed artificial gravity, and so have set one gee on both sides. The landscape is just under twenty square klicks. Thus, we have room for a small sampling of two or three of your experiments, no more.

"We can take a representative male and female from the others, upload their essence into a static matrix, and sequence their DNA and microbiomes. This will give us and you the ability to resurrect any one of these species sometime in the future."

"You can truly do this?" Liaise asked.

"We do it routinely," eThorpe answered.

Liaise laughed. "And you call us advanced. What you offer is extraordinary. We have invested millions of years with our experimental species. Your offer keeps that work alive."

"There is a problem," eThorpe said. "We have very little time. Since none of the Oort is corporeal, *we* will have to do the legwork of collecting the samples and doing the uploads. The sooner we start, the better.

"I will need the exact coordinates for a concentration of each of no more than three species we will transfer to *Andromeda*, the exact coordinates of the others, and a list of what animals besides the sapiens themselves you want. For example, we viewed one of the saurian species that tamed pterosaurs. If we bring them to *Andromeda*, we will have to bring at least one male and one female pterosaur. Are there similar relationships with other species?"

"That saurian species is the most advanced of the twenty-three species we have created," Liaise said. "We would like to see them established in your landscape. Rather than several species, which would be more than confusing for each of them, we think deploying only the advanced saurian species would be ideal. One of their communities has twenty-five each adult males and females and a mix of fifty children. Each of the adult males and each male child has bonded with a pterosaur.

"They breed the pterosaurs in captivity and bond each with a young male saurian shortly after the reptile's birth. The saurian and pterosaur grow up together. If I understand your starship layout, this would be a fascinating addition to your landscape."

"What about the normally predatory nature of pterosaurs?" eThorpe asked.

"In the wild, yes, but these are conditioned from birth. They and their saurian partners are virtual symbionts. We will also need to transfer an appropriate sampling of the wild animals they prey on, as well as the native plants they eat."

"Fine, we agree," eThorpe said. "Now we need to find a method of transferring the saurians, their mounts, and the other beasts into *Andromeda*."

"The males are fierce warriors. If we attempt force, we'll have a problem," Liaise said.

"We'll solve that with a knockout gas. I'll gather a team that will administer the gas, move both the saurians and their mounts through the portal, move the other beasts, and then transport and set up their yurts. They'll awaken to their own village in a strange location, but with everything intact."

Liaise nodded in agreement. "It will be a shock, but ultimately part of their development."

✳

eThorpe returned to *Andromeda* and met with Thorpe in his office. He explained the plan in outline.

"That's brilliant," Thorpe said. "In one fell swoop, you save the most advanced sapient species, preserve the rest, and find an effective use for our landscape. To tell the truth, after we had completed construction of *Andromeda*, I started to wonder why we had included the landscape side. Now it becomes useful in a way I never imagined."

"I will put Braxton in charge of the transfer. Let's see what ingenious solution he develops to transfer adult pterosaurs with a ten-meter wingspan and weighing in at two hundred fifty kilos."

Keid Sphere—The Saurian Compound

Braxton hovered *PS David Scott* six kilometers above the saurian village the Oort had designated. As of that moment, none of the warriors had spotted them.

Riding with him, eBraxton kept a sharp lookout on all sensors for pterosaurs with or without riders. Under eBraxton's control, Mother moved in a slow circle, capturing a series of detailed holoimages of the compound.

"Okay, we've got the images," eBraxton said. "Let's go to our excavation point."

Braxton brought the *Scott* to the point, 200 kilometers away from the settlement.

"Don't forget that a warrior on his mount can get here from the village in ninety minutes," eBraxton said.

"So, let's keep the noise down while we take care of business," Braxton said with a chuckle.

He dropped *Scott* to ground level, tossed the hyper-disk into the clump of gum trees, and walked down the ramp to the ground. He waved to eBraxton.

eBraxton signaled their team on *Andromeda*. "Activate the portal and join Braxton."

The portal opened sufficiently large to accommodate a tracked backhoe, a specialized tree digger, and a bunch of smaller machines designed to extract plant material without damage. Fifty men and women, Human and Asterian, stepped through and scattered about, collecting bushes complete with root systems, edible plants, tubers, and hundreds of other things listed in their Link instructions. They moved freely back and forth through the portal, transferring pallet loads of green stuff. The tree digger pulled fifty trees, roots and all, each with a five-meter dirt ball, and carried them through the portal.

On the other side, under the dome of *Andromeda's* landscape, more people and machines set trees and bushes in holes and replanted tubers and other plants. They followed the positioning of trees and other plants from the holoimage eBraxton took of their settlement. When they finished, the compound on *Andromeda* had the identical layout of trees, shrubs, and plants as the settlement inside the Keid Sphere.

"Now we need critters," Braxton said.

He had the M-Class ships standing by on *Andromeda*. The ships arrived at different locations covering the entire region where the saurians lived. Each ship flew around until it found several beasts or even a herd. Right in front of the animals or herd, it dropped an activated portal leading directly to *Andromeda's* landscape side. Then the vessel herded the animals through the portal. It took a bit of practice, but in an hour or so, each of the vessel crews could locate an animal or small herd, drop a portal, and drive the animals through the portal—all in just a few minutes.

By day's end, *Andromeda's* landscape side had all the animal stock Braxton needed to ensure the livelihood of the new residents.

*

"The next step will be more of a challenge," eBraxton told his flesh-and-blood counterpart. "We have nozzles installed on the bottom of *Scott*. We can cover a ten-meter-wide swath with a gas that will put any living creature asleep for several hours, depending on how much it inhales before going unconscious. We have injections to administer, if any of the subjects begins to awaken too early."

Braxton looked thoughtful. "We have everything from little kids to two hundred fifty kilo pterosaurs. I trust someone smarter than me calculated the dosages."

"Does Daphne count?"

"She may be the smartest of us all—except for Sally and Brad, of course," Braxton said. "Those two are total wonders. How much longer till nightfall?"

"An hour. These guys retire immediately after dark sets in, so let's give it an hour and a half."

*

Braxton set the spray flight pattern on automatic, with Mother supervising. He took a half hour to spread the gas. Then he set the spacecraft down near the edge of the village and turned over the controls to eBraxton. He slipped on a gas mask and exited the spacecraft. He placed a hyper-disk on the ground and opened the portal.

The first gas-mask-equipped team through the portal carried holocams to record where each saurian and pterosaur lay. As soon as they left the immediate area, the second team—also masked—stepped onto the ground. The members tagged every saurian, small and large, and every pterosaur, and moved them through the portal to a central location in the new village. For the larger animals, they used a crane with a sling to load them onto antigrav pallets. The largest pterosaur was sleeping just outside the leader's yurt. It took ten men to get him on a sling and lift him onto an antigrav pallet. The third team commenced taking down the yurts and rebuilding them in the new location exactly as they were. The yurts also required antigrav pallets. With a bit of ingenious packing, they could load a complete yurt, hide, sticks, and all, onto one pallet. They moved twenty-six yurts, one for each family, and a larger one that seemed to be an assembly hall. The fourth team picked up everything else, noted their positions, and moved them through the portal.

Dobson had his medical people standing by to administer injections as they became necessary. Halfway through the setup on the *Andromeda* side, the largest pterosaur, that had been snoozing outside the leader's yurt, opened a saucer-size eye and tried unsuccessfully to raise a five-meter-wide wing. A guttural scree died in its throat as it struggled again to lift a wing and raise its head. Dobson ran over and jammed a needle into its leg. The result wasn't instantaneous, but within a minute, the huge flying reptile closed both eyes and dropped back into a deep slumber.

The old village was completely empty. Even the ashes from the fire were gone. Braxton walked through the village one final time, making sure they left nothing behind.

Then he walked the new settlement, yurt by yurt, checking everything against the holoimage that floated in front of him. He moved a couple of items and stopped to pat the lead pterosaur's meter-long horn that balanced its beak in flight.

What a magnificent creature, he thought. Before this is all over, I just might try flying one of these guys myself.

PS Andromeda—The Landscape Side

Gelong's prodding awakened Toby from a deep slumber. He sat up, rubbing his eyes, trying to capture the remnants of a strange dream while rubbing Gelong's horn. The great flying reptile could not have fit into Toby's yurt, but his head did nicely.

Toby turned to his mate, Hobar. "You're sleeping late," he said.

She yawned, stretched, and nuzzled his snout. "I had a strange dream," she said sleepily. "Strange beings carried me away, but then you were there, and Jama, and Gelong was there, and everything was fine again."

Gelong bumped Jama in his ribs, and the young male saurian awakened. "Hey," he shouted, "cut that out!" He got up and left the yurt to empty his bladder and greet Suma, his personal pterosaur mount. He ran back into the yurt almost immediately.

"It's all wrong!" he yelled. "It's all wrong!"

Toby slipped on his weapons belt and sandals and left his yurt. It was like Jama said, everything was there, but it was all wrong. Other tribe members walked into the open, sleepily looking about. Toby whistled, and Gelong approached him. He tossed a saddle over the reptile's back in front of its wings, cinched it down, placed a halter over Gelong's head and around his beak, and clicked softly as he mounted the huge creature.

The great reptile rose into the air with zero forward motion, and then spiraled upward, reaching for altitude. Toby looked down. The landscape was unfamiliar. Rocky mountains dominated one horizon, and some kind of lake dominated the other. A ball of fire shone in the sky above. He turned Gelong toward the water and urged him along. He slowed as they passed the boundary between land and water. Suddenly, Gelong crashed into an invisible barrier and started tumbling toward the ground. Great warrior-bird that he was, Gelong recovered a hundred meters above the ground and swooped away from the invisible barrier.

Toby gave Gelong his head. The great reptile flew at an angle toward the barrier until his left wing touched it. Then he ascended, stroking the barrier with his wing as he flew. The barrier curved inward until, as Gelong reached half his five-kilometer maximum altitude, it formed an overhead roof. Then it curved down until it reached the ground about six minutes away from their starting point at normal cruising speed.

My dreams were real, Toby thought. This is someplace else. This is not home.

As Gelong brought Toby back to the village, he spotted game and rich fields of edible plants and tubers. He landed and gripped

Hobar, nuzzling her snout gently. "I don't yet know what happened," he whispered, "but we will have enough to eat while I figure it out. I'll keep you safe, no matter what."

"Listen up, People," he shouted. "Gather around." He raised his arms to quiet the crowd. "We have been transported from our home to this strange landscape. Someone tried to make it look like home, but it obviously is not. It is bounded by an invisible barrier so that we are effectively prisoners. Our prison is large and supplied with plenty of game and growing plants for food. But we are prisoners, nonetheless. I will try to discover what happened. In the meantime, be cautious, and above all, be vigilant. Teach your mounts to avoid the barrier, or you will fall from the sky and die. Teach the young men and their mounts how to avoid the barrier. It is hazardous. Gelong and I nearly fell from the sky this morning."

He walked to his yurt with Hobar. Feeling inspired by the adventure and danger, he asked, "Are you receptive, my Love?"

"I am," she answered, patting the egg in her pouch.

✳

"They seem to be adjusting," Braxton told Thorpe.

"I think it's too early to tell," Thorpe said. "I was watching this morning. The leader already discovered the limits of their new world— it nearly killed him."

"We still have half a month before Keid-C blows," Braxton said. "Let's see how they come along. By the way, I want to learn to ride a pterosaur." He grinned at Thorpe. "These guys are primitive, but they're by no means dumb. We need to find a way to bring them into our world. I think we owe them that much. When we're out of this mess, I'm going to talk with the Oort about that."

Chapter Twenty-One

PS Andromeda—Bio Labs

Daphne gathered her people around her in *Andromeda's* main Bio Lab. They were a mix of female and male Humans and Asterians.

"We have an interesting and challenging task before us," she told them. "You know that Keid-C will most likely produce a superflare sometime after the next three weeks. The Oort created twenty-three individual species of sapiens scattered around the equatorial band. One of those, a saurian species, is significantly more advanced than the others. We have already brought an entire village to our landscape side, where we hope they will prosper. That leaves twenty-two other species that we will try to rescue during the next two weeks." She stopped to let the idea sink in.

"It won't be like the saurians, and even there we rescued only a hundred or so. We will visit each species, capture a male and female, and bring them back here. We will sequence their individual DNA, sequence a microbiome between each pair, and upload their individual essences into a static matrix. Then we'll destroy the samples."

A general growl of protest rose from the group. A Human female spoke up.

"We're going to kill them?" she asked.

The group responded with shouts of horror.

Daphne had not expected this reaction. "People, we do this regularly with uploads. No one actually dies—we hold their essence in stasis."

"It's not the same thing," the girl said. "They don't have any choice."

Daphne needed to squelch this immediately. "What's the alternative?" she asked. "Each species has thousands, perhaps tens of thousands, of individuals. When Keid-C pops its superflare, they all will die—every one of them, no exceptions." She paused to give them time to think, to imagine the carnage.

"Our intervention will save two individuals *and* the entire species. Keid-C will kill everyone except the two we save. We'll collect what we need to ensure their ultimate survival. Once we do that, their remains are not important."

The girl opened her mouth to speak, but an Asterian colleague tugged her back into her seat. She didn't look entirely satisfied, but she was no longer protesting.

"It's not easy," Daphne said, "but it's the only way to save millions of years of effort by the Oort. We'll be as humane as possible, but all of you need to understand that we will necessarily frighten many individuals as we collect the male and female pairs.

"We've divided you into three groups, two with specific sector assignments, and one to remain here to process the samples as they arrive."

"At least call them people," the girl protested with sufficient volume for Daphne to hear her.

"You," Daphne said, pointing at the girl, "please join me up here. You will be part of my group. We will process the *people* as they arrive."

She addressed the group again. "Your coordinates should place you very near concentrations of people. Remember, these are primitive beings. Their males, and sometimes females, are ferocious fighters.

They will kill you if they can." She looked pointedly at the girl. "You are carrying EMDs set to stun. Use them if you have to."

"An M-Class vessel will flood the area with a gas to render the population unconscious. It will drop a hyper-disk, signal you, and depart. You will pass through the portal, select the first male and female you see that appear healthy and fit, and return them here to the lab. Make sure you collapse the portal after you." Daphne looked around the room.

"Do you have any questions?" She smiled at the girl standing beside her. "Thank you for making a good point."

A male Asterian raised his hand. "Won't just two samples severely restrict the eventual gene pool?"

"Good point," Daphne said. "Under normal circumstances, yes it would. If and when we set to reestablishing one of the species, we will use our ability to manipulate DNA to artificially generate a significant gene pool." She smiled at the crowd. "I trust this answers your question."

An Arcan female raised her hand. "What about all the other living things—plants, animals, everything else?"

"Fortunately," Daphne answered, "all those data are in the Oort archives. It may not be fully up to date from a development perspective, but that won't matter. We have what we need to reproduce whatever we might need."

Keid Sphere—The Equatorial Band

The first group received its GO! signal. The group leader activated the portal, and the members stepped through onto a tropical island surrounded by a warm ocean whose gentle waves washed up on the island's sandy beaches. Several dozen hominids lay collapsed on the sand. For clothing, they wore breechclouts, nothing more. A young Human man and woman, for that's what they looked like, lay side by side near the water. The group medic administered a sedating injection to each, and two of the men picked them up and carried them through the portal. The group followed, and the leader collapsed the portal behind them.

*

A similar scenario happened twenty-one more times, although none was on a tropical island. They retrieved primitive simians, other hominids that looked like Humans, primitive felines, felines that looked like Asterians, canines that might have looked like the Oort when they were flesh-and-blood, and several saurians, none so advanced as the species that resembled the Arcans, now living in *Andromeda's* landscape side.

On one occasion, the group stepped through the portal into a forest clearing that was home to a developing feline species. The unconscious population scattered around the village in the clearing looked very much like the Asterians in the group. Just as the medic injected the nearest male and female with an additional sedative, and two of the male Asterians picked up their limp forms, a group of hunters burst through the forest boundary.

When they saw what they thought was carnage in their village, they reacted instantly with a howl of protest and unleashed a flight of arrows that killed two Humans outright and injured both Asterians carrying the sedated forms through the portal. One large feline ran toward the portal, swinging a saber while the rest formed a semicircle facing the portal. Before anybody could stop him, the big feline ran through the portal.

The remaining group members drew their EMD weapons and disabled the hunters. Moments later, the unconscious form of the big feline tumbled back through the portal, followed by his saber. Then Daphne stepped through, EMD gun in hand, and waved at everyone.

"It's safe now," she said. "Come on back."

✳

All *Andromeda* crew members were equipped with real-time backups. The two Humans killed by the feline attack awoke in the restoration lab with their memories intact right up to the moment of their deaths. They said later it was a traumatic experience, but one they were glad they had.

✳

On a lab bench, the lab techs laid out side by side each pair brought back from the equatorial band. A lab tech drew their blood and ran it through a DNA sequencer. Because these were new species, the sequencer would take several hours to complete the sequence. Another tech attached multiple wires to each skull and uploaded their essences into individual matrixes. After verifying the viability of the uploads, the tech put the matrixes into stasis for long-term storage. The first tech opened the male's stomach and extracted a large gut sample that he placed in the microbiome sequencer. This process would take two to three times as long as the DNA sequencer.

The two techs went on to their next couple.

It took several days before each of the species was safely ensconced in *Andromeda's* static upload storage and their DNAs and microbiomes were sequenced and stored with them.

PS Andromeda—Oort Matrix

Back in the Oort vault, eThorpe briefed the Oort on his progress with their twenty-three-species experiment. "We moved about one hundred of the advanced saurian species to *Andromeda's* landscape side. They're adjusting. We have stored the other twenty-two species in our vaults. Now it's your turn. Keid-C may produce its superflare in less than ten days. We need to get you—all of you—into *Andromeda*."

"It's not that simple," Liaise said. "I told you earlier that not all of us are convinced about the superflare. We have reached a compromise between us. Simply stated, we will clone ourselves. One version will go to *Andromeda*. The other will remain here."

"What do you mean by *here*?" eThorpe asked.

"Right here in this vault. If it is just another flare, we will continue on as before. If it really is a big deal, this vault probably will survive—and if it doesn't, our clones will carry on."

Before he left, eThorpe dropped a closed portal inside the vault.

※

Back on *Andromeda*, eThorpe worked with Sally and Brad to set up an escape proof Matrix for the Oort. It was sufficiently large to accommodate all 1,000 Oort individuals. The archives had been copying ever since they first agreed to do it. They were close to being finished. Sally and Brad set up a wideband connection between the

Oort matrix and the archives so they would have full, continuous access.

Five days remained before the first possible eruption of the superflare. eThorpe visited the vault. "Liaise, it's time," he told the Oort. "The archives have copied completely. If you hold out any longer, you might not survive."

"We're holding onto our freedom as long as possible," Liaise said.

"You're not giving up your freedom, my friend," eThorpe said, "you're just relinquishing some if it for a short time. It's way better than the alternative. Over the course of our interactions, I've come to appreciate who and what you are. You have become a friend. You need to act now, Liaise."

"I agree, eThorpe. I want our friendship to continue, and I see only one way for that to happen."

Liaise consulted with his colleagues and then returned. "We have cloned ourselves," he said. "I represent the clone—and myself as your friend. We are ready to pass through your portal into the matrix."

eThorpe activated the portal he had placed in the vault earlier, and a thousand cloned Oort passed through into the matrix on *Andromeda*. eThorpe then collapsed the portal and deactivated it. It was now just another piece of flotsam and jetsam that littered the data flow inside the sphere. He retraced his path to the Keid City office, passed through the adaptor, and entered his personal matrix. Someone disconnected the adaptor and carried his matrix through the portal back to *Andromeda*.

Thorpe collapsed the portal to Keid City and pulled *Andromeda* a full AU out from the sphere. Only hours remained.

Keid Sphere

Keid-C had been a flare red dwarf for millions of years. Sitting at the center of the massive Dyson Sphere the Oort had constructed around the star millions of years ago, it put out well-behaved flares from time to time, flares easily absorbed by the inner sphere.

This time, the star's surface roiled more fiercely than it had previously. Its surface pressure increased so that it held onto flares that might have relieved its pent-up energy. Magnetic currents caused by large-scale circulation inside the star's 400,000-kilometer diameter changed from the patterns it had held for millions of years. A large magnetic vortex formed at the star's north pole. For several days, the star's intensity grew as its size swelled.

Deep inside the vault in the sphere, the Oort saw what was happening. They churned out Task Runners to reinforce points they identified as weak. They increased the velocity of the magnetic super-fluid in the twenty massive tubes forming a cage around Keid-C. The superfluid carried away some of the excess heat, but the additional velocity put a strain on the entire structure. The inner sphere had to absorb the rest of the excess. It had a 250 percent excess capacity to handle the regular flares Keid-C put out, but this was far beyond the inner sphere's capacity.

The Oort increased the structure's rotation to give it more stability. This increased the pull of gravity along the twenty-nine-and-a-half-million-kilometer-long, one-and-a-half-million-kilometer-wide equatorial band. Weather patterns changed dramatically. Storm cells packing 200 kilometer-per-hour winds raced across the countryside, building up huge static electricity charges. Massive lightning strikes enveloped forty-four trillion square kilometers of equatorial band, and crashing thunder filled the air in every cranny of the band.

✳

The simian humanoids Jocara and Kenred had discovered earlier hunkered forlornly in the middle of their clearing, weighed down by nearly twice their normal weight. Their individual huts and the communal hut had collapsed from their own weight, and wind howled through their clearing, carrying away anything not tied down. Lightning crashed around them continuously, and the resulting thunder made it impossible to think, let alone speak. The shaman stood to his feet, leaning into the wind, arms outstretched, grasping for the power the gods had given him. The roiling heavens answered with a bolt of lightning that struck him down and killed everyone in the clearing except one wailing infant struggling in its dead mother's arms.

✳

High wind swept away the teepee dwellings in the feline village Jocara and Kenred had found. Weighing nearly twice their normal weight, the residents slipped into the forest for shelter from the torrential rain and murderous wind, but discovered that the trees themselves were crashing to the ground. Lightning struck all around them, splitting large trees and killing several who grasped those trees for protection. Crashing thunder terrified the women and children, while the men tried in vain to pull together some form of protection from nature gone crazy. Hearing a thunderous roar, the village shaman leaped to his feet and climbed atop a large boulder. He faced the sound, arms outstretched. Moments later, the ground ahead of him lifted ten meters into the air as a ground swell passed like an ocean wave, smashing trees and killing the entire feline colony.

✳

The saurian warriors took to the air on their mounts at the first sign of atmospheric disturbance, led by the warrior they all looked up to. They weighed more than normal, making gaining altitude difficult. Within minutes, cloud-to-cloud lightning bolts filled the angry sky. A lightning bolt struck the leader, knocking him off his mount. His pterosaur, feeling the loss of weight and recognizing what had happened, swooped down to catch him. A ferocious wind gust cast them both toward the ground. The lead warrior succumbed in the air from the lightning strike. His mount struck the ground and perished. As if angry at their deaths, crashing thunder shattered the surrounding countryside. All around the village, lightning set the gumtrees afire, so that within minutes a maelstrom of raging flame engulfed the entire region. Nobody survived.

✳

Suddenly, the islanders felt very heavy, like rising on a big wave in heavy surf. The sky filled with roiling black clouds illuminated by continuous lightning bolts. The thunder was deafening. Then the wind picked up, blowing onshore from the ocean. Wind speed increased steadily as ever larger waves pounded the sandy shore. Far out to sea, the islanders spotted a line stretching left and right as far as they could see and coming in their direction. In the deeper ocean water, the tsunami remained little more than a ripple, but as it approached the island, it piled up until it reached a hundred meters in the air. The terrified islanders ran from the beach as fast as their extra weight allowed. The giant wave crested at the waterline and crashed over the island, stripping it bare and killing everyone who lived there.

✳

Keid-C swelled and roiled for several more days, and the tube structure still held. The Oort still hoped.

Finally, Keid-C belched forth a gigantic flare from the north pole vortex, nearly fifteen thousand times more intense than any previous flare. Moving at 6,700 kilometers per second, the super-flare reached the first longitudinal tube in two seconds, and the remaining seventeen, a split second later. It smashed through them as if they were Tinker Toys. Because the tubes were longitudinal and stacked at the pole, the destruction of the tubes there caused their destruction at the south. The inner and outer spheres lost their stability, and the inner sphere crashed into the outer sphere, completely obliterating that portion of the equatorial band that lay in the inner sphere's path.

Because of the outer spheres' strength, the collision caused the inner sphere to collapse, forcing the remaining fifteen longitudinal tubes to rupture. The momentum of the collision drove the outer sphere away from the collision, bringing the opposite side closer to Keid-C. This ruptured the equatorial tubes, and the outer sphere lost all structural integrity. The equatorial band broke into millions of smaller pieces, flinging landscapes, oceans, and where they existed, sapient beings, terrified thinking people, tangentially into the void.

✳

PS Andromeda hovered one AU from the Keid Sphere, well above the Sphere's ecliptic. She focused all her sensors on the Sphere's surface. Nine minutes after the inner sphere collided with the outer sphere and the sphere started its breakup, *Andromeda's* Bridge holo-screen displayed the first images of the catastrophe. Large sections of the equatorial band broke away and headed tangentially away from the Sphere at what appeared like slow motion, but actually was eighty-four kilometers a second, ten kilometers a second more than the orbital velocity before the Oort increased the sphere's rotational speed.

With nothing holding the top and bottom of the sphere together, both halves separated at the equator and slowly pushed out and away from Keid-C. The massive I-beams that held the tubes and spheres together broke apart. Immense pieces, hundreds of kilometers long, sped along their tangential paths at speeds approaching eighty kilometers a second. The top and bottom of the sphere split into several smaller pieces, and sped away along their tangents, slower than the equatorial pieces, but still many kilometers a second.

The inner sphere shredded into millions of pieces as the I-beams and tube sections tore through. The trajectories of these pieces pointed in every direction as the debris spread in an expanding cloud around the star.

Thorpe sat in his Captain's Chair, watching the carnage. His close team members, including their uploads, stood nearby.

As the debris cleared, Keid-C came into view, glowing red hot and roiling—very much like it had always been.

"No one has ever seen something like this," Thorpe said, "probably in all the history of the universe." He sighed. "It was magnificently horrific. The effort of millions of years gone in a flash—in a single moment of time." He looked around at his friends. "You will see many things in your long lives, but this…this moment, this cataclysmic instant, will stand out from everything else you will see and will ever encounter."

Epilog

Keid-C Space

The Oort watched chaos engulfing the sphere. All their attempts to correct the instabilities came to naught. As Keid-C's heat output increased dramatically, the Oort boosted the fluid flow in the tubes and rotation of the sphere to eighty-four kilometers a second. The consequences for the equatorial band were catastrophic. When Keid-C finally belched out the superflare, the Oort realized the game was over. They pulled themselves into their reinforced vault and severed all outside links.

When the I-beam infrastructure fractured and large pieces headed in every direction, the reinforced vault broke loose from its confinement without sustaining significant damage, on a path toward the constellation Eridanus, as seen from Earth.

Inside the vault, 1,000 Oort uploads considered their situation. Internal sensors told them they were free of the Keid Sphere, and were headed generally toward Eridanus at eighty-two kilometers a second—slow by cosmic standards. The superflare had destroyed their comms and external sensors. They were isolated and alone.

Keid-C Space—One AU from Keid-C

As the debris field approached *Andromeda*, Thorpe dropped the starship into a nullspace loop. For three days, the ship remained suspended, not going anywhere, just waiting for the debris to pass. Crew members kept coming to the Bridge, concerned about *Andromeda's* safety and worried about the sphere's fate. On day four, Thorpe reentered normal space. The ship hovered well above the ecliptic, one AU distant from Keid-C. Watchstanders and onlookers crowded the Bridge, relieved that the starship was safe, and horrified at the fate of Keid Sphere.

The star appeared by itself on the Bridge holoscreen. It was a normal red dwarf, bright red, somewhat more agitated than normal. The debris field was gone.

With a deep sigh, Thorpe turned to Jocara. "Are you ready, Girl?"

Jocara turned to face the main console. Her excitement was palpable. She pointed *Andromeda* generally at the Cosmic Microwave Background Cold Spot and ordered, "Mother, set a course for Eighty-two Eridani to arrive forty-five degrees above the ecliptic at one AU."

✳✳✳

Please Post a Review for
KEID: A Lost Civilization

Authors rely on reviews, so I really appreciate your posting a review on Amazon and Goodreads. To post a review, scan the pertinent QR code below and follow the prompts. You will be prompted to log onto the platform. If you are not a member, you will need to sign up. It's free. Amazon will require a minimum $50 purchase volume during the past twelve months. Goodreads has no requirement. Thank you very much for going through this effort!

Scan to review on Amazon

Scan to review on Goodreads

Excerpt from
Slingshot
The Starchild Saga Vol 1

by

Robert G. Williscroft

PROLOGUE

LOCKHEED ELECTRA—ABOVE THE WESTERN EQUATORIAL PACIFIC

"I'm tired, Fred. How much farther to Howland?"

She peered out through the Lockheed windscreen at the endless expanse of Pacific Ocean in front of her.

"Three hundred miles, Doll, just three hundred miles more on this leg. How're you doing up there?"

The lanky, soft-spoken man looked over his left shoulder at the dungaree-clad woman grasping the control wheel in front of her. In response, she rubbed her hand across her forehead and squinted into the reflected glare from the ocean surface far below. She glanced at her watch and then at the array of instruments in front of her.

"Hundred fifty knots, Fred. How do you make the fuel?"

Fred manipulated the circular dials of his navigator's slide rule.

"Fine, Girl. We got more than enough."

He twisted around and peered into the periscopic sextant mounted in the cabin overhead. After jotting down a few numbers, he noted the time and checked a volume on the small table jutting out from the bulkhead in front of him. Then he turned, scowling, and took a second sighting of the sinking sun behind them. A few moments later he laid aside his reference book and said, "Drop down a thousand feet, will you? We seem to be bucking a pretty strong headwind up here."

The silver bird dipped its nose in response. The altimeter needle spun until it pointed to 11,000 feet. With her right hand, the pilot picked up a pair of binoculars and scanned the horizon in front of her. Fred took another sight on the sun and plotted his results. She turned around and looked at him expectantly.

"We're goin' the right way, Doll. But these running fixes—you know the assumptions you have to make...drop another thousand feet, will you please?"

Blood red water astern swallowed the sinking sun as inky blackness spread across the sky before them. She had planned it this way, one last evening star fix to establish more accurately their position before setting a final vector for Howland Island just a few miles north and east of where Equator and International Date Line cross.

July 2, 1937, was drawing to a close; but it would start all over again as soon as she crossed the 180th meridian. Outside, twilight quickly deepened to tropical night. A million stars twinkled to her left and overhead in patterns long familiar, while she had to will the bright points off to her right into recognizable patterns.

"Amelia, Doll," Fred turned to look at the pretty pilot wearing a leather skullcap, flaps dangling near her chin. "We got a problem, Girl."

She looked at him with a steady gaze, saying nothing.

"That head wind," Fred paused to push a pencil back to the center of his table. "It was a good deal stronger than we estimated. There's still a lot of water ahead of us, Doll, a lot."

She raised an eyebrow.

"Marginal," he said. "The fuel's marginal."

She pursed her lips and scanned the horizon once again in the growing darkness.

"You won't find it," he sighed. "It's still four hundred fifty damn miles out there."

On they flew into the darkness—one hour, two hours. On Fred's chart their plot line crept closer to a dot labeled Howland Island, but that was countered by the fuel gauge needle creeping toward empty.

Fred took another sighting. This time his fix seemed a bit farther from the last than it had from the preceding one. He turned and said into the darkness, "I think we picked up a westerly. Looks like our luck is holding." Then he scanned the horizon before them through his binoculars. "But no sign of the *Itasca*," he said and began fiddling with his transmitter dial.

"KHAQQ calling *Itasca*. We must be on you but cannot see you… gas is low.…"

Static was the only response.

"Damn fool instrument!" Fred snarled, as he tried to zero into the homing signal he knew was being transmitted by the Coast Guard Cutter. "I guess we should have brought that new-fangled high-frequency receiver after all. It really didn't weigh that much." He grinned at Amelia's silhouette. "Good thing for the westerly, Girl. We need a kick in the rear!"

"A westerly," the woman's voice echoed from the pilot's seat. In her mind she could see the warning printed near the chart margin: *NOTE 3—Surface winds to 10,000 feet generally easterly in this area. Westerly winds usually signal bad weather.*

She glanced at the altimeter; it read 10,000 feet.

Might as well take advantage of the wind, she thought, as she pushed the control stick forward and brought the aircraft down to 6,000 feet. Around them stars disappeared as they dropped through a cloud deck. The aircraft shuddered as a gust of wind hit it. Amelia's arms tensed as she fought to keep the plane on course. Rain streaked the windscreen, illuminated by the cockpit's dull red glow. Outside was like a coal sack. She glued her eyes to the artificial horizon bobbing in front of her.

"Do you think this is wise?" Fred spoke matter-of-factly.

"We've got to make up some miles," she responded, a slight edge creeping into her voice as a strong gust buffeted the aircraft. "We've seen worse, Fred."

"Hang tight!" she said sharply, as the plane dropped suddenly in a vast air pocket. She poured on power, pulling back on the stick as the altimeter needle spun dizzyingly. Fred held his breath, hypnotized by the spinning dial. He sensed, rather than saw, the struggling woman beside him. As the needle slowed down, he let out his breath with a sigh.

"Some turbulence!"

She wasted no time answering him. Instead, she used precious fuel bringing the aircraft back to a safer altitude. At 6,000 feet she leveled off. "How much further, Fred?"

"Hundred fifty, two hundred miles. It's hard to tell with this wind and no stars to sight."

The cockpit lighted up brilliantly. A second flash illuminated a gigantic thunderhead towering in front of them.

"Better avoid that one," Fred advised.

The artificial horizon tilted right. Noonan's pencil rolled off his desk as the aircraft banked left. Again, the clouds lit up. From the picture frozen in his mind, Fred could see they were flying through a clear valley between two massive thunderheads.

Suddenly, the whole sky flashed around them; the plane jerked hard enough to clear Fred's desk. Swerving out of its left turn, the aircraft banked sharply to the right, almost standing on its wing. Inside, Amelia struggled desperately to regain control. She flicked her eyes across the gauges in front of her, already knowing what she would find.

"We've lost the right engine, Fred!" She glanced over her right shoulder, eyes big and round. "More than that," she added through clenched teeth. "I think the wing is damaged as well." She fought to keep the control stick from pulling forward out of her grip. "Strap in, Fred. This is going to be rough!"

As he struggled with his straps, another brilliant flash filled the sky. Once again, the whole plane shook, but when the flash was gone, the right wing continued to flicker.

"I have to ditch her!" Amelia's voice sounded shrill in the noise around them; it contained a hint of fear. Fred reached out and gripped her shoulder. She turned and saw his grin in the reflected glow of the instrument panel, highlighted by the flickering from outside.

"You're the best, Doll!" He winked. "Dinner's on me as soon as we hit Honolulu."

The damaged wing prevented her from leveling off. The best she could do was to keep the plane's spiral from becoming too steep. The altimeter blurred. They both began to hear the sound of driving rain against the aircraft skin; the flickering on their damaged right wing disappeared. Again, the sky flashed. Frozen before them, tumultuous waves stretched several hundred feet below. Amelia Earhart pulled back mightily on her control stick, trying to bring the nose up. She wrenched the wheel to her left, jammed her left foot forward.

Neither she nor Fred Noonan saw the waves rush up to meet them. Their damaged right wing caught the water first, flipping the plane up and cart wheeling it to the right.

"Fred!"

He lost his grip on her shoulder as the aircraft struck. Darkness closed in around them, but they could not feel the ocean pour in through the smashed windscreen. In the silence that followed, they felt nothing at all.

✳

Sixty miles to the northeast a small group of men glanced from a lantern-illuminated runway on tiny Howland Island to a lightning-outlined squall off to the southwest. All they saw was a group of lightning-illuminated thunderheads...but as long as they lived they would remember.

CHAPTER ONE

EQUATORIAL PACIFIC—SOUTHEAST OF BAKER ISLAND

Margo stopped kicking her feet as the ominous gray shapes flashed into her peripheral view. Long, tawny hair floated past her head as her feet dropped below her slim, brightly clad body. She took a deep breath and floated slightly upward. A hint of fear crept into her mind as she turned toward three gray, sleek predators cruising just inside the limit of her vision, about twenty-five meters away.

A gentle touch on her shoulder startled her. She turned to see Alex Regent tapping the depth reading on his dive-console with his index finger. Margo reached down and grasped her console, turning it so she could read her depth: twenty-five meters. She had drifted upward five meters since seeing the sharks.

Margo exhaled angrily and let some air out of her breathing bag. She knew better than to lose track of her depth. Out there her life depended on a constant awareness of exactly how deep she was. Together she and Alex sank back to thirty meters. Off to their right, the three gray shapes drifted with them. Would she ever get used to it, she thought, as she released a bit of air into her bag to stop her descent.

"Alex," she said.

There was no response.

"Alex!" She tapped the back of her console several times.

"Alex!" Nothing but silence.

Alex placed himself in front of Margo and looked into her facemask. With his right hand he formed a circle with thumb and forefinger. His three other fingers extended straight up.

Margo returned the sign indicating she was all right while nodding vigorously. Then she pointed to her ear and lifted her console, tapping the back. Alex fumbled at his ear, and then tapped his console, and then shook his head.

Great, Margo thought, *EFCom is busted just when we really need it. Not busted,* she corrected herself, *just a submerged antenna.* She pointed to the three menacing shapes off to her right. Alex turned and scanned around them. Above and just behind them the blue-painted hull of their boat bobbed in the gentle waves. About twenty meters ahead of them hung a smooth, horizontal fluorescent orange tube about one meter in diameter. To the left it stretched into the gloom; to the right it angled downward. The fluorescent tube was attached to a slender cable angling up to the shadow of a buoy just beneath the surface to their right. Alex turned back toward Margo, making an exaggerated shrug.

Margo reached for her dive-console again and pressed a button located prominently on its face. The three sharks turned and commenced a meandering movement toward the two divers. Their front fins extended stiffly downward at about forty-five degrees. Their backs arched slightly, and their blunt snouts moved back and forth as they approached.

Margo felt her hair stand up on the nape of her neck. She turned to Alex and motioned him to her side. Alex withdrew a telescoped baton from its holder at his waist and extended it to its full one-and-a-half-meter length. He checked the safety lever near its handle, and with his thumb he flicked the lever so it pointed forward. As the sharks drew nearer, he held the stick out in front of him, pointed in their direction. Margo glanced around them again and pushed her console button once more. Alex waved the stick about slowly, and then steadied up on the nearest of the three menacing monsters.

Suddenly, with blurring speed, the nearest shark attacked. Alex struck out with his stick, the jolt of its impact rocking him backwards. A sharp crack was followed by a hissing sound as carbon dioxide rushed into the shark's body. In the same moment, flashes of silvery-black streaked from several directions. One of the remaining sharks was struck broadside by a dolphin's blunt nose. In a flash, it disappeared.

The animal Alex had injected rolled on its side and began a crazed, uncontrolled spiral toward the surface thirty meters above them. On its way up, it was hit several times by charging dolphins. It expired of massive embolisms before reaching fifteen meters. In the melee, the third shark vanished.

Margo reached out for Alex, grabbed a handful of breathing bag, and pulled him close to her. She placed the flat of her full-facemask against his and looked deeply into his eyes, as close to a kiss as she could come under the circumstances. Even down here they were deep blue. Several bubbles escaped from the positive pressure maintained inside their masks and shimmered their way toward the surface, expanding rapidly as they rose.

Like an old-time scuba diver, Margo thought, watching the rising silvery spheres. Instinctively she checked the volume in her breathing bag and glanced at the gauge on her tiny, ultra-high-pressure air flask. She found she was holding her breath, and as she felt the need to breathe, a gentle pressure developed against her back. She pulled back and turned to confront a two-and-a-half-meter-long dolphin nudging her from behind.

It was one of four that had responded to her sonic signal—George, her favorite. The other three dolphins crowded in around the neoprene and nylon suited divers, jostling each other for attention. Margo rubbed the head dome of each and indicated to Alex that he should do the same. Then the two of them turned their attention back to the tube suspended in front of them.

Alex swam to the angled portion and began to search along the tube's length, descending slowly. Margo dropped her arm from George's neck and kicked in Alex's direction, keeping him in sight, but staying between him and the surface. The four cetaceans arrowed toward the surface and grabbed a gulp of air, then settled back down, playfully cycling between Alex and Margo, gently jostling them. About thirty minutes later, Alex motioned Margo to join him. She released a bubble of air from her bag and dropped down beside him. Her console showed a depth of fifty meters. Alex pointed to a five-centimeter rip in the bottom curve of the tube's fluorescent covering.

Margo reached into a deep pocket located on the left leg of her suit and withdrew a role of patching tape. Alex stretched the edges of the tear, and Margo applied a strip of self-sealing tape along the opening. Then she located a small pneumatic valve on the top of the tube and attached a hose from her spare air tank. On a signal from Alex she released air into the tube, forcing water out through a one-way valve on the underside. She stopped when bubbles escaped from the lower valve.

As the tube rose slowly, Margo held on, keeping track of their progress on her console. They stopped rising when the gauge read thirty meters. Margo felt the tube—it was taut and solid. She tapped the back of her console, listening for the faint rush of sound in her ears. Nothing. She pointed to the back of her console and then her ear, and shook her head. Alex offered another of his exaggerated underwater shrugs and grinned, although the only part of the grin she could see was his crinkled eyes. She grinned back and pointed toward the suspension buoy and their boat, making an angled upward sign with her free hand. Alex nodded, checked his console, and they both headed back, slowly rising as they swam.

Margo saw Alex check his console from time to time, making certain they kept below the ever-changing ceiling limit it calculated for him. Since she had remained shallower than Alex for most of the dive, she knew she would be safe following his lead. She looked around at the four dolphins. Her earlier fright was gone, and she simply enjoyed George's protective nearness and the playful bumps and nudges from the others.

On the surface finally, Alex dropped his facemask down around his neck, fully inflated his bag and grinned at Margo. "Close call down there!"

Margo shoved her facemask down and patted the glistening snout that appeared in front of her. "Thanks, George. I love you too."

The dolphin mewed a pleased response, lifted his body out of the water and backed away, chattering as he went. The other three animals circled at and below the surface, keeping watch over their human charges.

"What happened to the EFCom?" Margo asked. "I expected it to come back on line as soon as the antenna surfaced."

"Broken antenna wire, I imagine," Alex answered.

"Storm damage, I'm sure," said Margo, as they turned and headed toward the waiting vessel.

"Probably," agreed Alex. "But that wasn't a burst seam," he added.

"Yeah, maybe the sinking tube snapped the wire."

Actually, tube flotation chambers flooded on a regular basis. They had patched a full ten percent of them since the project started. But it was a bit unusual to find a rip on the tube bottom, and the Electrostatic Field Communication ("EFCom") transceivers on the buoys almost always survived.

You have just been reading from Chapter One of Robert G. Williscroft's exciting Science Fiction novel, RAN: A Civilization in Hiding, *the thied book in* The Oort Chronicles. *Download a copy of* RAN *or order a hard or softbound copy or an audio version from your favorite online bookseller.*

About the Author

Dr. Robert G. Williscroft is a retired submarine officer, deep-sea and saturation diver, scientist, author, and a lifelong adventurer. He spent twenty-two months underwater, a year in the equatorial Pacific, three years in the Arctic ice pack, and a year at the Geographic South Pole. He holds degrees in Marine Physics and Meteorology and a doctorate for developing a system to protect scuba divers in contaminated water. A prolific author of both non-fiction, submarine technothrillers, and hard science fiction, he lives in Centennial, Colorado.

Dr. Williscroft is a member of Colorado Author's League, Independent Association of Science Fiction & Fantasy Authors, Science Fiction & Fantasy Writers Association, Libertarian Futurist Society, Los Angeles Adventurers' Club, Mensa, Military Officer's Association, U.S. Sub Vets, American Legion, and the NRA, and now spends most of his time writing his next book, speaking to various regional groups, and hanging out with the girl of his dreams, Jill, and her two cats.

Scan for more information: 

Other Works by this Author

Please visit RobertWilliscroft.com to discover other books by Robert Williscroft. Scan for more information.

Current Events:

The Chicken Little Agenda: Debunking "Experts'" Lies

Children's Books:

The Starman Jones Series:

Starman Jones: A Relativity Birthday Present

Starman Jones Goes to the Dogs (2026)

Biographies:

Mission Possible (by Gladys L. Williscroft)

Sŭbmarine-ër (by Jerry Pait; compiled by Robert G. Williscroft)

Short Stories:

Reality Hack

First Contact

The Cold Spot

The Virus

Novels:

Mac McDowell Missions:

Operation Ivy Bells

Operation Ice Breaker

Operation Arctic Sting

Operation White Out

Operation Vela Redux

Operation Alfa Rogue (2026)

The Starchild Saga:

Slingshot

The Daedalus Files

The Starchild Compact

The Iapetus Federation

The Oort Chronicles:

Icicle: A Tensor Matrix

The Oort Federation: To the Stars

RAN: A Civilization in Hiding

KEID: A Lost Civilization

Beyond the Beyond (2025)

Connect with the Author

I really appreciate you reading my book! Here are my social media coordinates:

Facebook: *https://www.facebook.com/robert.williscroft*
X/Twitter: *@RGWilliscroft*
Amazon author page: *https://buff.ly/2N5ZnlG*
Blog: *https://ThrawnRickle.com*
LinkedIn: *https://www.linkedin.com/in/argee/*
Book website: *https://RobertWilliscroft.com*
Newsletter: *https://eepurl.com/guZ5uv*

GLOSSARY FOR KEID

Amred— (1) The home nation of Kenred Zlaxiz, on the planet *Arcan* in the *Ran* star system. (2) The language spoken by citizens of Amred and by the Space Push Consortium (*SPC*) and its astronauts.

Arcan— (1) A planet in the *Ran* star system. Major nations: *Amred*, *Ceffid*, and the Geroptic Nation. (2) An individual from the *Ran* star system. Evolved from lizards, they are Human height and weight, females are somewhat smaller, heads are similar to Humans, but with a slightly protruding snout that varies from individual to individual. Legs are like Humans but shorter; arms are like Humans. Hands and feet have six digits. Body is covered with green scales that ripple in color, revealing emotions: pink—sorrow, red—fear, orange—anger, yellow—irritation, pale yellow—astonishment, blue—excitement, lavender—joy, pale blue—humor, multiple colors—uncertainty. Female has a marsupial-like pouch with four teats. They produce leathery eggs (typically two, but up to four) each year that they place into their pouches where the male fertilizes them. If they wish no more young, they discard the eggs. When the eggs hatch, the young attach themselves to a teat for three months, after which the mother removes them from the pouch and begins to care for them like a Human mother would her weaned child.

Aster, Aster System—A star eighty-four lightyears from Sol in the constellation Aries. It has two Earth-like planets in its life zone, *Frohlic* and *Rogan*.

Asterian— (1) An individual from one of the planets around the star *Aster*. (2) The common language spoken by all Asterians, both *Frohlicans* and *Roganians*. (3) The Asterians were bipedal humanoids with a feline heritage. They have six digits on each hand and foot. They are shorter and stockier than the average Human, with skin tone ranging from light to dark tan. Their faces are much like Human faces with flattened noses and very thin lips. Their ears articulate like cat ears, and their head hair looks like Human hair. Their genitalia, mammary glands in females, vestigial mammary glands in males, and body hair look Human, but they also sport a five-centimeter tail from their tailbone.

Carbyne—Has a chemical structure with alternating single and triple bonds: (-C≡C-)n. This structure of carbon gives an impressive Young's modulus (stiffness) of 32.7 TPa, which is forty times that of diamond, and thirty times that of carbon nanotubes.

Carbynophene—Made by sandwiching a forest of vertical *carbyne* segments between two *graphene* sheets. It is 200 times stronger than steel.

Casimir field—In quantum field theory, the Casimir field is the physical force arising from a quantized field. It is named after the Dutch physicist Hendrik Casimir, who predicted them in 1948.

Ceffid— (1) The home nation of Jocara Porovik, on the planet *Arcan*. (2) The language spoken by its citizens.

Databank—An electronic or digital repository for data.

Dyson Sphere—In 1960, American physicist Freeman Dyson suggested a method for harvesting the vast amounts of energy a star puts out: Surround the star with an artificial shell. In honor of him, such a shell is known as a Dyson Sphere.

E-disk—(Escape-Hyper-disk) A specially designed *hyper-disk* that senses the holder's environment and will open a portal and whisk the holder to safety when conditions warrant.

EMD stun weapon—An Electro Muscular Disruption stun weapon, much like a Taser.

Frohlic—The original planet of the *Asterians*. It orbits closest to *Aster* in the life zone.

Frohlican— (1) A member of the *Asterian* race from the planet *Frohlic*. (2) The language spoken by all Frohlicans.

FTL—Faster Than Light.

GEO—Geosynchronous Earth Orbit (pronounced geo or G-E-O).

Graphene—Has an intrinsic tensile strength of 130 GPa with representative engineering tensile strength ~50-60 GPa for stretching large-area freestanding graphene and a Young's modulus (stiffness) close to 1 TPa.

Holovision—Analogous to a current television image, but instead is a three-dimensional, color, holographic image.

Hyper-disk—A 5-cm disk with a dull metallic side and a deep black side connected to a *Portal Locus* through *nullspace*. Rubbing the metallic side activates the portal.

Icicle—The original uploaded Braxton Thorpe in *The Oort Chronicles* volume one, *Icicle—A Tensor Matrix*.

Keid Sphere—The *Dyson Sphere* around the star Keid-C.

Lagrange points: In celestial mechanics, the five points near two large bodies where the smaller orbits the larger, where the balance of gravitational forces allows a much smaller object to maintain its position relative to the large bodies. L1 is between the two large bodies close to the smaller one. L2 is on the far side of the smaller of the two large bodies. L3 is on the far side of the larger of the two bodies. L4 leads the smaller body in its orbit around the larger body. L5 trails the smaller body in its orbit around the larger body. These are named after the 18th-century Italian astronomer and mathematician Joseph-Louis Lagrange, who first determined their existence.

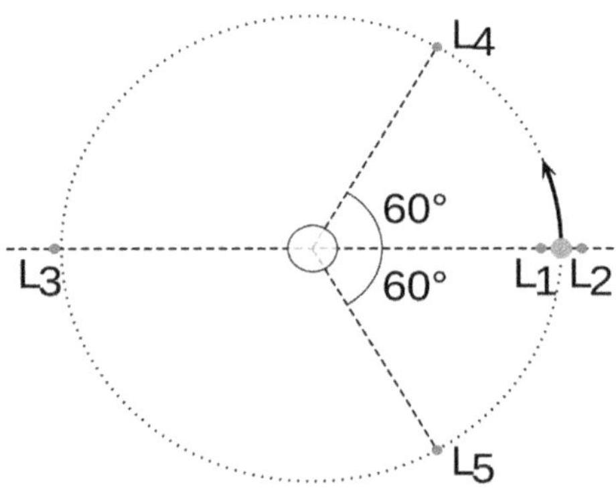

Lagrange L1 point: The *Lagrange point* between the larger and smaller body in a system. In our Earth-Moon system, about 60,000 km toward the Earth from the Moon.

Lagrange L2 point: The *Lagrange point* beyond the smaller body in a system. In our Earth-Moon system, about 60,000 km beyond the Moon.

Lagrange L3 point: The *Lagrange point* beyond the larger body in a system. In our Earth-Moon system, in Moon's orbit on the other side of Earth.

Lagrange L4 point—The *Lagrange point* in the orbit of the smaller body leading the smaller body in a system. In our Earth-Moon System, about 400 thousand km from Earth and Moon, leading Moon in Moon's orbit.

Lagrange L5 point—The *Lagrange point* in the orbit of the smaller body trailing the smaller body in a system. In our Earth-Moon System, about 400 thousand km from the Earth and Moon, trailing Moon in Moon's orbit.

LANR—Lattice Assisted Nuclear Reaction. Formerly called cold fusion.

Launch loop—A method for launching Human and freight payloads into space without using rockets. Constructing the World's first Space Launch Loop is the theme of *Slingshot*, the first novel in *The Starchild Saga*.

LEO—Low Earth Orbit (pronounced L-E-O).

Liaise—The name the Oort chose for himself when communicating with eThorpe.

Link—An electronic device for hooking up to any available network. It has various configurations, from a wristband, to a piece of apparel, to a surgically implanted device. It has both aural and holographic displays.

MABU—*Moxie* Automated Breathing Unit. Consists of a *Moxie* oxygen generator, a carbon dioxide scrubber, and an electronic mixing valve that maintains the proper oxygen percentage and gas pressure.

Matrix— (1) Within the framework of this novel, a box shaped to fit into an electronics rack that contains complex electronics that can form its own electrical pathways over time. It contains the self-aware essence of an uploaded person (or cat). Plural herein is matrixes. (2) a mathematical expression of n dimensions (where n > 1) whose elements are tensors with n-1 dimensions. For example, a two-dimensional matrix with columns and rows has one-dimensional tensor elements that are the point intersections of each column and row. Plural herein is matrices.

MBH—Mini Black Hole

MBH Drive—A subluminal spacecraft with a rapidly rotating Mini Black Hole (*MBH*) at its core. It has a circular plasma path lined with 100-Tesla electromagnets surrounding the *MBH*. A dense plasma focus generates a plasma stream in the ring. The magnets accelerate the stream to near light speed and bend it into a circle. Upon reaching terminal velocity, the plasma stream splits off continuous particle pairs. As each pair passes a designated drop point, one of the particles drops into the *MBH* event horizon. Governed by the Penrose process, the *MBH* loses a minuscule amount of angular momentum, while the remaining particle gains that angular momentum plus an additional 27 percent. This continuous process develops an enormous amount of energy that powers the extraction process and supplies all the power needed to drive the spacecraft.

MERT Drive—An *FTL* drive consisting of passing one *MERT portal* through another, and then the second through the first, and so on, to leapfrog quickly through normal space.

MERT portal—MERT = Morris-Einstein-Rosen-Thorne. A *Casimir field* that contains a stable wormhole with the ability to position one end of the wormhole manually.

Microbiome—The total of all the trillions of microorganisms inside a living being.

Microbot—Within the framework of this story, dust-mite-size robots that scavenge for raw material, modify that to useful material, and construct or repair the *Dyson Sphere*.

Mother—The controlling AI computer for *MERT Drive* ships.

Moxie oxygen generator: (Moxie = Mars OXygen In situ resource utilization Experiment.) A 21st-century device used on early Mars exploration visits to convert carbon dioxide to oxygen.

Nanobot— Nano-size robots controlled by programs generated by the *Nanocosm*.

Nanocosm—A device capable of translating simple English directions into highly complex, wide-ranging instruction sets to *nanobot* swarms that build whatever the original instructions dictated.

Nullspace—Within the framework of this novel, stands for non-space. The interior of a *wormhole* or a series of connected *wormholes*.

Oort— (1) Collective name for all the uploaded individuals dwelling in the *Keid Sphere*. (2) As flesh-and-blood beings before they uploaded, they came from a canine background, but never revealed their actual former appearance.

Oort Cloud—An extended shell of icy objects that exist in the outermost reaches of the Solar System at distances ranging from 10,000 to 100,000 AU. Named after astronomer Jan Oort, who first theorized its existence. A similar cloud around any star.

Portal Locus—The origin end of a *MERT portal*.

PS—Phoenix Starship

Q-carbon—A carbon phase that is harder than diamond, ferromagnetic, glows when exposed to energy, and back-converts to diamond with a simple melting process.

Ran, Ran System—A star 10 lightyears from Sol in the constellation Eridanus. It has one Earth-like planet in its life zone, *Arcan*, and several other planets.

Rogan—The planet orbiting *Aster* at the outer edge of the life zone. *Frohlic* colonized Rogan long ago.

Roganian— (1) A member of the *Asterian* race from the planet *Rogan*. (2) The language spoken by all *Roganians*.

SPC—Space Push Consortium. The public-private *Amred* company that runs the combined *Amred* and *Ceffid* space programs.

TBH boots—Jet boots developed in 1967 by three NASA scientists, David Thomas, John Bird, and Richard Hellbaum. NASA tested the jet boots Earthside back then, but they were not introduced into current use until a few years before Thorpe was revived. They're simpler and less cumbersome than any of the old Manned Maneuvering Units. They fit like calf boots, but with completely flexible ankles. The boot uppers are two stiff, shaped polymer bags containing pressurized hypergolic fuel components. The toe of each boot contains a microswitch that controls a fuel valve, and produces ten newtons of force. The wearer bends the knees for appropriate thrust.

Tensor—A mathematical object analogous to, but more general than, a vector, represented by an array of components that are functions of the coordinates of a space. In the within context, an upload can generate a tensor to use as a messenger or to accomplish something at a distance.

Wormhole—A hypothetical structure connecting disparate points in spacetime. It is based on a special solution of the Einstein field equations. A wormhole can be visualized as a tunnel with two ends at separate points in spacetime (i.e., different locations, different points in time, or both).